Tara Sue ~~~~~~~~~~~~~~~~~~~~~~~~~~~~~~~~~~~~~~~ nty years later, after penning several traditional romances, she decided to try her hand at something spicier and started work on *The Submissive*, she soon followed that with *The Dominant*, *The Training*, followed by *Fire*, *The Enticement*, *The Collar*, *The Exhibition*, *Master*, *The Exposure*, and *The Flirtation*. The series has become a huge hit with readers around the world and has been read and reread millions of times.

Tara kept her identity and her writing life secret, not even telling her husband what she was working on. To this day, only a handful of people know the truth (though she has told her husband). They live together in the southeastern United States with their two children.

Find out more about Tara on her website www.tarasueme.com, or visit her on Facebook www.facebook.com/TaraSueMeBooks and on Twitter @tarasueme.

Praise for Tara Sue Me's breathtakingly sensual Submissive series:

'I HIGHLY recommend *The Submissive* by Tara Sue Me. It's so worth it. This book crackles with sexual lightning right from the beginning . . . It has heart and the characters are majorly flawed in a beautiful way. They aren't perfect, but they may be perfect together. Step into Tara Sue Me's world of dominance and submission. It's erotic, thrilling, and will leave you panting for more' *Martini Reviews*

'For those *Fifty Shades* fans pining for a little more spice on their e-reader . . . the *Guardian* recommends Tara Sue Me's Submissive Trilogy, starring handsome CEO Nathaniel West, a man on the prowl for a new submissive, and the librarian Abby, who is yearning for something more' *Los Angeles Times*

More praise for Tara Sue Me:

'Unbelievably fantastic! . . . Nathaniel is something special, and he has that . . . something "more" that makes him who he is and makes me love him more than all the others. Beneath the cold and detached surface there is a sweet and loving man, and I adored how Abby managed to crack his armour a tiny bit at a time . . . I can't wait to continue this beautiful story' *Mind Reader*

'Tara Sue Me's *The Submissive* was a story unlike anything I'd ever read, and it completely captivated me . . . It's an emotional, compelling story about two people who work to make their relationship exactly what they need it to be, and how they're BOTH stronger for it' *Books Make Me Happy*

'I am awed by Tara Sue Me . . . a very powerful book written with grace and style. The characters were brought to life with a love story that will leave you wanting for more' *Guilty Pleasures Book Reviews*

'Very passionate . . . The characters are very easy to relate to and there is a depth to their feelings that is intriguing and engaging . . . intense and very, VERY H-O-T' *Harlequin Junkie*

'This is the kind of erotic writing that makes the genre amazing' *Debbie's Book Bag*

'Titillates and captivates from the very beginning' *Romantic Times* (top pick)

By Tara Sue Me

In The Lessons From The Rack Series
Master Professor
Headmaster

In The Submissive Series
The Submissive
The Dominant
The Training
Seduced By Fire: Partners In Play
The Chalet (e-novella)
The Enticement
The Collar
The Exhibitionist
The Master
The Claiming (e-novella)
The Exposure
The Flirtation

HEADMASTER
TARA SUE ME

HEADLINE
ETERNAL

The right of Tara Sue Me to be identified as the Author of
the Work has been asserted by her in accordance with the
Copyright, Designs and Patents Act 1988.

Published by arrangement with Berkley,
An imprint of Penguin Random House LLC

First published in Great Britain in 2018
by HEADLINE ETERNAL
An imprint of HEADLINE PUBLISHING GROUP

1

Cataloguing in Publication Data is available from the British Library

ISBN 978 1 4722 4274 7

Typeset in 10.45/15.7 pt Fairfield LT Std by Jouve (UK), Milton Keynes

Printed and bound in Great Britain by CPI Group (UK) Ltd, Croydon, CR0 4YY

Headline's policy is to use papers that are natural, renewable and recyclable
products and made from wood grown in well-managed forests and other
controlled sources. The logging and manufacturing processes are expected
to conform to the environmental regulations of the country of origin.

HEADLINE PUBLISHING GROUP
An Hachette UK Company
Carmelite House
50 Victoria Embankment
London EC4Y 0DZ

www.headlineeternal.com
www.headline.co.uk
www.hachette.co.uk

To my family.
For everything.

ACKNOWLEDGMENTS

If you know me, you know I'm not much of a plotter. That fact has never bothered me before, but halfway through writing this book, I started doubting if Lennox and Marie would have a Happily Ever After. Doubt can be a scary thing, but only if you let it get to you.

Thankfully, I'm surrounded by people who not only support me but remind me that books don't get completed by worrying about them. You can only finish a book by sitting your butt in a chair and writing.

So thank you to both my cheerleaders and taskmasters. You know who you are.

Thank you to Mr. Sue Me, who understands my need to sometimes have my head in the clouds, and therefore keeps us both grounded.

And many thanks to my readers. Without you I'd be unemployed, and even on those days when doubt creeps in, I never forget that I have the Best. Job. Ever.

Prologue

WINNIE'S JOURNAL

I saw him as soon as he walked into the room. How could I not? He was by far the hottest man at the party. The way he strolled in, with that swagger only the most confident men have. I'm sure if I had been able to look anywhere else except at him, I would have seen other women similarly obsessed. His dark hair, dark eyes, and that mouth? Hell, that wasn't even taking into account his hot-as-hell, fuck-me-all-night body.

But when I had a chance to look at something else, it wasn't to the other women, it was over to Marie, and then I knew I was in trouble. We'd never wanted the same thing before.

CHAPTER

One

The one thing Mariela could count on to never let her down was dance. Dance was the one thing she could turn to and lean on when things were hard. The one thing guaranteed to make a day better or to take away all her stress. Through thick and thin, life's ups and downs, it had always been her rock. Until today, when the rock crumbled.

She took a deep breath, moved into position, and jumped and turned in a coupé jeté en tournant. Finding her technique lacking, she repeated it again and again until, exhausted, she leaned against the barre and let a string of curses fly.

"Bad day?" someone asked from the hallway.

Mariela lifted her head and forced a smile at Andie Lincoln, RACK Academy's newest chef. "You could say that."

"In that case, I came just in time. Come with me, I need someone to try my icing and tell me if it sucks."

Mariela pushed back from the barre and wiped the sweat from her forehead with a nearby towel. "Isn't that what we have men for?"

"Yes. Well, that and sex. But Fulton always likes everything I make, and Lennox just kind of looks at me like I've grown a second head and says he doesn't understand why I feel the need to improve upon perfection." She tilted her head. "So now that I think about it, nah, that's not what we have men for. We only have them here for sex."

Mariela laughed, glad that Andie had shown up to drag her away from a disappointing ballet session. "Okay, let me clean up and I'll be right there."

"Just come like that. No one's here yet."

Mariela looked down at her leotard and tights. Not really dining room apparel, but then again the students for the fall session wouldn't arrive for another week. She threw her towel back over the barre. "You're right. What kind of icing are we talking about?"

Andie started chatting about buttercream versus cream cheese and, to be honest, Mariela zoned out a bit. Cooking and baking were not her things. That's what chefs were for.

Andie pushed open the two wide wooden doors that led into the dining area. "Okay, go have a seat and I'll bring the samples out to you."

Mariela looked around the area and breathed a sigh of relief at finding there was no one else in the dining area. And by no one else, she meant the headmaster, Lennox MacLure. Other than Andie and Fulton, he was the one other person on the island that housed the academy. The other staff members would be arriving tomorrow.

4

Unfortunately, she hadn't sat down for more than two minutes before Lennox walked through the door. She dropped her head and pretended to be horribly curious about the pulled thread on her tights.

She expected him to ignore her. After all, that's what he did best. But even with her head down, she could sense him approach her.

"Marie," he said, calling her by the nickname only he ever used.

She looked up and, like always, he took her breath away. Dark and dashing, as her best friend Winnie had described him. She had been right, with his black-as-sin hair and gray eyes, he looked like he belonged between the pages of a historical romance, starring as an evil pirate or maybe an unrepentant rake.

"Lennox," she said, cringing because she knew her raspy voice gave her away.

"You are aware the dining hall has a dress code?"

She waited for him to smile and tell her it was a joke, that of course he wasn't going to enforce the dress code when there were only four people on the island. But the smile didn't come and neither did the *hahaha, I'm just joking* follow-up.

"What?" she finally asked.

"The dress code," he snapped. "You're in violation of it."

"Oh my god. You're serious."

"We have rules and regulations for a reason."

"Right, but since there are only four of us here . . ." She trailed off, assuming her intent would be clear.

"You thought you didn't have to follow the rules?"

She couldn't believe he was being such a dick over something so stupid. "Yes," she said, just to goad him. "That's it exactly. I figured since there were only four of us, you wouldn't care if I wore a leotard and tights into the dining room. I mean, seriously, who do you think it will bother? Not Fulton or Andie. And you typically don't give me the time of day. I could probably sit on your desk, buck naked, and you wouldn't lift an eyebrow."

"I would have thought by now you'd be well acquainted with the expectations I have of my employees."

He knew just what to say to shut her down. There was little else he could have said that would cut as deeply as the unnecessary reminder that all she was to him was an employee.

"It's my fault, Master MacLure," Andie said, appearing with a tray in her hands. "She wanted to get cleaned up, and I told her it didn't matter since there are only four of us here."

Mariela stood up. "No, it was my fault. I knew better."

She turned and walked out, not waiting for either of them to say anything.

LENNOX WATCHED MARIE walk away with a lump in his throat the entire time. Yes, he was an ass. He shouldn't have reprimanded her for her casual attire, but hell, what was a man to do? She'd walked into the dining area in that dance outfit like it was nothing at all. How could she not know what the sight of those skintight clothes would do to him?

Hell, why did she think there was a rule that only street clothes could be worn in the dining hall? Technically, the rule stated no fetish wear was allowed, but that outfit she had on could in no way be considered street clothing.

Even though she'd left the room, he could still picture her perfectly. She was petite and he liked that about her. Liked that she was small and dainty compared to him. Fuck, what it did to the Dominant inside him to imagine her tiny body beneath him. How it would feel to take possession of her.

He clenched his fists as the image of her swam before his eyes. The outfit had left nothing to his imagination and even though he'd seen her naked before, to see her in dance attire like she'd worn today did nothing but mock him.

He pictured it all too clearly. Her lithe body, made strong by her dance routines. The muscles of her legs. How would they feel wrapped around him? His fingers itched to run over them, to feel their strength. No, more than that. To master her strength.

For he knew the rush that came with taking control of a submissive was only multiplied when her submission was coupled with a strength she had willingly laid aside. And he had no doubt that as small as she was in stature, Marie was a powerhouse. To be given her submission would mean to be gifted with the sweetest of all gifts.

Yet even though he knew how amazing it would be, he could not allow himself to take it. He knew she would give it to him. He'd known for a long time that he need only look at her and she'd be on her knees. But it was an offering he could not accept.

He no longer allowed himself to indulge in his Dominant nature. Ever. In fact, he'd buried it so deep within him and for so long, he wasn't sure he could revive that part of him. What he did know was that he could not take the chance of finding out. The last time he'd freed that need within him, the results had been fatal. He could not take that risk again. Especially with Marie.

If the end result was she thought him a coldhearted bastard, so be it. He could live with her scorn. What he could not live with was the responsibility for another woman's death.

"I feel as though I should apologize again, Sir," Andie said, and he realized he'd been staring at the empty place Marie had been sitting for several seconds. "But I'm not exactly sure what for."

"Has Andie been causing trouble again?" her Dom and one of his Master Professors asked, coming up behind her. "Do I need to take her over my knee?"

Lennox smiled as Fulton's arms came around his submissive, even as she swatted at him in mock outrage.

"What's this about again?" she asked. "When have I ever caused trouble?"

Fulton dropped a kiss on the top of her head. "The correct question is, when have you not caused trouble?"

Andie crossed her arms. "Mpph. I didn't know I caused you so many problems, Sir."

"You're putting words in my mouth, Andie. I didn't say problems, I said trouble."

"Pretty much the same thing."

"Hey look," Fulton said, obviously trying to change the subject. "Are those icing samples?"

Andie reached for the tray and held it out to him. "Yes. I was going to have Mariela help me decide which one tasted better."

Fulton grabbed a spoon from the place setting already on the table and took a bite of each one. "Mmm, I don't know. They're both really good to me. Boss?"

Lennox dutifully took another spoon and tasted them. "These

are both excellent, but so is the icing you've been using. Why mess with a good thing?"

Andie shook her head and mumbled under her breath while cleaning up. She gathered everything together and started for the kitchen without saying anything further.

"Andie?" Fulton asked as she walked away.

"Sex," she called over her shoulder. "Just sex and nothing else."

"What was that about?" Lennox asked Fulton as she left through the door that led to the kitchen.

"Damned if I know. I gave up trying to figure women out ages ago. It only gives you a headache." Fulton scratched his head. "But she said 'Sex and nothing else.' That has to be good, right?"

"You would think."

"Wish she'd have left some of that icing. Think I'll go in the kitchen to see if I can get some more."

Lennox snorted. "Good luck with that."

AN HOUR LATER, Mariela had taken a shower and changed into her regular clothes. She wasn't surprised when Andie knocked on the slightly open door of her office.

"Hey, girl," she said, pushing the door open wider. "Come on in. Have a seat."

"I'm so sorry about Lennox. I had no idea he'd throw such a fit." Andie sat on the loveseat, tucking her legs underneath her.

Mariela sat beside her and waved her comment away. "Don't worry about it. I'm used to it."

Andie nodded. Mariela had shared most of her history with

both Andie and Fulton when they'd stopped by her apartment a few weeks ago to show off Andie's collar. Mariela had kept some of the story to herself. The new couple didn't need to know everything.

Andie still didn't seem convinced. She shook her head. "It doesn't matter if you're used to it. He was a total ass to you. Seriously, would he have said anything to anyone else if they'd come into the dining hall dressed like you are, with only four people on the island?"

"Seeing as how you're the only one of the remaining three who could possibly even fit into a leotard or tights, I'd say he probably wouldn't have said anything. Though Fulton is a definite. If he showed up in my outfit, I know Lennox would say something."

Andie reached out and touched her shoulder. "Let's take a minute to imagine Fulton in a leotard and tights."

"Pink?" Mariela asked.

"Is there any other color?"

They giggled for a few minutes over the idea of Fulton in a pink ballet outfit. Andie looked over to the barre.

"Did you ask for Lennox to install that for you?" she asked.

"No, he actually did that on his own, believe it or not."

"I believe it. I think he cares more than he lets on."

Mariela shook her head. "It doesn't matter if he cares or not. What's he going to do about it? Even if he were to come to me and confess his undying love—and I know hell would freeze over before that happened—he won't be whole until he admits he's a Dom as well as a man." She sighed. "And I don't think that's ever going to happen."

It had been three years since Winnie's death. Three years. She had thought he would have returned to the lifestyle long before now. Yet outside of establishing the BDSM academy, he didn't seem to have taken any steps in that direction. She couldn't understand how he could ignore that part of himself, especially since he was surrounded by it daily.

"Do you know, I don't think you've ever told me how you and Lennox first met," Andie said.

"The first time I was actually introduced to him was at the dinner party where he first met Winnie." She remembered that day so vividly. Standing there beside Winnie and being introduced to him. Finally, she had thought, she could meet the man she had wondered about for so long. But of course, he only had eyes for Winnie.

"But you knew who he was before then, right?" Andie asked.

"Yes." She hesitated for a minute, waiting to see if Andie wanted more information.

"Come on," Andie finally said. "I know there's more to it than that. Tell me all about it."

Mariela took a deep breath and let her mind wander down the paths of her memory. Paths that she had not traveled down in quite some time.

"I first noticed him at a play party," she started. "It was a new group for me and I didn't know very many people. He was there. I wish you could've seen him then. How he was before he pulled back from the lifestyle. He was doing a demo scene and he was magnificent."

She could still remember how he stood there without his shirt on. Could still picture the way his muscles moved as he worked with a submissive. He had been a sight to behold.

"Of course, I asked who he was. I was told that Master Mac-Lure was the club's most eligible Dom. Intelligent, good-looking, wealthy, and one hell of a Dominant. All the subs wanted him. Male and female. I think I spent the entire night watching him do one thing or the other."

"How long was this before the dinner party where you were introduced to him?"

"Six months maybe?" She tilted her head to the side as she tried to think back. "I went to every play party after that first one. Just hoping to get a good look at him. He went to several of the meetings, but never with the same submissive. Oh no. Not Lennox. He had his choice of partners vying for his attention. I guess he probably would today as well."

Andie nodded. "He would according to the gossip I hear from the students in the kitchen."

"I bet you hear a lot." Marie shook her head. "But all that stopped after he met Winnie. They hit it off right away and that was all she wrote. From then on it was Winnie and Lennox."

"Did she know how you felt about him?"

"I don't know. I never told her that I had admired him from afar or that I had a crush on him. Besides, he never looked at me the way he looked at Winnie. And that hasn't changed."

So why hadn't she given up? Why was she still half in love with him after all these years? Why had she jumped at the chance to work at his academy when he called her up and offered her a job so soon after its completion?

Because some part of her held on to the hope that someday he would want her, that he might desire her in that same way.

"There's no delicate way to ask this," Andie said. "So I'll just be blunt. What does he do for sex? I mean, I find it hard to believe he's been celibate for so long."

Mariela knew she wasn't able to hide either her wince or the bitterness in her voice. "I can't say for sure, but I know he heads to the mainland a few times a month. It's always overnight on a Friday and he's back on Saturday. I assume that's what he's doing. Though I don't know anything about who he might be meeting there."

She'd thought about sneaking out to spy on him, follow him to see where he went.

"There's no good way to follow him," Andie said. Obviously her mind was as devious as Mariela's. "Since it's an island, he'd see another boat behind him." She thought for a second and snapped her fingers. "I know! Have you thought about telling him you need to go to the mainland? That way you can ride the boat with him and maybe follow him when you get off?"

"Yes, but then I think about being on the boat with him. Knowing, or at least being fairly certain of, what he's getting ready to do . . ." She shook her head. "I can't do it. I can't be so close to him, knowing that there's another woman waiting for him on the other side."

"I can understand that."

"I can't help but wonder about her. Is it always the same woman? Or does he have a handful that he rotates through? What's the sex like? Is it rough? Does he dominate her, just a little? Or is it strictly vanilla?"

"You have to stop. You can't torture yourself like that."

But Mariela couldn't stop—and it felt so good to be able to share her thoughts with someone else, she didn't want to stop. "And then, after I ask all those questions, I look in the mirror and ask myself, why not me? Is it so impossible that he could find something in me to interest him?"

"Because you're worth more than that and you deserve better. You want to be more than a convenient way for a man to scratch an itch."

"I can't help but think that sometimes maybe scratching the itch is enough. I mean, it's more than I'm doing now."

Andie pressed her lips together in a line. It was so hard for Mariela to believe that a few months ago, Andie had enrolled at the academy as a virgin. Now she was sitting in Mariela's office offering her sex advice. The universe was certainly funny sometimes.

"I know what you need," Andie finally said with a nod. "Yes, indeed. This is perfect."

"I can't wait to hear, Oh, Wise One," Mariela said, and she was teasing, just a little.

"Joke all you want, but this is foolproof."

Mariela lifted an eyebrow.

"You need a plan," Andie said confidently. "A master plan of seduction."

WINNIE'S JOURNAL

Holy hell and a half, Marie knew him! Okay, truthfully, she'd never met him, but she knew who he was. Lennox MacLure. Real estate mogul. Except she had an odd look on her face when she admitted she knew who he was, like there was more to the story than that. But she wouldn't tell me. I didn't understand, she'd never withheld information from me before.

Then she told me he wasn't my type. Well, screw her. She only said that because she wanted him for herself. I could tell by the way she looked at him. But the thing was, I knew she wouldn't do anything about it, so I decided to march up to him and introduce myself.

CHAPTER

Two

On a scale of one to ten, Mariela put the idea of a seduction plan at around a six. She didn't think anything too scripted would work. Besides, hadn't she been working from a plan for the last couple of years?

But Andie looked undeterred. In fact, she looked downright excited.

"Where's some paper?" Andie jumped off the loveseat and jogged to the desk. "And a pen. We have to write this down."

Mariela found she couldn't roll her eyes and tell her to drop it. Poor Andie was way too positive *this plan* would be the thing that turned Lennox around. No, she couldn't tell her to stop, but she could tell her the truth.

"I really don't think this is going to work," Mariela said. "Trust me. I've done it all."

"Not like this you haven't." Andie had found a pad of paper

17

and turned to a clean page. "You see, I bet you've always worked on trying to get Lennox to notice you."

"Isn't that the point?"

"Eventually. But what we need first is for him to understand that he needs to accept his Dominant nature." Andie wrote furiously on the paper.

Mariela had to admit it sounded like a good place to start. And, truth be told, she hadn't approached Lennox from that angle. It might be worth at least *hearing* Andie's plan. "Go on."

"He's a man," Andie spoke without looking up. "So we have to keep in mind that whatever we do, you need to let him think it's his idea. He'll balk if he realizes it's someone else's plan."

"That's a man for you."

"Exactly. The second thing to remember is we have to take baby steps. No big leaps. He isn't going to go from nothing to a full-fledged scene, you know?"

Mariela nodded, a bubble of excitement starting to grow in her belly. "Makes sense."

"The third and last thing before we get into the actual plan is that we have to expect setbacks and not let them get us down."

"That's a hard one."

"Right. But probably the most important." Andie looked up. "You've said he's been in denial for a long time and that means his patterns of behavior are seriously ingrained. Setbacks are going to happen."

She knew Andie was right, but she also knew how hard it was not to feel discouraged when he acted cold toward her. She had to remember she was in this for the long haul.

"I guess when any setbacks crop up, I'll have you here to support me and not let me quit."

"Now you're starting to get the idea." Andie had a mischievous gleam in her eye. "Now, step one. Do you think he needs to direct a scene?"

Mariela shook her head. "I think we need an even smaller first baby step. I'm not sure the last time he *watched* a scene."

Andie gave a low whistle. "That bad?" At Mariela's nod of confirmation, she continued. "Okay. So step one should be him watching a scene."

"We should jot down any ideas we have for how we're going to accomplish these things."

"Yes." Andie wrote something else down. "I think that one should be relatively easy. We have the new students coming in. We can arrange for all the instructors to be busy and he's the only one who can be in the classroom making sure no one gets hurt."

"Yes, that's the perfect first step. It'll be just far enough outside his comfort zone to stretch him, but not so far that he'll have to refuse."

"This is going to work. I can feel it."

"I hope so." Mariela had to admit, it was the most optimistic she'd been in a long time. Heaven alone knew why she hadn't given up hope entirely way before now. She'd actually tried to break away once. She left for the summer two years ago, never planning to return to the island, but she didn't last a month before she was back and near Lennox once again.

"Step two is him directing a scene?"

"I think so."

19

"Possible ideas are either do something with the students again or maybe Fulton can approach him about something involving us. We don't want to use the students too much or he might catch on."

"You're going to bring Fulton into this?" She wasn't sure what the Master Professor would think.

"Maybe not the whole game plan, but definitely some parts of it. I think if it were only the two of us, Lennox might catch on that we're up to something, but if we bring Fulton in?"

"Okay, you have a point."

"Should we ask him how he feels after each step?"

"If we do, it has to be in a roundabout manner. You know, something like, '*Oh my god*, are you okay?' More that kind of thing instead of, 'Tell me how it felt when the Dom used the flogger the way you asked.'"

Because Mariela knew how the latter would go. She could hear him. *"Not another damn therapy session, Marie."*

Andie tapped the pen on the pad. "See? Here's where it gets a bit iffy. After he directs a scene, what's the next step? Will he be ready to be an active participant in one?"

"Smaller baby steps," Mariela reminded her. "I say we find a way to have him assist in a scene. That way he's not the lead, and if we make it that it's his idea, he's only helping. In his mind, that would be far different than being in a scene for his own pleasure."

"Good point, and it may be that we have him assist in several scenes before we think about trying to set him up on one where he's the only Dom."

Mariela nodded. "We'll have to play that part by ear. Adjust if needed."

"Yes, and hopefully, by the time he's assisted in a few scenes, he'll be ready to play one-on-one. We can see how things are going and decide if we want to bring another submissive in or if you want to do it."

Would they even get to that point? Mariela had her doubts. Sure, the plan looked good on paper, but there were so many pieces and so many things along the way that could go wrong. Plus the big question mark was how was Lennox going to act? If at any point he made up his mind he didn't want to do something, there would be no persuading him and the plan would go straight to hell.

"You're worried," Andie said. "Don't be. We have this all under control. And with the two of us as masterminds, I promise it won't be long before you have him eating out of your hands."

"I hope so." But she still wasn't sure.

"I don't even want to know what you two are plotting, do I?" Fulton asked from the doorway.

"Probably not," Andie replied. "Probable deniability and all that."

"Probable deniability? Lord help me, woman, you aren't going to have us wind up in jail, are you?"

"Oh no. I'm not planning anything illegal," Andie said.

"Let me ask another question. You aren't going to get us fired, are you?"

"Mmm." Andie put a finger to her lips. "That's more likely than jail time, but still an unlikely possibility."

He crossed his arms and cocked an eyebrow at his sub.

Andie held her hand up, as if taking an oath. "I hereby solemnly swear, I am planning something for the betterment of mankind and, if it goes according to plan, it will improve the academy as well. Trust me."

"Okay, but if I hear anything that sounds remotely like it's a bad idea, you're going to tell me everything."

"Deal."

"Mariela?" Fulton asked.

She blinked innocently. "I can neither confirm nor deny I have anything to do with this."

"You don't have to confirm it, it's written all over your face."

"Damn, and I thought I washed that off this morning."

Andie ripped the paper she'd been writing on from the pad, folded it, and handed it to Mariela. "So," she said, looking at Fulton, who didn't miss the handoff. "What's up?"

He looked at his watch. "We need to head out if we're going to have dinner at that place on the mainland you wanted to try and still have time to run by the market and get back before dark."

Andie looked at Mariela. "Date night before the staff comes back."

She waved the couple out the door. "You two go. Have fun. Get a hotel room for the night if you want."

But Andie hesitated, looking up at Fulton and asking a silent question. He nodded.

"You could come with us if you wanted to. Just dinner and the market," Andie said.

"You just said it was date night, so no. I won't intrude. Besides, I don't like the mainland."

Though she thought it was awfully nice of Andie to think of her, she'd been the third wheel enough. A lifetime of memories threatened to overtake her, but she forced them back into the past where they belonged. No more. She had promised herself she would never be the third wheel again.

And it wasn't a lie that she didn't like the mainland. It would be just fine for her to never leave the island again. The mainland held too many memories. On the island, it was easier to shove them away and leave them in the past. But the mainland was a different story. On the mainland, they would refuse to stay buried.

Maybe it made her weak. Maybe it said something about her character, but regardless, she wasn't going to face them today.

"If you're sure?" Andie slid her hand in Fulton's. He leaned down and whispered in her ear. Probably about how she rarely left the island. She'd told Fulton and Andie part of her history with Lennox and Winnie, but she'd left out that part. Fulton would know, though. Simply from working with her for years.

"Positive. I'll be just fine here. I have some work I need to take care of and a few plans to think through." She gave Andie a wink.

"Okay. Bye!" Andie called over her shoulder as Fulton led her out the door. Mariela couldn't help but smile as Andie giggled over something Fulton said. Those two were made for each other. You only had to look at them together to see it.

Mariela sat down with a sigh and straightened out the paper Andie had jotted their plan on. Would it work? Was it enough to revive a long dormant Dom? And if so, was it enough to possibly have him notice her in a sexual way for the first time? Why did she possibly think this would work now when nothing she'd ever tried in the past had?

She sat staring at the paper for a long time, and it wasn't until she heard footsteps in the hallway outside that she realized it was Friday night.

And Lennox was headed to the mainland.

* * *

LENNOX DIDN'T MISS the fact that Mariela was still in her office as he walked down the hall on his way out of the academy. He had waited until Fulton and Andie left because he didn't want to be on the same boat with them. He thought briefly about stopping and apologizing to Marie, but decided not to. Considering where he was going, he didn't think it wise to see her first. Maybe that made him a coward, but he knew he'd either see pity or disgust in her eyes and he didn't think he could bear either.

If he stopped and thought about it, he might feel bad. That's why he kept moving. He viewed his Friday nights off the island as a necessary evil. Something he had to do to ensure he didn't give in to his Dominant tendencies.

Because he knew he could not give in, he could not let the beast inside of him go. Could not set it free. Therefore, he had to do the next best thing. And that was to release his sexual tension with a willing woman, one he had no claim on.

He wasn't proud of his nights away from the island, but he had long ago decided they were better than the alternative. Because he could in no way allow too much time to pass between nights where he sought some kind of physical satisfaction.

As he normally did when traveling on personal business, he bypassed the academy boat and took his own. Once he was on his way and plowing through the water, he thought about Marie. He wondered what she would think of his Friday night activities. No doubt she would not approve. He wished he was whole, that he could be with somebody like Marie.

But the truth was, he never had been and never would be. Oh, he had thought Winnie was the answer to his dream. The bitter truth was, she turned out to be his nightmare instead. Even so, that did not excuse what happened to her, and he would spend the rest of his life trying to make up for that.

Her death had led the way to the opening of the academy. It was ironic when he really considered it. How personal tragedy had turned into both his salvation and his punishment. For in running the academy, he hoped to ensure that the tragic ending of Winnie's life would not be repeated on his watch.

He'd put aside his real estate empire to build and run the school. He'd told himself it was yet another part of his penance. In time, he'd grown to enjoy his work. He felt as if he was doing his part at the RACK Academy to properly train those who enrolled, while at the same time he never had to actively participate.

Though what he was thinking when he hired Winnie's best friend, he wasn't sure. He snorted. Yes, he did. He knew exactly why he hired Marie. Because he wanted her, but wouldn't take her. So he did the next best thing; he kept her in his sights. Ensured he knew who she was playing with. Who she was in a relationship with. In short, he kept her close, so he could know all there was to know about her without the possibility of a relationship.

He wondered sometimes if he was being unfair to Marie. She didn't appear unhappy, at least most of the time. There were times, more times than he would like to admit if he was being honest, that he saw a sadness in her that matched his own. He wasn't stupid or blind; he knew she wanted him. Hell, he wanted her. But he could not let that happen.

He reached the mainland and collected his car from storage. He closed his mind off as to where he was going and just drove.

If he thought about it too much, he would be ashamed. And yet even still, as he approached the familiar building, he grew hard. Damn traitorous cock. It was the only part of his body that would be happy tonight.

He sat in his car for several long minutes after he arrived, wondering if he should alter his plans for the evening. Get a hotel room. Get himself off with his hand. Unfortunately, he knew from experience that wouldn't be enough. In the end, he got out and walked inside, just like he knew he would.

The door wasn't locked; it never would be to him. Whoever was working inside tonight had both expected him and seen him as he approached. He stepped inside and found the owner of the club, Rachel, waiting on his arrival.

It wasn't that unusual of an occurrence. She typically greeted him every few months, to ensure his needs were being met and that he was satisfied.

"Mr. MacLure," she said. "So pleased to have you visit tonight. Come this way."

Rachel was a beautiful middle-aged woman who ran the operation of professional submissives. He insisted on being called Mr. MacLure as opposed to Master MacLure. At times he thought it was silly, but it helped everyone to remember who he was. And more importantly, who he was not.

He followed her into her office, a sleek, modern number with contemporary furniture. It was a bit too cold and clinical for his taste, but he didn't visit the place for its decor.

She waved to the chair in the sitting area of her office. Once he was seated, she took her spot across from him.

"We've been doing this for a long time," she said, by way of introduction.

He nodded, unable to see where she was headed. "Yes. And I would like to think our association has been mutually beneficial."

After all, he paid a near fortune for the entry fee into the club of her professional submissives. No one dared to call them prostitutes, at least not in Rachel's presence. If you did, you only did it once. He'd gone to great lengths to check that the women who worked for Rachel did so of their own free will and that they were not coerced at all. In fact, he knew that most encounters didn't end in sex at all.

"That it has, Mr. MacLure, that it has."

"You need to tell me something?" he asked, sensing that was the case, and that whatever it was, she didn't really want to deliver the information.

"Yes." She looked away from him and gazed out the window. In the distance, he saw the lights of Portland.

"Whatever it is, surely it can't be that bad." He tried to keep his voice light. From what he could tell based on Rachel's actions, she was loath to tell him.

"I've recently become engaged," she said, and he noticed the huge diamond solitaire on her left ring finger for the first time.

"Congratulations."

"My fiancé . . . well, he's an understanding man, but he's not overly excited about . . ."

"His wife running a group of professional submissives?" he guessed.

"Yes." Her cheeks colored slightly and he found that amusing.

Not in all the years he'd known her had he ever witnessed her blush. "But it's more than that. He's been offered a job in New Orleans, so we'll be moving before the wedding."

"I see," he said, and he did. While he wouldn't have a problem with his wife doing what Rachel did, he could understand that some men might. Of course, all that really didn't matter in the end since she'd be moving to the other side of the country.

"I thought it best to go ahead and let all my clients know now. I'll still be here for the next few months. So if you need to make an appointment between now and then, I'll be here for you. Well, not me, but you know."

"Yes, of course." He knew exactly what she meant. And he also knew he wouldn't return after tonight. This would be his last Friday night trip off the island.

"You won't come back, will you?" she asked, with a slight tilt of her head.

He wasn't surprised she picked up on his thoughts. After two years, they knew each other fairly well.

"Probably not."

She nodded. "For what it's worth, I'll miss you, Lennox. You've always been a good man and a gentleman."

Her words stung even though he knew that wasn't her intent. Stung because, of all the men in the world, he was the least gentlemanly of all. If she could see inside his head, she'd know how depraved he really was. If she could see into his past, she'd likely go running in the opposite direction.

"Thank you," he forced himself to say.

Rachel smiled at him and he wondered why he had never noticed just how beautiful she was until now. Had he grown so isolated in his grief and penance that he didn't even look at women any longer?

No, that wasn't the case. He looked at Marie. A lot.

Damn it. He'd worked hard to never think of her when he was here. He wasn't ashamed of what he did here, but he didn't want any association of this place with her. He thought it would sully her somehow.

He stood up. "I think I'll leave early tonight."

Rachel frowned. "I should have told you after. I'm sorry. I ruined your evening."

"No, that's not it. I'm just . . ." He groped for the right words. "Not in the right headspace." That was as good of a reason as any.

"Penny will be sad to hear that. She was looking forward to serving you tonight."

He chuckled. "I'm sure she'll survive not having to blow a has-been Dom."

Rachel bit her lip as he turned to walk out the door. He'd just put his hand on the doorknob when she called out to him.

"Yes." He turned around.

"It's none of my business and I wouldn't say anything except that I probably won't see you again."

He waited. He had a fairly good idea about what she was going to say, so he braced himself for the well-meaning but totally useless advice so many people wanted to toss around.

"I lost my first husband shortly after we were married," she said, and he blinked. That was not what he'd expected her to say. "We were sightseeing in New York. It was a random mugging gone horribly, horribly wrong. I used to think a part of me died that day, and for the longest time I was convinced they should have buried me the same time they buried him."

She stopped and wiped the tears that gathered in her eyes. He wished he had a handkerchief or something useful, but all he could do was wait for her to continue.

"I don't know your history," she said. "That's one of the reasons why our arrangement has worked so well. But I see in you a grief that I know all too well. I'm not going to tell you to get over the loss and live your life, because I'm sure you're sick of hearing that. I'll just tell you that I know where you are. I've been there and I've made it through to the other side." She reached into her desk, took out a card, and wrote something on it. "This is my cell phone. Call me if you need to talk or just need someone to listen."

He was so shocked that she hadn't told him to get over it and to be thankful he was still alive that he walked back to her and took the card. He'd been in therapy for years, had talked to numerous people, listened and half listened to a dozen more, but never to anyone who had actually been through anything similar to what he had been through.

"Thank you," he said, and meant it. As he took the card, his gaze fell on her new engagement ring. He put the card in his pocket, and told himself he'd throw it away when he got back to the island. Because as much as he appreciated the gesture, Rachel wasn't like him. Her situation, though similar, was nowhere near the same.

By her own account, her first husband's death had been a random mugging gone bad. She hadn't caused it. The death of her husband didn't stain her hands. And that was the difference. That was why he couldn't get over Winnie's death and go on with his life. Because every time he looked in the mirror, he was confronted with the truth.

Winnie was dead because of him.

WINNIE'S JOURNAL

His voice . . . gah . . . I could seriously listen to that man read from a phone book. Everything about him is a walking advertisement for sex. Raw sex. Dirty sex. Keep-me-in-bed-all-day-and-all-night-too sex.

But it wasn't just his voice. I was mesmerized by his hands, especially his fingers. One look and I couldn't stop thinking about how they would feel and what they could do to my body. And his eyes . . . When we were introduced, his eyes had this look, like they knew exactly what I was thinking, but more than that, like he approved.

And, of course, I can't forget his mouth. When he said my name, the corner of his mouth lifted in a sexy half smile. My knees just about gave out. I looked at

Marie to see if she was affected the same way, too. What I saw shocked the hell out of me.

I wanted to climb on top of his body and do wicked, wicked things, but Marie . . . she looked like she wanted to kneel before him and do his bidding.

CHAPTER
Three

The first day of class for a new session of students always carried an air of excitement, and the newly arrived fall class was no different. Mariela actually thought the level of excitement felt higher than normal, but had to admit, part of that stemmed from Andie.

"This is so fun," her friend said, practically bouncing as she oversaw breakfast preparations. "I mean the weekend was fun, too, when they all arrived, but to know that class starts today?"

Mariela let her chat. She'd arrived at the dining hall earlier than usual to see if Andie needed help, but so far she was doing fine on her own. Mariela peeked out the door as one of the wait-staff entered the dining hall. Lennox had enrolled eighteen students for the fall, slightly higher than last fall's sixteen.

They wouldn't make it to her class until later in the week, but she had met several of them over the weekend since she acted as advisor to a number of the submissive students present.

Speaking of submissives, she needed to prepare for her introductory demo. She'd made the mistake of asking Lennox to help her over the summer and had been shot down. It was not a mistake she was going to make twice. David Nader, a Dominant on staff and a fellow instructor, had always assisted her in the past. He could do so today, too.

Right as she was getting ready to tell Andie that she'd see her later, the door opened and Fulton came in. Andie skipped over to him, rose up on her toes, and kissed him. He smiled and grabbed her by the waist, swinging her around.

"Seriously, you two," Mariela said with mock disgust.

"Hey," Fulton said to her, not releasing his hold on Andie. "I'm glad you're here. I wanted to ask you something."

"Sure. What's up?" Mariela knew Fulton didn't have much time. He would be doing the new student introduction in a little over an hour. Which meant she had about an hour and a half before he'd need her for the demo.

"I know this is last minute, but I was thinking Andie could do the class demo this morning." Fulton glanced over at his submissive. From the look on her face, he hadn't discussed the possibility with Andie.

"What?" Andie asked.

He shrugged. "I figured why not? You did demos with me over the summer when you were a student, so this won't be a big deal. Besides, Mariela always does them. I thought maybe she'd like to take a break."

Andie's gaze narrowed. "I think that's something you should ask a person before you go around assuming things."

That was another thing Mariela liked about Andie—she was a spitfire who had no problem telling it like she saw it. She didn't back down from anyone, and the only time she appeared even remotely submissive was when she was in a scene with Fulton.

Fulton, for his part, looked crestfallen as he turned to Mariela. "I didn't think you'd mind. You've seemed a bit distant lately. . . ."

Mariela knew she had been. She wasn't sure why, or at least why things had started bothering her so much now. Maybe it was because she'd been in Andie and Fulton's company almost exclusively in the weeks leading up to the fall term. She didn't like the thought that being around a happy couple would bring her down, like she was jealous, but that could very well be the case.

Even now, with Andie's mild rebuke, she could see the excitement in her friend's eyes at the thought of doing the demo. When was the last time Mariela had been that excited about a scene? She honestly couldn't remember.

"It's okay. I have been distant lately." She took a deep breath. "And I would actually really like for Andie to do the demo. If she doesn't mind."

"No. Not at all." Andie took Fulton's hand. "Do you need me to tell Master Nader?"

"I can do it on the way to my office. You two go get ready." Mariela turned to leave, but not before she saw Andie once more kiss her man.

If she thought she might have been moody and distant before talking with Andie in the kitchen, once she made it back into her office after stopping by Master Nader's, she was even more so. She gave the barre a long look, but for some reason it didn't beckon her today like it normally did.

Three months ago she'd have changed clothes and danced whether she felt like it or not. But today . . . today she gave in to the overwhelming urge to sit at her desk and mope.

She rested her chin in her hands and looked over the paperwork she should tackle. There were people to call to set up the ball the academy hosted after every term. The fall term was always a little bit more special than either the spring or summer because the end-of-term ball fell near Christmas.

Lennox wasn't one to celebrate the holidays, but he didn't mind if the rest of the staff did. Mariela had always loved Christmas and she usually adored overseeing the decorating of the academy. At the moment, though, she just couldn't bring herself to get excited about twinkling lights and greenery.

"Marie?"

She didn't have to look up to know it was Lennox who'd called her name.

"Master MacLure," she said in response.

"Aren't you doing the first-day demo?" He cocked an eyebrow at her, like he'd just caught her with her hands in the cookie jar.

"Why?" she asked. "Were you going to volunteer to do it with me?"

"You know me better than that."

"Right. The Dom Who Isn't. Forgive me, I forgot. So, let's see. If you aren't interested in running the demo with me, you must have stopped by because you want to watch."

He didn't say anything, and his silence made her more upset than if he'd challenged her.

"That's it, isn't it? You like to watch." She was probably shooting Andie's plan all to hell, but she found she didn't care. "You can't man up enough to actually participate, so you'll get yourself off by watching."

He stood there, still and quiet as a statue. She stood up and walked in front of him.

"Tell me, Lennox, does it excite you to see me on my knees? Does your mind come up with all the naughty things we could do together, but that you won't let yourself do?"

"Stop it, Marie."

But she was too far gone to stop now. She reached out to touch him, but pulled back when he flinched away. "Do you miss fucking a real flesh-and-blood woman or is your fantasy life enough? When you're jerking off, who do you see? Is it me, Lennox?"

She knew she'd pushed him too far with that last remark. His jaw tightened and he fisted his hands. "You are my employee, Marie. This is a highly inappropriate conversation."

"We work at a BDSM academy. Answer the question."

His lips tightened into a thin line and she thought he wouldn't say anything, but then he spoke and she wished she'd been right.

"No, I don't see you at all."

LENNOX KNEW HE'D hurt her with that remark. He'd seen the pain in her eyes seconds before he turned and walked away. It seemed as if he couldn't be near her or talk to her lately without being an absolute dick. He didn't know what his problem was, but he needed to get over it. Marie was too kind and meant too much to him. She deserved better.

He walked into his office and slammed the door. Her words had been too close to the truth. He did like to watch. Oh sure, he told himself he was only following up with the instructors to make sure they all did what they were supposed to. But that was a lie, he'd handpicked his staff and they were top-notch.

All public rooms in the academy were fitted with cameras, a safety feature he'd insisted upon and one that everyone knew about. Without stopping to think, he flipped his laptop on and pulled up the live feed of the camera in the classroom.

Immediately, he saw why Marie wasn't doing the demo. Fulton had enlisted Andie. He turned the laptop off.

You're a sick pervert spying on your employees. Winnie was right about you all along.

He picked up a pen, planning to write a few notes about some improvements he'd noticed were needed, but found he couldn't focus on the task. He tapped the pen against his desk, trying to figure out what was bothering him.

Tap. Tap. Tap.

Listening to the sound of his pen, he knew what was off. Marie should be playing some god-awful music that she insisted helped to get her in the proper mind-set to dance. A quick glance at the clock confirmed it, ten minutes until nine. Unless there was something going on, she started the music at eight forty-five and danced from nine until ten.

Because even though there wasn't a camera in her office, most days he walked past her door in order to catch a glimpse of her.

But she wasn't playing anything today, which probably meant she wasn't going to dance and it was all because of him.

Now you're not only a sick pervert, but you're also an asshole.

He stood up. He should go apologize. Immediately. He should have done it as soon as he saw what his words did to her. It had been a mistake not to and he had to go correct it.

His phone rang at the same time someone knocked on his door and he mumbled a curse. With a heavy sigh he accepted the fact that apologizing to Marie would have to wait.

A WEEK LATER, Mariela sat in her office, closely observing the couple sitting in front of her. Watching the hesitant way they interacted with each other, she could tell she had her work cut out for her. "Why don't we start by one of you telling me why you're here."

Dana, the submissive, looked down at her lap while her Dominant partner, Brian, looked bored. Neither one of them answered, but Mariela didn't repeat the question. She might not be addressed as *Master* by the students, but they weren't about to run over her either.

She crossed her legs and leaned back in her chair, ready to wait for however long it took. It felt like forever, but in reality, it was likely only about thirty seconds before Brian sighed and said, "Master Matthews told us to come see you."

"Yes," Mariela said. "I am aware of that. I'd like to hear from you why he told you to do so."

Silence greeted her again. Dana played with her nails, but Mariela could see that she was biting her lower lip.

"We'll start with you, Dana," she said, and the student's head

41

popped up in surprise. "What do you think was Master Matthews's motivation in having the two of you speak to me?"

"I guess he thought we'd work together better after talking with you," Dana replied.

"Do you not work well together now?" Mariela asked.

Dana glanced at Brian before answering. "It's hard to submit to someone you hardly know."

"True," Mariela said, deciding not to add that the student should have known what she was getting into when she applied to the academy. "However, you do know you're safe here, right? Anytime you're in a scene there's always an instructor present, and private play isn't allowed."

Dana nodded and crossed her arms across her chest. "It's still odd."

Mariela stood up. "Let me see how the two of you move together. Stand up and get into position to dance."

Brian groaned, but stood up. "I knew we were going to have to dance at some point."

"Yes," Mariela said. "You're very smart figuring out that the dance instructor would have you dance."

They looked awkward standing there with their arms around each other, and awkward just wouldn't do. Mariela grabbed two blindfolds. Brian shook his head when he saw her walking toward him.

"I'm training to be a Dom," he said, like she didn't know.

"Excellent." Mariela tied the blindfold around Dana's eyes. "I'm sure you've gone over the benefits of experiencing firsthand what a sub feels. However, this lesson isn't directly about dominance or submission."

He didn't protest any further when she tied the blindfold around his head. Once they were sightless and in position again, she put a hand on Dana's shoulder.

"Dana, a lot of the dancing revolves around you, just like when you're in a scene. Brian can only lead if you follow. He can only dominate you if you submit to him."

Dana nodded.

Next, Mariela placed a hand on Brian's shoulder. "Your main job isn't just to lead, it's to be in touch with your partner, to sense how she's doing. I've blindfolded you so you can focus on your other senses for a time."

Mariela stepped away and turned on some music that was both soft and slow.

"Now I want you to dance," Mariela said. "Start slowly. It takes some time to grow accustomed to being in the dark. I'm watching you, so I'll let you know if you're in danger of running into something."

They started off just as awkward as when they had first gotten into position together. Brian's fingers tightened around Dana's waist as he attempted to lead. Mariela let it continue for a minute before stepping in.

She placed her hand on top of his. "Easy. You can't force it. You need to focus on what Dana's body is telling you. Since you can't see her, you have to rely on touch, and that's difficult to do when you have a death grip on her hip."

He relaxed his fingers.

Mariela smiled. There was hope for this guy yet. "Very nice. Now as you step, use your fingers to get a sense of what's going through Dana's mind. Is she resisting? Is she relaxed? Can you

43

feel the sway of her hips as she moves with you? Take the information you get from her body and use it to make your next move."

Mariela stepped back again and let them dance once more. They moved together much better this time. As she watched them dance, she felt the self-satisfaction she always did when she helped someone. True, Dana and Brian were only students and not in a committed relationship. But hopefully the tools she gave them today would stick with them so they would be prepared in the future for a real D/s relationship.

"Very nice," Mariela said as the song came to a stop. "Don't take the blindfolds off yet." She paused the music so it wouldn't interrupt her and walked back over to the couple. "Dana, you need to let go and rely on Brian to be the leader. You're trying, I can tell, but it's not quite there yet. Picture yourself being cradled in his embrace. Let go and let him take over. His only concern right now is you and his entire attention is focused on you."

"Okay," Dana replied in a whisper.

Mariela stepped back and started the music again. "Let's try it again."

LENNOX STOOD TO the side of the open door, watching as Marie worked with the young couple. He'd received his share of questioning looks when he'd told colleagues he was hiring a dance instructor for the academy. But he'd known back then it was an excellent idea and anyone who had doubted the advantages would surely be a believer after watching Marie interact with the students.

He waited while Marie finished with them. They left moments later, walking past him with a "Good afternoon, Sir," and looking far more relaxed together than they had when he'd seen them the day before.

Then he stepped into Marie's office, which was much larger than anyone else's because he'd insisted she have a barre and a small dance space. He remembered her look of surprise the day he'd shown it to her and how it struck him then how much he enjoyed doing it for her.

"Master MacLure," Marie said. "I didn't expect you to come by."

He nodded toward the door. "I wanted to get your thoughts on Dana and Brian."

She thought about her answer, pushing the hair that had fallen in her face out of her way. "They're not there yet, but they'll get there. It'll just take patience and a little bit of work. I think they made good progress today, but I'd like to get Master Matthews's opinion the next time he works with them."

"I'll see to it that he follows up with you." He turned to walk out, stopped, and looked back at her. "Excellent work today, by the way. I know I don't say it enough, but the academy wouldn't be as successful as it is without you."

Marie's jaw dropped for a split second, but she recovered quickly, though her cheeks flushed the slightest hue of pink. "Thank you, Sir."

He smiled and winked. As he walked away, he tried to put his finger on what exactly it was that happened to make him feel so . . . buoyant, for lack of a better word.

Thinking back, he believed it had to do with what Marie said about a Dom. How their entire attention was focused on the submissive. It wasn't anything new, or something he hadn't heard two thousand times. In fact, he'd often said it himself.

No, it was that a part of him realized what he'd been missing. Someone to protect. He'd thought he could channel his Dominant side into the academy and that would be enough, but it wasn't. He needed that personal connection. That intimacy with another person.

And as much as he could try to deny it, he highly doubted he could ignore that need for much longer.

WINNIE WAS WAITING *for him when he made it to the cabin, but not the way he'd told her to be waiting. He'd left specific instructions. E-mailed them. And he had the confirmation that she'd read them.*

It wasn't that he was surprised she wasn't naked and kneeling in her art studio. Rather, he was disappointed. For the last six months he'd been waiting for the other shoe to drop. It appeared today was the day.

"Is there a problem?" he asked her.

She had a tiny drop of black paint on her right cheekbone. She'd probably been painting all day. More of those dark and depressing landscapes if he had to guess. All her work had been so dismal lately. He remembered when her paintings reflected her joy.

There was no joy in her work now. He'd asked her recently why that was and what happened to the joy. She'd shrugged and said she couldn't paint what she didn't feel. Then she'd sighed heavily and said of course he wouldn't understand, since he wasn't an artist.

Frankly, if being an artist meant sitting in a dark room all day painting depressing pictures, he was glad he wasn't one. Of course, he kept that to himself because being an artist also apparently meant you had fragile emotions and the tiniest thing could crush your creative spirit, leaving you in a funk for days.

"I got your e-mail," she said, answering his earlier question.

"Then I would have thought to have you waiting for me in a different manner."

"God, Lennox." She rolled her eyes. "Does it always have to be about the kink with you?"

That hurt more than he let her know. "No, but it hasn't been about the kink for a long time."

"I just don't have time for that right now."

"You don't have to have time," he said. "Not if it's a part of who you are."

Lennox jerked awake. It seemed his subconscious didn't want to relive that day any more than he did. He rolled over to check the time. Four thirty. He groaned, knowing he wouldn't be able to go back to sleep.

He stayed in bed for a few minutes, but eventually got up and stepped outside onto his balcony. It was one of the few luxuries he allowed himself. After Winnie's death, he'd so often felt fenced in. He viewed adding the balcony to his apartment in the BDSM academy he was building as a necessity.

The fall session had been going on for two weeks and the September air held a chill of the coming winter. He turned to go back inside and put a shirt on, when a movement on the docks caught his attention. Who would be out this early in the morning?

Whoever it was at least had enough sense to carry a flashlight. The movements seemed familiar and he recoiled a bit when it realized it was Marie.

He couldn't stop his feet from hurrying in her direction even if he'd wanted to. He stopped by his closet long enough to pull on a sweater and a pair of jeans and then he was out the door, headed to the docks. Numerous questions ran through his mind as he made his way across the lawn.

Did Marie suffer from insomnia? Did she walk the docks a lot this early in the morning?

Though he tried to tell himself he was only checking on her because he was her employer and he wanted to ensure she was okay, he knew better. Marie was a beacon of light in his otherwise dark and dour world and he needed that light like plants needed the sun.

And just like the sun, he could bask in her light, but he could not allow himself to get too close or she'd burn him alive.

He'd finally apologized to her, but things remained tense between them. He missed how easy things used to be with her and wondered if they'd ever be like that again.

By the time he made it to the dock, she'd settled into one of the few chairs that were positioned along the water. Her head jerked up at the sound of his approach, but it was too dark and he was too far away to see her reaction to his arrival.

"I couldn't sleep either," he said by way of introduction. "I saw you out here and thought you might like some company."

She turned her head toward him and the ocean breeze ruffled her hair. She brushed it out of her eyes before answering. "I don't mind," she said. "But I would have enjoyed your company more if you'd brought coffee."

"Right. Coffee. I knew I was forgetting something."

Now that he was by the sea there was a breeze, and he had to admit, coffee would have been a really good idea. But he didn't want to go back inside to get some for fear she'd leave in his absence.

"Do you come down here often?" he asked. "I mean this early?"

She shook her head. "Only when I have trouble sleeping and, fortunately, that's only a few times a month. Usually I either walk down here or dance."

"You didn't want to dance?"

She didn't reply, and the silence became a bit uncomfortable. He tried to figure out what about his question could have upset her, but he had no clue. Should he apologize?

"I can't dance," she said before he could decide.

"What?"

"I haven't been able to dance lately. It started a few weeks ago, not long before classes started. I thought it was just a thing and I'd get over it in a day. Then I thought maybe a day or two. But now, it's been so long . . ." She looked away from him and toward the ocean. "Sometimes I fear I'll never dance again."

Marie not dancing didn't make sense. He didn't think she could be alive and not dance, it was so much a part of her. "But the classes?"

She waved her hand. "That's different. That's work. I can do work. What I can't do is dance for me. Alone."

"Has this ever happened before?"

He knew her answer as soon as the question left his mouth. He knew, too, that she didn't want to say.

"Yes," she whispered.

"I understand," he said, having experienced the same thing. "How long did it last, before?"

"A few months."

Obviously, it wasn't anything she wanted to continue to talk about. Normally, he would share in that thought, but this morning he had something he needed to ask her about. Something he'd been tossing around in his mind for quite a while, but wasn't sure how to broach.

"I need . . . I would like your opinion on something." He balled his fist, as a way to get through the pain of talking about her.

"Really?" She snorted. "That's a new one. I don't remember you ever needing my opinion on anything before."

Ouch.

"That's because I've never done anything related to her," he said.

"She has a name, you know." Anger flashed in her eyes briefly. "Do you ever say it or even think it, or is she always just *her* to you?"

Her question took him aback. As he thought about it, he realized he hardly ever did say her name. In fact, the only time he could remember recently that he said it was in the hospital, after Andie's boating accident.

"I say it," he said. "Sometimes, though, it hurts too much."

"I think it's like a Band-Aid, just rip it off and do it. Eventually, it'll get easier and easier."

But he didn't want it to get easier. He needed the pain, he welcomed the pain. The pain reminded him of what he had done, it never let him forget. He had never been able to explain that to his therapist, so he doubted he could get Marie to understand either.

"I'll try. I promise."

That seemed to make her happy or at least she didn't have the anger in her eyes anymore.

"So what did you want to ask me?"

He took a deep breath. "The cottage on Cannon Beach? I've wondered for a long time what to do with it. Should I sell it? Rent it out?" He shook his head. "I've been at a total loss as to what to do with the property. But I think I know, and I want your opinion."

Next to him, she had been the person closest to Winnie. In many ways, she was actually the closest person to her. Winnie had been an only child and both of her parents had died when she was a teenager. Marie had been a close friend since they were young. He wondered what secrets Marie had that she'd never shared.

"You have an idea for the property?" she asked.

"Yes. I can't sell it. I know that much. And I don't want to rent it out. I just can't imagine anybody else living there. I'm not going to live there. But it seems a waste to have such a nice piece of property sit empty."

The entire time he'd been talking, Marie had been nodding along with him. In agreement with everything he had said. He wished it was lighter outside, so he could see her expression when he finished what he was going to say.

"I thought, maybe, I could turn it into something for the community, an art center. With classes and courses for anyone of any age and at any level. Maybe even have an art gallery. I don't know. It could have her name, that way it'd be like she was giving back to the community."

Marie was silent. He wasn't even sure she had moved a muscle since he'd started talking. The silence grew to be too much, so he rushed on.

"I know it would take a lot of work and I'd have to hire staff. I'm here all the time, so I couldn't oversee it. But I think . . . I think it could work. The property would need some restoration and renovation. It's been sitting empty for too long." He took a deep breath. "So that's it. That's what I was thinking."

Again, nothing except complete silence from Marie. She hated the idea. She must. Why else would she just be sitting there, saying nothing?

"If you don't think it's a good idea or if you can think of something else to do with the property . . ."

She sniffled. Very quietly, but it was definitely a sniffle.

"Marie?" he whispered.

And then it wasn't a sniffle, but a full-fledged sob. He wasn't sure why she was crying. He hated it when she cried. Did that mean she hated the idea?

He cleared his throat to say something, but he forgot what it was, because the next thing he knew, Marie had launched herself out of her chair and was practically in his lap, wrapping her arms around him.

"Lennox," she said. "It's the most perfect idea. I love it and I know Winnie would have loved it, too."

She liked it? That's why she was crying? But no, now that he knew she liked it, he could hear the smile in her sobs. And with her practically in his lap with her arms around him, it was the most natural thing in the world to return her hug.

It'd been too long since he'd held a woman. Sure, he had danced at the end-of-session balls a few times, but that was structured and in a public setting. Plus, it normally involved students. Marie was not a student, and though they were outside where anyone could see them, he was pretty sure they were the only two people awake on the island at the moment.

Most importantly, there was nothing the least bit structured about the way his hand moved up her back so he could tangle his fingers in her hair. Or the way he dropped his head to her neck in order to smell her skin.

And pressing his lips to the spot just under her ear, to see if she'd tremble? Definitely not structured. Though by that time, he didn't care because she had trembled at his kiss and he wanted to make her do it again.

In the back of his mind, he told himself this was Marie and he'd kept his distance from her for all these years for a reason. He just couldn't remember what those reasons were at the moment. Not when she was so soft and inviting. He pulled back for a minute, but didn't release her hair. He couldn't. It was so silky, and it'd been so long since he'd had his fingers buried in a woman's hair.

She stared at him with a dazed look, but he saw the hunger she couldn't hide and he knew she wanted this just as much as he did. His gaze dropped to her lips, so full. What would they taste like? For years, he'd refused to think about her lips, because he knew as soon as he did, he'd have to taste them.

She gave a slight whimper as he lowered his head. He wondered if she'd been curious about how he tasted, too. He told himself it would only be a quick kiss. Just a small sample to satisfy his need for her.

But as soon as their lips touched, any thoughts of a quick kiss disappeared. She pulled him close and he palmed her back, while keeping her in place with the hand in her hair. His last kiss had been with Winnie and kissing her was nothing like kissing Marie.

Winnie had been refined and controlled, and toward the end, she didn't even want to kiss. Marie was her polar opposite. She kissed as if she'd never have another kiss and she wanted this one to be enough to last forever.

She teased him with her tongue and moaned when he parted his lips to deepen the kiss. He was vaguely aware of her hands clasping him tightly, but he didn't care because in that moment, he never wanted to let her go.

Kissing Marie was better than any fantasy he could have imagined and she tasted sweeter than anything he had a right to experience. She shifted to get closer and, in doing so, she pressed against his erection.

And with that one touch, every reason he'd ever had for keeping Marie at arms length fell on him with the weight of a fifty-pound rock. She was everything he could never have, and to be kissing her the way he was gave her the wrong impression.

He pulled back, amid her protests.

"Marie, we can't."

"I think we just did."

He moved her off his lap and onto her feet. "Then we can't do it again."

"Tell me why." She spoke softly, and he hated the hint of hurt in her voice. "Why we can't when it's obvious we both want it."

Because of a million reasons, he wanted to say. But how could he explain that he could never be the Dom she needed? If he knew one thing after working with Marie for all these years, he knew she would never be satisfied without kink. In a bitter and ironic twist, it mirrored his relationship with Winnie, and that had proven that no good could come from trying to become something you're not.

"Because it won't work," he said. "That's why. We might be happy for a bit, but it wouldn't last."

Already, he could sense her shutting herself off. She pulled her coat tighter around her body. "You don't know that. You can't know that unless we try."

"I'm not going to *try* with you, Marie."

"Because I'm not good enough?"

He saw the pain in her eyes and it ripped a hole in his chest. Though he couldn't give her everything she wanted, he knew in this, he could give her the truth.

"No, because I can't lose you, too."

MARIELA WATCHED IN shock as Lennox stood up and walked back to the academy building. Her fingers drifted to her lips and she knew if she concentrated enough, she would still be able to feel his lips against hers. Over the years, she'd wondered what his kiss would be like. Though she'd imagined it hard and demanding, it was so much more. His lips had been strong and insistent as they moved with hers. With his kiss, he'd claimed her, even if only for that second. Kissing Lennox had been better than she'd imagined it would be, and for one small moment, she'd allowed herself to think that they might actually have a chance.

That was the bad thing about hope. When life kicked your ass and you knew you were a fool to think something better might happen.

Yet as she watched him disappear into the early morning fog, hope refused to die. Because as much as it hurt when he walked away, she'd been in his arms, she'd felt the heat of his embrace, and the desire in his kiss. She now knew that no matter what he said, he wanted her as much as she wanted him.

And that was the good thing about hope.

She looked at her watch and waited for ten minutes before returning to the academy. On the off chance that anyone was up this early, she didn't want any rumors about her and Lennox. Heaven only knew how much *that* might set him back. As it was, she probably needed to have a chat with Andie to see if they needed to change their seduction plan.

A noise from behind her caught her attention and she turned to see what it was. Not too far from the docks was the island's lighthouse where Fulton lived. It seemed as if Andie had spent the night and was heading over to the main building to start on breakfast. Mariela watched as Andie kissed her Dom good-bye, and when she turned toward her, Mariela waved to catch her attention.

Andie said something to Fulton over her shoulder and he nodded, keeping an eye on her until she caught up with Mariela.

"Why don't you go ahead and move in with him?" Mariela asked when Andie fell into step beside her. "Don't you spend every night there anyway?"

"Only the ones that he doesn't spend with me." Andie shot her a smile. "We've talked about it. I'm thinking I might move into the lighthouse after the first of the year."

They walked in silence for a short while until Andie spoke.

"You're up and out a little early, aren't you?" She looked Mariela's way when she didn't answer right away. "Oh my god. Are you blushing?"

Mariela felt her cheeks heat and she knew she was. "Probably."

"Probably, my ass. Tell me. Tell me everything."

Mariela took a deep breath and told Andie everything about

what had just happened with Lennox. She didn't leave anything out, partly, she thought, because talking about it made it seem more real.

When she finished, Andie had a wicked gleam in her eye. "It's time to put the first stage of the plan into motion."

BY MIDMORNING, LENNOX gave up all pretense of work. He didn't know what he was thinking anyway—had he actually believed he would get anything accomplished after kissing Marie?

He'd listened for her footsteps out in the hallway to alert him that she'd made it inside, and was disappointed when they didn't come. Eventually, he went into the dining hall and discovered she'd been in the kitchen talking with Andie. He didn't want her to see him watching her, so he took his breakfast back to his office and ate there alone.

Unable to work and tired of pretending, he decided to take a boat and go off the island to the cabin. He could start making plans for what he needed to do in order to convert it. Plus, it had been a few months since he'd last visited. It probably needed a good cleaning. He really wanted to ask Marie to accompany him, but he knew that probably wasn't a good idea after the kiss.

"Boss?" Fulton asked from the doorway.

"Master Matthews," he said, ready to get his mind on something else. "What can I help you with?"

Fulton looked a bit apprehensive. "I wouldn't ask you, but there's no one else."

Dread started to seep into his veins. He wasn't sure what was going on, but if Fulton was concerned, he was worried.

Fulton stepped inside and closed the office door behind him. "The students are going to be running through an impact scene. We've already gone through it a few times, so they don't need instruction, just someone in authority to be in the room. I've had an urgent issue come up at the lighthouse and it has to be dealt with now."

"And Master Nader?"

"He had that doctor's appointment to take his mother to."

That's right, Lennox remembered when he'd asked him if it was okay to take the day off. "I assume Andie is too busy with lunch?"

Fulton nodded. "And not that I don't trust her, but it's not a responsibility I want to place on her just yet."

"And Marie?"

"I asked her first, but she has a conference call scheduled."

"And she can't reschedule?"

"I did ask that, Sir. But she said this was a supplier for the Holiday Ball and she'd been trying to get on this guy's calendar for a month and she'd reschedule as long as I agreed to personally cut down and arrange all the greenery and flowers." Fulton winced. "I thought I'd ask you first because I suck at that floral shit."

Lennox almost told Fulton to reschedule the session, but he stopped himself. He was the fucking headmaster of a BDSM academy. Surely he could watch a session just to make sure no one got hurt. Couldn't he?

"You know what?" the other man said. "Don't worry about it. I'll just cancel and reschedule."

He sighed. "No. I'll do it."

"Are you sure?"

"Yes. What time?"

"Thank you, Sir," Fulton looked greatly relieved. "I appreciate it. Dungeon classroom B at eleven. It'll run until noon. I usually give a time check about halfway through. Thank you again."

Christ, the way Fulton was thanking him, it was like Lennox had agreed to give him a kidney. Was it really such a big deal that he observe a scene? He tried to recall the last scene he'd witnessed and he was shocked to find he couldn't remember.

He waved Fulton away and tried not to notice how the thought of even just watching a scene excited him. A glance at the clock told him he had thirty minutes before he had to head down to the dungeons. It had been months since the last time he went into one of the dungeons.

It had been the night of the anniversary of Winnie's death and he'd gotten drunk off his ass, like he did every year. Except this year he'd decided to add fuel to the fire and visit the dungeon level. Why he did it, he still couldn't really figure out. It was one of those things that only made sense when you were drunk.

He also remembered Marie finding him, and he'd been rude to her. He ran his fingers through his hair. Why that woman put up with him, he'd never know. She had to be a saint. Even more so, how was it possible she still seemed to want him after he'd been so boorish for so long?

He pushed back from his chair and decided to head down to the dungeons early. To acclimate himself. He walked past Marie's office, but the door was closed. Maybe her call had started.

Once he made it down the stairs, he entered the class dungeon with a bit of trepidation. He wasn't ignorant of the things said about him or his lack of participation. Hopefully, his presence wouldn't be a distraction to the students or his instructors.

Before the students arrived, he walked through the space, re-acquainting himself with where the first-aid supplies were, and he made sure an area had been set up for aftercare. He was pleased but not surprised that Fulton had everything in order.

"Oh, sorry. I didn't know anyone was here."

He turned at the sound of the feminine voice and found one of the students standing naked in the doorway. Actually, *standing* wasn't the right word. *Posing* might be more accurate.

Her name was Susan. She'd applied to the academy several times in the past, but he'd never offered her an invitation for enrollment before this term. Her application indicated she'd done some modeling and, truthfully, that was the main reason he'd turned her down.

It was wrong and judgmental, but somehow in his mind he'd convinced himself that anyone in the arts or entertainment industry would not be a good fit for the academy. Of course, he only had Winnie to base that on. Earlier in the summer, though, he'd been around Andie's ex, Terrence. Terrence was an actor as well as a Dom and being in his presence helped Lennox to see his flawed logic.

So he'd made a last-minute decision to allow Susan to enroll, and another Dom with her so there would still be an even number.

She walked—no *sauntered*—into the room. "I heard a rumor you might be joining us today."

God, she was sure of herself. He had anticipated her beauty, and she certainly was a stunning woman. What he had not antic-ipated was the visceral reaction he had toward her. At the moment, his cock didn't care that she was a student, that he was the headmaster, or that he'd sworn off relationships, especially those kinky in nature.

No, his cock only cared about one thing.

But his cock was also used to disappointment and it looked as if today would serve as another lesson.

"Susan Mims, right?" he asked, making sure he kept his eyes on her from the neck up.

She stopped. "You know me by sight? You, Mr. Headmaster? I'm honored."

It didn't escape his attention that she had yet to address him as either "Sir" or "Master," which was a clear violation of academy protocol. On one hand, he was only there to be a warm body at this scene. On the other, it was a rule. As a warm body, he shouldn't say anything. As the headmaster, he had to address her infractions.

He couldn't help but think she was baiting him. He had pegged her as a bratty sub, and now he saw that his initial assessment was correct.

But to draw her attention to the rule meant he had to enforce it if necessary and discipline her if warranted. He suddenly saw why filling in for Fulton was a very bad idea.

"I'm the one who ultimately decides who is enrolled at my academy, Miss Mims. It's not so surprising I can tell eighteen students apart. Especially since nine are women. And while 'Mr. Headmaster' has a nice ring to it, I believe you know better. There's a proper way to address me and that's not it."

"Well, that certainly puts me in my place, doesn't it? I guess I'm not so special after all."

"No. You're especially not so special that you may feel entitled to drop the proper forms of address. You won't get another warning."

She didn't look overly abashed to be called out on her behavior. "You're right and I apologize. Do you prefer 'Sir' or 'Master MacLure'?"

"Either one is acceptable, as I'm sure Master Matthews has told you."

Fortunately, he was spared any further communication with Susan by the arrival of a group of students. He nodded as they entered and moved aside so they could make their way to the various stations Fulton had set up earlier.

Several minutes later, Susan's partner hadn't made it to the room and Lennox glanced at his watch. Four minutes. The Dom in training was cutting it close. He wondered if he'd have to step in and scene with Susan, when the young man dashed into the room.

"So sorry, Master MacLure," he said. "I had a note that a package was waiting for me, but when I stopped by the office, no one could find it or remembered writing the note in the first place."

Someone in the class—Susan, Lennox believed—snickered.

"And did it not occur to you, Mr. Powell, that perhaps it would be in everyone's best interest for you to wait until your lunch break?" Lennox asked, narrowing his eyes at the student.

Powell was a first-time applicant. A recent college graduate who had been highly recommended by several Doms Lennox knew on the mainland. While he might one day make a great Dom, it appeared he needed a lot of work.

Susan mumbled something from the back of the room.

"What was that, Miss Mims?" he asked. "Did you want to make a comment?"

"No, I'm good," she said, her pointed look a clear challenge even as several students gasped.

Cold fingers of panic encircled his heart, but he refused to let the class see his struggle. "I believe I've already corrected your lack of respect today, Miss Mims. I let you off with a warning. I will not be as lenient this time." He crooked a finger at her. "Come here."

WINNIE'S JOURNAL

In what has to be a cruel joke of the universe, Marie confirmed my fear. MacLure is a Dominant. Damn it all. Now what?

I should have let Marie have him—she's into that kinky shit. And she's totally into him. He would be a better fit for her than he would be for me. I should have stepped aside. I know that would have been the right thing to do. The best thing for everyone involved.

But then he asked me out. Me. Not Marie. I honestly did think about telling him no. In the end it was Marie who changed my mind. She told me to go for it.

God help me. I am.

CHAPTER
Four

Mariela tapped her foot as she waited for Andie to pick up her phone, all the while keeping one eye on the live feed from dungeon classroom B.

"Hello," Andie finally said.

"Andie, thank goodness. I thought you would never answer."

"Sorry, trying to get lunch ready. What's up?"

On her computer screen, the student was making her way to Lennox. There was no sound, but she didn't need it to guess what had just gone down. Nor did she need it to know that Something Very Bad was about to happen.

"We've got Code Red or something brewing downstairs."

"Code Red?"

"It seemed better to put it that way than to yell, 'Abort! Abort!'"

"Damn. Are you talking about the plan? What's going on?"

Susan was now kneeling in front of Lennox and he was talking.

"Susan Mims must have done something and it looks like Lennox is going to punish her."

"Oh, shit. Shit. Shit," Andie muttered.

As Mariela watched, Lennox left his place at the front of the class and walked to one of the well-stocked cabinets. He didn't immediately search the cabinet, but looked up, directly at the camera. She wondered if he knew she was watching because it certainly felt as if he was staring straight at her.

His expression was so tortured, it made her chest hurt. The pain was made worse by the fact that it was all her fault for agreeing to go along with Andie's plan. Damn it. She had gotten him in this position and she needed to get him out.

"What do we do? We can't go in," Andie said. "And they won't leave until he's finished. What's happening now?"

"He's opening the cabinet." Mariela kept an eye on the screen, even as she considered what Andie had said. She couldn't think of a reason to burst into the dungeon. And like Andie had said, they weren't coming out anytime soon. Unless . . .

"Fire alarm!" she shouted in the phone. "I'll go pull it!"

"Yes!" Andie agreed, but Mariela hadn't waited for her agreement. She left her office and was headed down the hall to the nearest alarm pull. She made it in mere seconds and didn't think twice before activating it. Even so, the high-pitched beeping made her jump.

She ran back into her office, just in time to see Lennox directing students out of the dungeon, making sure everyone had a robe or a blanket to cover themselves with. Satisfied, she killed the feed and turned her laptop off before joining the students and staff in the hallway.

Andie caught up with her. "Oh my god," she said, as they stepped out on the main lawn. "I'm not sure our plans could have gone worse."

Mariela agreed, but she didn't say anything since she was too busy looking for Lennox. With Fulton and David both out of the building at the moment, she was next in charge. She finally found him near the drive, his hand in his hair, talking on the phone.

"I need to go to him," Mariela told Andie.

"Okay, I'm going to call Fulton and let him know we're all right."

She hoped Andie didn't tell her Dom everything, but she couldn't worry about that yet. Lennox was gesturing with his free hand as he spoke to whoever was on the other end of the line. He saw her coming, said something else she couldn't make out, and disconnected.

"Marie," he said.

"I came to see if you needed my assistance while we're a bit short staffed."

"Yes, that's what I was just telling the monitoring service. They're insisting the alarm was manually pulled and I don't see how that's possible when there were so few people with the opportunity to do so."

Damn it to hell and back, she'd not thought through her plan to save him very well. She bit her lip, hoping she looked thoughtful and not guilty. The cameras had probably caught her pulling the alarm. She needed to get to those files before he did.

"Is there any way a fuse could have blown or a wire short-circuited or something?" she asked.

"Not according to them." He sighed. "I need to make sure everyone's out of the building. Can you do a head count and see if anyone's missing? I'll get started on clearing everything for us to get back inside. Maybe Andie can see if Fulton could help me with that?"

"I'll get right on it, Sir."

"Sir," he mumbled under his breath. "Speaking of which, you're Susan Mims's advisor."

It wasn't a question, but she nodded anyway.

"She has a problem forgetting to use proper terms of address. She's due a punishment, but I'd like for you to talk with her first."

"Of course, Sir." So that's what had happened in the dungeon. "I mean no disrespect by asking, but are you going to be the one who punishes her?"

"I don't see another viable alternative, though I'm going to follow up with Fulton and David to see if they've experienced anything similar from her."

She nodded. In the end, she hadn't saved him from anything. At best, she'd bought him more time. She debated for a few seconds if she should get the camera files now when he was obviously occupied elsewhere. After all, it really didn't matter if everyone was out or not, it hadn't been a real fire. But there were too many eyes, and now she had to speak with Susan, so she went back to the larger group. Hopefully, there would be time later to grab the files.

As it turned out, it was much, much later before she had a chance to pull the damning video from the server. Fortunately, it didn't appear that Lennox had been back to his office before she made it to hers. She breathed a sigh of relief even though she knew that nothing was ever really deleted. Hopefully it wouldn't prove important enough for anyone to dig into the incident more deeply.

A knock on the door drew her attention away from her laptop. Susan. She had a feeling this would be a very interesting talk.

"Come in," Mariela said.

Susan walked in and draped herself across the loveseat. Mariela had met with Susan once before, back when classes first started—she thought she might be a bit of a bratty sub. Which was fine, some Doms liked that in a sub. Mariela didn't think Lennox was one of them, however. He'd sent her a brief message a few minutes ago saying Susan had always used correct protocol when speaking with Fulton and David.

Mariela had a pretty good idea as to why she pushed things with Lennox, but she wanted to hear Susan say it first.

"Miss Mims," Mariela said. "Master MacLure asked me to meet with you today. Can you tell me what happened this morning?"

"I'm sure you've heard what happened."

"Yes, but I'd like to hear your side."

"My side? It's really very simple. I don't have any issues with protocol." Susan smiled and leaned forward. "I decided not to use it because I figured out how to get something out of Master MacLure that no one else has been able to."

The little bitch.

"So you were aware that not addressing him properly would lead to some sort of consequence?"

"Very much so. How long has it been since he's done anything remotely close to punishing someone? A long-ass time, that's how long. Or at least that's the rumor going around."

And Mariela and Andie had basically handed him to her on a silver platter.

"You deliberately baited him to get him to punish you?" Mariela asked.

"Yes, and it worked until that damn fire alarm was pulled."

"Miss Mims, one of the principles of RACK Academy is respect for others. Your actions this morning show a decided disregard of the others involved in the scene. Not only did you disrespect Master MacLure, but you disrespected your entire class."

"I felt it was worth it to have his hands on me."

Mariela felt like such a hypocrite. How could she say anything to this woman about respecting others when her own actions didn't? When she herself longed to feel Lennox's hands and had done underhanded things in an attempt to draw his interest? The only difference was Mariela hadn't been caught.

"Be that as it may, that is not the type of action we encourage, endorse, or will allow to continue. If it happens again, you're out." She really wanted to send the woman packing now, but Mariela knew she had to follow the proper channels. "As for what Master MacLure had planned for you, I'm sure you'll be receiving more information shortly."

Susan nodded, looking more unsure about herself than she had when she arrived. "Am I free to go?"

"Yes, of course."

LATER THAT NIGHT, Mariela was in her apartment on the island, drinking her second glass of wine and wishing she'd poured whisky instead. She hadn't seen Lennox at all after her talk with Susan. She'd had dinner with Fulton and Andie, and Fulton had said he'd shut himself in his office and hadn't been seen since early afternoon.

When Fulton said Lennox hadn't been seen all afternoon, Andie had glanced her way with a look of remorse. So much for the plan. Thus far it hadn't gone very well. Maybe it'd be more accurate to call it a complete and utter failure.

From what she'd guessed, Andie hadn't told Fulton what they had planned or their unexpected involvement in the day's events. She secretly hoped it'd stay that way. There was little doubt that Fulton would stop their plan in its tracks and, as bad as today had been, she wasn't ready for that to happen.

The knock on her door startled her. Curious as to who might have come by to see her, she rose and went to answer. She opened the door and managed to cover her surprise at finding Lennox there.

"Master MacLure, how nice to see you this evening. Come on in."

"Thank you."

"Would you like a glass of wine?"

"Yes, I think I would."

She went into the kitchen and poured him a glass. He waited beside her mantel holding an old picture of her and Winnie that was on display there. He looked up as she walked in and put it back down.

She handed him the wineglass. "Here you go. Want to sit down?"

"Thank you," he said, settling into a corner of her couch. "How did your talk with Susan go?"

"About the way I thought it would."

"And how was that?"

She took a sip of wine. "I'm not sure what you plan to do with her, but I strongly recommend you not be the one to punish her."

He lifted an eyebrow. "Oh?"

"Yes, Sir."

"Why is that?"

"Because that's what she wants. She wants you."

"You must be mistaken."

She rolled her eyes. "Really, Lennox. How out of touch are you? Think about it from her point of view. An elusive Dom. He never plays. You rarely see him. And suddenly he's in your classroom? Come on. I bet every submissive in that classroom wanted the same thing. She was the only one brave enough to do something about it. It's like when a woman tells you she can't orgasm. You take it as a challenge."

"And you think I should just ignore her disregard for protocol?"

"Of course not. I'm suggesting you let Fulton or David deal with it. If you do it, you're playing into her hands."

He at least seemed to be thinking about what she said. Whether he would take her advice was something else entirely. He finished his wine and she offered to pour him another glass, but he politely declined.

"I better not, but thank you." He stood up. "I should be going."

It was driving her crazy that he hadn't brought up the fire alarm. Shouldn't he have at least mentioned it? At least in passing or something? He was almost at the door and, damn it, he wasn't going to talk about it at all.

Just as his hand touched the doorknob, she blurted out, "Did you ever find out anything about the fire alarm?"

Lennox cleared his throat and turned around. "Interestingly enough, the files that contained the security footage have been deleted from the system's hard drive."

Yes! She'd been successful! She forced herself not to smile. "Oh."

"But what the person who deleted them didn't know is that all security videos are copied and sent to my personal hard drive."

The wineglass almost slipped from her hands. She was totally screwed. It hadn't even occurred to her that he would have something like that set up. His expression gave nothing away.

"So you know that . . ." she started.

"That you pulled the alarm?" The corner of his mouth lifted slightly. "Yes. Good night, Marie."

She stood, dumbfounded, as he left and silently closed the door behind him. He knew? He knew she pulled the alarm and he wasn't going to call her on it? Hell, it appeared as if he wasn't even going to bring it up. What did that mean?

She poured another glass of wine, knowing she was getting ready to face another night of insomnia.

WINNIE'S JOURNAL

I did it! I went out with Lennox! We had such a great time, I decided it didn't matter that he was into kink and I'm not. It's just a variation of sex, right? I mean, how bad can it be? Seriously, sex with Lennox? There's no way it can be bad!

I'm going to talk with Marie and see if she can fill me in on this submissive stuff. She's all into it. Heck, she'll probably love the fact that I'm telling her I identify as a submissive. I know Lennox will be thrilled.

I'm so excited!

CHAPTER
Five

Early the next morning, Lennox called Fulton and David into his office. Fulton, who typically got up early in order to send Andie off, was all smiles, but David obviously needed coffee before he became human.

Lennox directed him to the freshly brewed pot and then waited for him to pour a cup and have a few sips before he started speaking. He began by giving them a rundown of what happened the day before. Though he left out the part about Marie being the one to pull the alarm.

He explained what Mariela had discovered and shared her opinion on Susan's discipline. He wrapped up by confirming that neither man had ever had a problem with her in the classroom.

By the time he finished, David looked more alert. "I agree with Mariela," he said and, beside him, Fulton nodded. "I don't think you need to be the one to punish her. Especially if that's the reason she was acting out."

"I agree in theory." Lennox pulled up Susan's file on his laptop. "But I'm afraid it'll be seen as me being weak if someone else administers the punishment and I don't want to give anyone that impression."

"No one who knows you will think that," David assured him.

"The students might think that," Lennox said. While he didn't want to punish Susan, he knew whatever action he took had to be done swiftly and in a manner that was full of confidence. He was grateful to Marie for pulling the alarm, as it got him out of a bad position, but damn, it'd left him in a mess. "The other thing is, I don't want to bring attention to Susan's motives."

"What you could do," Fulton said, his hands wrapped around his own cup of coffee, "is have David or I be the one who actually punishes her while you're in the room, overseeing everything."

It wasn't a bad idea. Lennox thought it had a lot going for it. It was decisive and would get the point across and he wouldn't have to lay a hand on Susan. The more he thought about it, the more he liked it.

"That's a really good idea," David said, echoing Lennox's own thoughts.

"Don't act so surprised," Fulton said. "I do have them on occasion."

David flipped him off.

"That's what we'll do then." Lennox looked at his two most trusted staff members, outside of Marie. "Which one of you will volunteer to be my hands?"

"I'll do it," David said. "I'm afraid Fulton might have gotten too soft since he's in love and shit."

Fulton pointed at him. "I'll bring Andie in here and she can verify I'm no softie."

"That's enough," Lennox said. "If you're finished comparing dick sizes?"

"Sorry, boss." Fulton punched David's shoulder.

Lennox rolled his eyes. "David, I'll let you go inform Susan of our decision. She should be at breakfast now. Tell her to be in dungeon classroom B at eight thirty sharp. Let's get this out of the way."

LATER THAT AFTERNOON he walked down to Marie's office, a fistful of papers in his hand. He'd received them the day before and wanted to share them with her. He'd planned to schedule a meeting, but Marie hadn't attended Susan's punishment session and he hadn't seen her at lunch.

She couldn't hide from him forever.

Her office door was closed, but he heard nothing coming from the other side. She probably wasn't in a meeting. He knocked and at her softly spoken "Come in," he pushed open the door.

She was sitting at her desk and looked up in surprise at him. "Lennox."

"Why do I get the feeling that you're trying to avoid me?" He didn't wait for an invitation, but sat down in the chair across from her desk.

"I don't know. I promise I'm not."

He couldn't help but notice that her normally jovial eyes looked tired and sad today. She had dark circles under her eyes, too. In fact, when he stood back and looked at her as a whole, something didn't seem right.

"Are you okay?" he asked. "You look tired."

"I am. I didn't sleep well last night."

He nodded, knowing all too well how that felt.

"What brings you by?" she asked. "I'm assuming you did have some kind of reason other than to tell me I look like hell."

"I never said that. You're putting words in my mouth."

She didn't come back at him, she just stared at him.

He cleared his throat and brought out the papers he'd carried in with him. "Remember when I mentioned to you that I was thinking about turning the cottage into a public studio or gallery?"

At the mention of those plans, he finally caught a bit of a sparkle in her eyes. "Yes."

"I'd casually brought the idea up to a friend of mine. Actually, the man who helped me with the blueprints for this place." He looked around the office, proud of the academy he'd built. He especially liked Marie's office. He remembered her delight when she saw the barre he'd installed and how he'd insisted the walls be painted in her favorite color, a pale blue.

"I didn't ask him to draw anything," he said. "Truly we had just a casual conversation. But apparently he was inspired and he came up with a few ideas. I'd like for you to see them."

She cleared off an area on her desk. "Yes, I'd love to."

Happy that they were talking about something without arguing, he spread out the papers.

"This one," he said pointing to the first paper on top of the pile, "is a drawing of what the cottage looks like now."

Her eyes grew misty as she looked over the rendering of Winnie's cottage. She sucked in a deep breath. "Wow, it's been a long time since I've seen that place. Brings back memories."

"I'm sorry, I didn't mean to upset you." Damn it, he didn't mean to make her cry. He'd hoped it would be good for her, give them something to talk about.

"It's okay. Just the initial shock, you know?"

He did. All too well.

She ran a finger over the drawing, as if she was seeing it in her mind through her fingertips. "I remember when she bought this place."

Winnie owned the cottage when they met and had left it to him, but he'd never heard the story about how she bought it. "Tell me."

"We had just graduated from college. She had a trust fund that her parents left her and since she had graduated recently, she had access to it. She thought about traveling through Europe, but her financial advisor convinced her to look at real estate. He recommended a few properties and she hated them all."

He laughed, because it sounded so much like what he would imagine her doing. "Let me guess, he recommended city properties. Penthouses. Maybe some commercial properties. That sort of thing."

"Yes. And she would have none of that. We went to Cannon Beach one Saturday. She wanted to spend the afternoon painting and she begged me to come along. I figured why not, so I took a couple books, planned to spend the afternoon reading while she painted."

He wondered if she had painted with joy then. She would have been so young, before she met him. Before he took away her joy.

"We got to the beach," Marie continued. "But we never even had a chance to get her things set up. We were walking down the shore and she saw a cottage for sale. It was horribly run-down. Weeds had taken over the yard. It needed a new roof. You name it, it needed it. But she saw it for what it could become. She said there was something inside yearning to be set free. I told her it was a rat, probably a family of them. I never was as creative as she was. She was always like that, you know? Could see the good at the core, what something might be. And she was right, not only about that cottage—it ended up beautiful—but just about everything else."

Except she hadn't been right about him. She had sorely misjudged Lennox. But as Marie spoke, he pictured Marie and Winnie as young women in his mind. Both of them laughing, joking, having a grand time as they fixed up the cottage.

"We did a lot of the work ourselves," Marie said.

"She told me." He shuffled the papers, putting a new one on top. "She often talked about how much she enjoyed fixing the cottage up with you. That's why I think we won't change a lot of the outside."

He had been awed by the drawing his friend had rendered. Apparently, Marie felt the same. She gasped and her hand flew to her mouth as she studied the second picture.

"It's beautiful."

He nodded. "We leave the outside basically the same." He

pointed to an area off to the side. "Except we install a small garden here. She always mentioned she wanted to do that." He looked over at Marie. Her nod confirmed Winnie must have told her the same thing.

"Yes," Marie said. "She would love that."

"The inside of the cottage will need a little bit more work. I'd like to keep a bedroom."

"Just in case you need a place to stay when you're in town?"

"Something like that."

He was getting ready to show her the ideas his friend had sketched out for the inside when a loud crash out in the hall caused them both to jump.

"What the hell?" he asked, standing up.

Marie rushed past him and opened the door. "Oh no."

Lennox looked out into the hallway, and tried to make sense of what he saw. Andie had Susan pushed against the wall outside of Fulton's office. A discarded tray lay upturned at her side.

"I know fifteen ways to poison you that a medical examiner would never discover. Try me, bitch." Andie's grip tightened on Susan's shirt.

Marie gasped.

"Miss Lincoln," Lennox said in a tone of voice that had been known to put the fear of god in grown men.

Andie didn't budge. "Tell them. Tell them what I just overheard."

"Master MacLure," Susan said. "Thank goodness. This . . . this . . . *lunch lady* attacked me as I was going down the hall."

"I'm a chef, you no good sorry piece of—"

"Andie!" Fulton said from the end of the hall, walking toward them.

At the sound of his voice, Andie dropped her hands. Nobody said anything until Fulton made it to where they stood.

"Everybody into my office," Lennox said. He opened the door to his office and ushered everybody inside, away from the prying eyes of other students and staff that now filled the hallway. He had no idea what had happened between the two women, but he intended to find out. He waited while everyone took a seat.

"This will not turn into a shouting match. You will speak one at a time, when I ask you a question." Once everyone had nodded, he continued. "Andie, you were the most vocal outside, let's begin with you."

Susan raised her hand.

"Yes, Susan," Lennox said.

"Are you really going to listen to her, Sir? After what she did to me in the hallway?"

Lennox crossed his arms. "Miss Lincoln is a trusted member of my staff. Yes, I am going to listen to her. Just as I will listen to you when it's your turn."

Andie cleared her throat. "I was on my way to Fulton's office with a tray full of snacks, when my phone rang. It was Terrence." She looked sideways to where Fulton sat.

Fulton's expression grew hard. "You still talk to Terrence?"

Terrence was Andie's ex, but more than that, he was also one of Lennox's friends, who just happened to be Hollywood's latest golden boy. It was a bit understandable that Fulton wouldn't care for him.

"No, just today. I was so surprised to hear his ringtone, I stopped in the hallway to answer."

Fulton didn't seem overly pleased with this bit of information, but he nodded so she would continue.

"He said he'd had a meeting this morning with a reporter when he happened to mention he'd been in Portland recently." Andie frowned. Probably remembering exactly why he'd been in Portland. He'd been visiting her after she'd had a boating accident and ended up in the hospital. That had also been when she'd broken up with him for good. "The woman he was meeting with got all excited, she said she had a plant doing an undercover assignment at an exclusive adult-only castle. He figured this was the only castle in the area, so he tried to call you, Master MacLure, repeatedly, and when you didn't answer, he called me."

Lennox's stomach fell to his knees and he reached for his phone, remembering he'd turned it off before the session earlier with Susan. He turned it on and within seconds the screen was populated with missed calls. He cursed under his breath.

"Then," Andie said. "I turned the corner into this hallway and I hear her," she pointed to Susan, "on the phone saying the exposé on the headmaster was a bust, but she had an idea about filing assault charges on Fulton."

Fulton stood up. "What the fuck?"

Lennox held his hand up, trying to remain calm even though he was so angry he could have snapped his desk in half. "Susan?"

For her part, Susan looked completely unaffected. Lennox decided she must be more than a model; she was also a damn good actress.

"Let me get this straight," Susan said to Andie. "*You're* the woman who left Terrence Knight all high and dry? You're the one who broke his heart?"

"Yes," Andie said. "Not bad for a lunch lady, is it?"

Fulton put his hand on her shoulder and whispered something to her, though Lennox could see his own control was being tested. Susan looked Fulton up and down as if just noticing him for the first time.

"Damn," she said. "And here I thought it was the headmaster's pants I wanted to get in. Looks like I was going after the wrong Dom."

Andie shot out of her chair. "Listen here—"

She was cut off by Fulton grabbing her and slipping his hand over her mouth. "If it's all the same to you, boss, we're going to leave. If you need us, we'll be at the lighthouse. I don't think it'll be to anyone's benefit for us to stay for the rest of this."

Lennox nodded. Fulton was right. He waited until they left, then called David.

"Master Nader," he said, when the other man picked up. "I need you to go to Susan Mims's room and confiscate her computer and any papers you find. Call me when you finish."

Susan shot up, showing fear for the first time. "Hey, you can't do that."

"I just did." To David, he added. "I can't imagine anyone is in the right frame of mind for class today, so you can go ahead and dismiss them. We'll resume tomorrow."

"Should I stay?" Marie had been so quiet, he'd forgotten she was in the room.

"Yes, please," he said. "I don't think it's a good idea for me to be alone with Miss Mims. I need a witness present or else I have a feeling I'd find myself facing false assault charges."

Susan wisely didn't say anything; she crossed her arms and her legs, bouncing her foot up and down. Marie examined her nails—she looked calm, but he knew all too well how good she was at masking her emotions.

He wondered how he'd been fooled into thinking it'd be a good idea to let Susan enroll. He'd turned her down before. Had she always been planning on throwing him and the school under the bus or was it just this year?

He ran a hand through his hair. Damn it, he was getting too old for this. He enjoyed the academy, but maybe it'd served its purpose. Maybe it was time to let someone else run it. Someone who would actually participate in a scene. He had plenty of business investments on the mainland.

There was only one thing that kept him on the island. He glanced at her and found her watching him. Marie would never live on the mainland. She loved the island too much. And though he'd never admit it, he didn't want to leave her.

He remained standing while he waited for David to call back, the tension mounting as the minutes passed. Fortunately, it didn't take long. Ten minutes after he first called David, his phone rang with a return call.

"Yes," Lennox said, answering.

"It's a hot mess, boss."

Lennox closed his eyes as anger and rage pounded through his veins. "Tell me."

"I haven't even gotten to the computer yet, but her desk is filled with photos and papers she shouldn't have. And there's a notebook that has a rough draft of an article as well as an outline."

Lennox looked over to Susan. She'd stopped bouncing her foot and was biting her lower lip.

"Thank you, David."

He disconnected and leveled his gaze at Susan. "Oh, Miss Mims, you're going to wish you hadn't done that."

WINNIE'S JOURNAL

I wonder if I should ask Marie to teach me how to be a submissive? Do people even do that? I should probably talk to her about it, maybe ask what she thinks Lennox would expect.

But I saw the way she looked at him and I don't know if it'd be asking too much. He asked me out, after all. And I don't say that to be snotty or anything, but it's the truth. I'd like to think that if he'd asked her out, I would step aside and wouldn't interfere.

Marie is like that. She's so into making sure everyone is content and happy. At times I wish I could be more like her. I'm self aware enough to know that most of the time I'm only looking out for me.

If the roles were reversed, Marie would never ask me to teach her. I should probably ask Lennox to do it anyway. Besides, that would be a lot more fun!

CHAPTER
Six

With Susan out of the way and no longer causing trouble, life at the academy fell once more into a predictable schedule. Lennox sightings had been scarce—Mariela knew he'd been meeting with his lawyers about the entire Susan incident, and he rarely made it to the dining hall for meals.

One Friday afternoon, about two weeks after Susan left, Andie dropped by her office.

"Still not able to dance?" Andie asked, looking at the barre that was now a coat rack of sorts.

Mariela shook her head. It had gotten to the point where most days she didn't even try. The way she saw it, if she never tried, she would never fail. Of course, the flip side was she wouldn't know if she was inspired to dance if she never tried.

"No," Mariela answered. "Not yet, but then again, I haven't tried the last few days."

Andie nodded, but seemed distracted. Mariela wondered what was really on her mind and waved her to a chair.

"So," she said as Andie sat down. "What's up with you?"

"Not much, but I've been wondering what's going on with Lennox?"

Mariela laughed. "And here I was getting ready to ask you if you had seen him. I don't even see him at meals."

"He comes to the kitchen early, gets a tray, and takes off." Andie bit her lip. "I know he's been busy with his lawyers since that whole Susan mess, but Fulton said all that was finished days ago. I don't know what his problem is."

Mariela had a sinking suspicion she knew what his problem was. Her.

You're his problem. You know you are.

"We should move forward with our plan," Andie said, as if that would fix everything.

"I don't think so."

That obviously wasn't the answer that Andie had expected. She wrinkled her forehead. "Why not?"

"For several reasons, actually." Mariela hoped she could remember them all. "The whole thing with Susan made me realize that I can't watch him with another woman. And, since the next step would be him playing in a scene, I wouldn't want it to be anybody except me. And trust me, that is not going to happen." Andie looked as if she was going to interrupt, but Mariela kept talking. "Secondly, I don't think I told you, but he knows I'm the one who pulled the alarm."

"How?"

"Apparently, all the camera feeds are duplicated and files are left both on the hard drive and his personal computer. So while I was able to delete the hard drive videos, he still had them on his computer."

"Shit. Does he know that you know?"

Mariela nodded. Though they had spoken several times, he had never brought up the fire alarm again. She knew there was a reason; he wouldn't have mentioned it the first time otherwise. But she had to admit the not knowing and waiting was driving her batty. "Yes, he knows."

"Which is why you don't think he'll want to scene with you?"

"I don't think he's ready. I'm not sure he'll ever be ready. I think I need to accept the fact that he's not going to be the Dominant he once was. Or at least he's not going to act on it."

"I just can't imagine giving that part of myself up."

Mariela knew Andie was early in her submissive journey. It was all exciting and new, especially since Fulton had collared her. In her mind, it would always be that way, and Mariela honestly hoped it was. Maybe for them, it would be.

"I don't get how he's able to do it either. I know I could never be vanilla." Mariela shuddered just thinking about it.

"So what do we do?"

"I think we let it rest for now. Maybe try again next year."

She could tell Andie didn't want to give up. Her new friend wanted to help her get her man. The problem was, he wasn't her man. He had never been. And probably he never would be.

"Okay," Andie said. "I trust you. We have plenty of time."

They changed the subject then, moving on to the upcoming

ball. This would be Andie's first Holiday Ball, and she had already made several menu suggestions. Her excitement was contagious and within minutes they were both making plans and creating lists for everything that needed to be done.

"There you are," Lennox said sometime later, causing them both to look up in surprise at the man standing in her doorway. "Your Master has been looking for you," he told Andie.

Andie looked down at her watch. "Shit. I'm late."

Given that it was a long weekend, the students had left earlier in the day and most wouldn't be back until Tuesday. There were no classes until Wednesday.

"You guys going somewhere?" Mariela asked, doing her best not to look at Lennox.

Of course, it didn't work. Her body knew it had been a long time since they had been in a room together. She was acutely aware of his very presence, how he commanded the room, even with just three of them there. He was behind her, and she swore she could feel his presence.

"We're going to drive up and down the coast. No set schedule or anything. I haven't done much exploring of the west coast since I've been here and have been looking forward to it." Andie hurriedly picked up her papers, told them both good-bye, and left.

She expected Lennox to leave after Andie did, so she was surprised when he stayed in her room. She still didn't have the courage to look at him.

"Any plans this weekend?" he asked.

"No, nothing."

She was hoping with the island empty and no one around that

she might find an interest in dancing again. She was going to try anyway, force herself if she had to.

She turned to look at him. "I don't have to ask where you're going."

"Oh?"

"I'm guessing you're going to your normal Friday night hang-out." She wasn't sure why she brought it up. Why now, after all these years of saying nothing?

"You're mistaken, Marie." He sounded angry. "In fact, I haven't gone to my normal Friday night hangout in weeks."

"Is that right? Do you expect a gold star?" She thought back and realized it was true—he hadn't gone off the island for several weeks. Interesting.

"No, but I do expect you to talk to me with respect."

She didn't reply to that. She was curious about why he'd changed his routine. "Did you get tired of the anonymous thing?" She rolled her eyes at his glare. "Did you get tired of the anony-mous thing, *Sir*?"

She was being a huge brat, she knew she was. Probably because deep down, she wanted him to take charge and do something, damn it.

"Did it ever once occur to you that Doms don't like being with subs who are so blatantly disrespectful?" His voice was ice.

"Let's face it," she said. "I work at a BDSM academy. Most scenes I'm in, I'm working with newbie Doms who wouldn't know they were being topped from the bottom if I told them that's what I was doing."

"I don't doubt there's truth to that. In fact, I believe a thorough session with a belt would do you good."

She cocked an eyebrow. "You volunteering? Because we just might be the only people left on the island."

"No, I'm not volunteering. Though I do think I'll ask Master Nader to work on your lack of manners next week."

"Not man enough to do the job yourself?" She snorted. "Sort of makes me wish I'd let you try to lift a hand to Susan. You probably couldn't do it."

"As fun as this is, I am leaving the island. I'm going to the cottage." He turned to leave, but looked back over his shoulder. "I am man enough to do the job, but you aren't worthy of my belt."

She sat with her mouth dropped open in shock. How dare he? How fucking dare he? The longer she sat there, the angrier she became. She moved to where she could see the boat dock, and twenty minutes after Lennox left, she decided to do the one thing she never thought she'd do again.

She was going to go to Winnie's cottage.

WINNIE'S JOURNAL

He's going to do it! Lennox has agreed to train me as his submissive! He's also taken to calling me "Winnie girl." I don't know why my stomach gets all tingly when he says it.

One of my concerns was that he'd expect me to be submissive all the time. According to Marie, some couples are like that. But when I brought it up to him, he said he wasn't into that. That he only wanted a submissive in the bedroom. I think I can do that!

We're not going to start training yet, though. He said he wanted to wait until we'd been dating for a few months before he introduced kink into our relationship.

CHAPTER

Seven

Mariela's anger hadn't abated by the time she pulled into the driveway of Winnie's old place. Especially when she spotted Lennox's SUV parked outside.

The wind from the approaching storm blew her hair into her face when she got out of the car. She paid it little attention. Even less attention than she paid the light rain that began to fall. Oh, yes, this storm was going to get worse, and not just the one outside.

She didn't knock. Winnie had given her a key years ago. As quietly as she could, she unlocked the door and stepped inside, wanting to surprise Lennox. She didn't find him downstairs though. Which only left the room upstairs. Damn it.

She didn't want to go into Winnie's old studio, but she took the stairs two at a time. The top landing opened into what had once been a beautiful studio but now looked more like a shrine.

"I didn't think you ever traveled off the island," Lennox said, from a chair facing the window.

Talking to his back only made her angrier. "What the hell is your problem?"

"Right now my problem is an obnoxious submissive who won't mind her own damn business."

She took a deep breath. "Mind my own business, how about you stay around to finish a conversation."

"You came all the way here so we could continue our argument?"

She crossed her arms. "Yes."

"Liar."

"What?"

He slowly stood up and turned around. She'd thought he might have been drinking and half expected him to be drunk, but the man looking back at her was completely sober. Yet there was a wildness in him. His hair was tousled and his normally perfect shirt and tie were both askew. But it was his eyes. His eyes were raw and hungry. "I said *liar.*" He took a step toward her, and she felt the heat radiating from him. "Tell me why you're really here."

She would have taken a step back if she wasn't afraid she'd fall backward down the stairs. "I told you, I wanted to finish our conversation."

"We weren't having a conversation, you were insulting me. I want to know why you're really here and you're going to tell me. Now."

She had wanted to awaken the Dominant within him. She could see now she'd vastly underestimated what would happen when that beast stirred. "I . . . I . . ."

Fuck, why was she stuttering? She never stuttered. And this was Lennox. Lennox who never gave her the time of day.

"You want to know what I think?" he asked. "I think you believed if you baited me enough that I'd punish you. Pulling Susan's trick? Or did you believe that I would somehow magically be healed and you could pat yourself on the back for making me better?"

Tears filled her eyes. How could he be so blind? Had she not basically thrown herself at him for the last three years? It hit her then—it was never going to happen between them. Never. They were never going to be together and she'd been counting on that fantasy for so long, she didn't know how to live without it.

"You ass. You damn foolish ass." She didn't even try to stop the tears. "You have no idea, do you?"

He didn't say anything, he just stared at her.

"I don't want to fucking heal you to make myself feel better or to pat myself on the back. I wanted you, you asshole. I wanted you to want me."

Lightning flashed, illuminating the dim room momentarily, and she hated the darkness that followed the bright light because it hid his reaction.

"You don't want me, Marie."

"You don't get to tell me what I want. You think I didn't know who you were before Winnie introduced us? Do you honestly believe that just because that was the first time you met me that I didn't know who you were? You pompous ass. I wanted you long before you even met her."

He was a mess. A complete and utter mess and she'd spent

too much of her life trying to fix him. Well, she was done. Done. Done. Done. He was never going to change and it was time she accepted that.

"Know what?" she asked, decided and feeling fully alive for the first time in years. "I don't even care anymore. Screw you. I'll find someone who sees me as more than their dead girlfriend's best friend because you know what? I'm worth it."

She turned on her heel, determined to make it to her car before she broke down. She made it to the first step before he spoke.

"Stop."

She stopped, but she didn't turn around. "You don't control me, Lennox."

"That's one. Address me properly, sub."

She lifted her hand and flipped him the bird.

"That's two."

She still didn't turn around, although something in the tone of his voice made her knees turn to jelly. "Two what? You don't have the balls—"

She couldn't finish what she was saying, because he'd moved as quickly and as quietly as a ninja and wrapped his hand around her mouth. "Your safe word is *red*. Say it and everything stops. We go back to how we were before and we never bring this up. Understand?"

She tried to say something, but she couldn't with his hand covering her mouth, so she just nodded.

"You think you want me? You have no idea what I'm like."

She wanted to argue to tell him she did know, but the truth was, she didn't.

"But you're getting ready to find out."

He marched her down the stairs, through the short hallway, and into the cottage's small guest room. Once they made it to the middle of the room, he pulled her to a stop. "Strip."

"I think we should—"

"Quiet. You're not here to think. You've been doing enough of that lately. Tonight, I'm the one doing the thinking. Now strip. You don't want to find out what will happen if I have to say it again."

She was pretty sure she did, but more than that, she wanted to find out where this was going. What he was going to do. What he was going to do to her or what he was going to have her do. If she goaded him too much, he might decide to do nothing and she didn't think she could stand that.

With trembling hands, she slipped her tunic shirt over her head and let it flutter to the floor. She pushed her skirt down and stepped out of it, then she toed off her shoes. She stood in her underwear, wondering. . . .

"All your clothes, Marie. I want to see every last inch of you."

She didn't know why his command gave her pause. She was a submissive on his staff, of course he'd seen her naked before. Yet this seemed so much more personal and intimate.

She unhooked her bra and slid it from her shoulders. He remained expressionless as she pushed her thong down and stepped out. She felt exposed under his gaze and she closed her eyes, unable to stand under the weight of his stare.

He was so quiet and the rain was so loud, she jumped at the sound of his voice, inches from her ear.

"You may be right about me not knowing who you were before her, but you can be damn sure I never forgot you after. You think

I'm distant and cold because I don't feel anything and don't want you? Let me assure you, I feel deeply and I want you too much."

She gasped at his words. It couldn't be true. It just couldn't. Surely, if it was, she would have picked up on it before now.

"How—"

"Shh." He placed a finger over her lips and his voice sounded low and dangerous. "This is not the time for you to be talking. You wanted me to remember my Dominant side? To revive it? Guess what? I have and right now, it's all directed at you. One more slipup like that and you won't like the consequences. Understand?"

Her heart raced at the thought, even as a shiver ran through her body. "Yes, Sir."

"Very good. Now get on your knees."

With as much grace as she could with her body trembling so much in anticipation, she lowered herself to her knees. Would he touch her soon? So far, he'd mostly kept his hands to himself.

"You have no idea the things I want to do to you and that body of yours. Tell me, Marie, do you want to find out?"

"Yes, Sir." For the love of god, yes.

"Ground rules," he said. "For tonight, I'm not your employer. This has nothing to do with the academy. Anything we do, we do because we want to. Agreed?"

"Yes, Sir."

"Stand up."

She couldn't imagine why he wanted her to do so, she'd only just got to her knees. He moved from behind her to stand in front of her. Once more, his eyes were piercing.

After she stood, he placed his hand behind her neck. "I can't resist you anymore."

She whimpered because she wanted to tell him not to try, but he'd told her to be quiet. His fingers tightened around her neck.

"Tonight, you're mine. Say it."

"Tonight, I'm yours, Sir." Her voice was raspy, even to her own ears.

He didn't respond with words; rather, he pulled her to him and covered her lips with his. Before, his kiss had been intense, but she'd known he'd been holding back. Tonight, there was nothing held back. He was raw and unrestrained, and when he parted her lips and pillaged her mouth, she wondered what she'd freed.

She felt his desire and need to her very bones, but she didn't fear it. She relished it, rejoiced in it, and she wanted to give him everything she had. She moaned into his mouth and, though she thought for a second he might pull back, he didn't. He actually dropped one hand to rest right above her ass.

He broke the kiss, only to push her closer with a hand on her lower back, causing her to press against his erection. "You want this cock?"

It took all her self-control not to grind herself against it. "Yes, Sir."

"It's been too damn long since I've fucked anyone. I'm going to use you and use you hard. Tell me now if that's not what you want."

If he thought that was going to make her change her mind, he was dead wrong. She licked her lips. "Tonight, I'm yours, Sir. Use me however you need to."

She prepared for him to touch her or to tell her to get on her knees, but he did neither. He crossed his arms.

"Tell me why you pulled the fire alarm."

Her face heated. Damn him for bringing that up. And why now? Why now, when it seemed as if everything she'd wanted was finally within her grasp? But he stood there, his arms crossed and that stubborn look on his face and she knew that they had to get through this before they could continue with anything else.

"I was watching the live feed, Sir—"

"Why?"

She took a deep breath. Was she going to have to confess everything? "I wanted to make sure you were okay, Sir. I knew it had been a long time since you'd done anything related to a scene."

He nodded, his face showed no emotion. "Go on."

"I saw what happened. I knew you were going to punish Susan. . . ."

"And you thought I couldn't do it?"

"That was only a little part of it."

"What was the rest?"

She bit her lip. Fuck, this was embarrassing. And he was going to be pissed. She shook her head.

"Last warning," he practically growled.

"I didn't want you to touch her. She didn't deserve to have you touch her."

"Explain."

"Damn it, Lennox—"

He snapped his fingers. "Hush. Answer the question and only answer the question. And call me Lennox one more time and you'll be sorry."

She took a deep breath. "You haven't done a scene in years. *Years.* And I'll be damned if some submissive who thinks she's the end-all be-all is going to traipse into the academy and be the first one to kneel for you."

"Why do you have a problem with that? You think it should be you?"

She lifted her chin. "Of course," she said, and hoped he didn't ask her to explain.

"It seems it's your lucky night then, because we have quite a few things to settle between us. You spying on me, your blatant disrespect, and I believe you've only used the proper form of address twice since you walked in here tonight."

He was going to punish her? No fucking way. They hadn't been in a scene. "You can't do that, Sir." Though, she had to admit, she had just said she'd been spying on him.

"On the contrary, Marie. I most certainly can, but even more than that, I think you want me to." He nodded toward the bed. "Go lean over the bed."

Damn him for being right. She did want him to do this, but the most important thing was, he wasn't backing down. He'd told her what he was going to do and he was standing by it.

Finally.

She moved to the foot of the bed and closed her eyes because she feared that if she looked around the room, she'd see Winnie. This was her house. Mariela was in her guest bedroom. Naked in front of Winnie's lover and Dom.

She swallowed, trying to ignore the feelings of guilt that threatened to overtake her. The guilt that whispered how dare she act this way in her best friend's house. And told her that what she was doing was a betrayal of their friendship.

She heard Lennox move behind her and she wondered if he felt guilty.

"I don't have anything resembling a toy bag here," he said. "So I'll have to improvise."

No, she decided, from the sound of it, he didn't feel guilty at all. Then his hands were on her backside and they felt so good, she shoved anything remotely related to guilt or Winnie out of her mind.

"I'm not going to bind you," he said. "But you should know that I'm going to take my time. It's been far too long since I've punished anyone's ass and I'm going to enjoy every stroke I give you."

She wondered how many that would be, but didn't ask.

"The sight of your backside makes me so damn hard. I can just imagine how tight your ass would be around my cock." He pinched her butt cheek. "I might have to fuck you there first. Always liked the thought of punishment ass fucking."

She took a ragged breath. She hadn't planned on him being a talker, but it was seriously hot.

"Would you like that?" he asked. "For me to push my cock up your ass and fuck it hard and deep? Pound into it over and over?"

She could only whimper, because she couldn't remember ever being so turned on by words alone.

He slapped her butt hard. Twice. "Answer me."

"Yes, Sir. I would." And she'd love every second of it.

"Maybe later."

She heard the unmistakable sound of a belt being pulled out of pant loops and felt herself grow wetter. She hadn't noticed he had a belt on, but truly, his outfit hadn't been where her attention was focused.

For all his dirty talk just moments before, he was silent as he started spanking her with his hand. She shifted her weight a bit, because, oww, the man spanked hard. She sucked in a breath through her teeth.

It had been over six months since someone other than a Dom-in-training had spanked her. If she'd thought Lennox would be out of practice, he'd just proved her wrong.

"Shit," she grunted as a particularly hard smack of his hand landed just under her butt cheek.

"Unless you're thanking me or saying 'Please, Sir, spank me harder,' keep it to yourself." He didn't sound the slightest bit out of breath.

She shifted her feet.

"And stay still. Honestly, you're speaking out of turn and moving around. I have to say, Marie, this would not be a very good example for the students to see."

She didn't care about the students at the moment. They were the furthest thing from her mind. All she could think about was how she had never dreamed Lennox could spank so hard.

"It's not really a punishment if I go easy on you, is it?" he asked, and she realized she must have voiced her thoughts out loud.

"No, Sir."

"Did you think that because it has been awhile since I spanked someone that I'd forgotten how to do it?"

While they were talking, he continued raining hard smacks across her ass. Yet his voice remained steady and even. Unlike hers.

"No, Sir," she said, and she ended with a yelp as the belt landed on her backside for the first time.

He didn't talk anymore after that, which was fine with her.

The silence allowed her to disappear into her mind, to marvel that it was Lennox she was submitting to. That thought alone warmed her body and she gladly took everything he gave her.

She relaxed her muscles, absorbing the brief pain that followed the strike of the belt and enjoying the warmth left in its wake. He knew just how to spank in order to get the most reaction out of her. But she had moved beyond responding. She was free and Lennox was with her, urging her onward and upward.

More.

More.

More.

She wanted all of him. Every ounce he was willing to give her, she'd soak up. He was water and she was dying of thirst. He would sustain her if she just gave herself over to him.

She didn't have to contemplate whether she would or not.

"Marie," he said, sometime later and she jerked, becoming aware that he'd stopped.

"Mmm," she hummed and wiggled her backside. "Green, Sir."

"I think that's enough for now." He gave a low chuckle and stroked her back, massaging her and slowly bringing her down. When she was more alert, he sighed. "I can't remember the last time I sent someone into subspace."

Was it her imagination or did he sound sad? She decided it must be her imagination because when he told her to stand, he didn't sound sad, he sounded wicked.

"Turn around," he said, and her heart raced because there was nothing but lascivious intent in his voice.

She turned, slowly, drawing out the anticipation and enjoying the rush of excitement that followed his command. But when she turned, her jaw nearly hit the ground because he'd taken his clothes off and, holy hell, what the sight of him naked did to her body.

She'd known Lennox for years, longer than he'd known Winnie, and even though he'd been active in the lifestyle when she first became aware of him, she'd never seen him naked. She couldn't take her eyes off of him.

"Oh my god," she whispered, and for the first time since becoming a submissive, she strongly considered disobeying on purpose. Because whatever and however he'd punish her would be worth it for the chance to touch him.

"Surely you've seen a naked man before?" Lennox teased and then, probably to drive her completely out of her mind with lust, he took himself in his hand and pumped.

Her gaze was locked on his erection and the way he worked it. "Yes, Sir," she said in response. "But never one so magnificently put together."

Because he was, from the cut muscles of his chest to the curves of his biceps. She was certain his cock was just as incredible, but she'd only caught a glimpse of it before he'd taken it in his hand.

He looked faintly amused at her statement. "I don't think anyone's ever said that to me before."

"Then they were blind, Sir."

"You're very kind to an old man, Marie."

"Beg your pardon, Sir, but you know how you Doms get all bent out of shape when a sub says something negative about themselves?"

"Yes."

"I totally get that now, you shouldn't talk down about yourself."

He nodded. "Point taken. I'm the hottest thing to ever walk the face of the earth."

Who was this man before her? The one who was actually joking? She couldn't remember him joking on the island. She wasn't sure if it was the cottage or being naked or if spanking her had brought out this part of his personality.

She tilted her head. "Now you're just being cocky, Sir."

"Perhaps," he said. "But speaking of cock." He lifted an eyebrow.

Her belly was suddenly filled with flutters. "Yes, Sir."

"On the bed, on your back, with your head at the edge."

She had a fairly good idea of where this was going, so she licked her lips and got into the position he requested. He walked toward her, still fisting himself, and her mouth ached to taste him.

Finally, he stood at her head, his hand right near her mouth. "Open."

She parted her lips and waited. She'd thought he'd enter her mouth fast and hard, but he surprised her by taking his time. She licked the head of his cock and was rewarded by his groan of pleasure.

"Fuck," he said, pushing in slowly, inch by inch. "I somehow knew you'd have the sweetest mouth."

Positioned like they were, her body was completely available to him for his pleasure. He could touch or kiss her as he wished, or he could do nothing at all.

She hoped he did something.

Please.

"Spread your legs, Marie." He tapped them gently. "Let me see where I'm going next."

She parted her legs with a hint of a moan on her lips, but just a hint, because he chose that second to push deep into her mouth. She opened her throat for him and he took possession. His hissed pleasure only made her wetter.

He slipped a hand between her legs and teased her, his fingers dancing across her inner thighs. "Fuck, I can smell you."

It took all her years of training to remain still when what she really wanted to do was lift her hips up to his touch. If he'd just shift his fingers a tiny bit . . .

But he knew that and he didn't. He kept them right where they were, keeping her aroused, but not doing anything about it.

Much sooner than she anticipated, he groaned and withdrew from her mouth. It occurred to her that he might be struggling with keeping his control as well.

"I have to stop," he said, breathing heavily. "It's been too damn long."

"Please, Sir," she couldn't help but beg.

"Please what?" he asked, as if he didn't know.

"Take me. Use me. Fuck me."

"Marie," he chided. "Are you telling me what to do? Because that's bad, and bad submissives don't get my cock."

"Sorry, Sir."

"That's more like it." He stepped back from the bed. "Flip your body around so your ass is at the edge of the bed."

She positioned herself the way he asked and it wasn't until she did so that she noticed she was at the perfect level for him.

He leaned over her and she felt the heat from his body. "There's so much I want to do to you and we have all night, but I need to take the edge off first. Your job is to remain still and quiet. And no coming. I haven't decided if I'm going to let you come tonight or not."

Was he serious?

But one look at his expression told her he was completely serious. Still, what would be the worst that would happen if she came?

"I know what you're thinking," he said with a self-satisfied grin.

"I was unaware that you were a mind reader, Sir," she couldn't help but say.

He slapped the inside of her thigh. "Are you being disrespectful, Marie? Thinking that maybe since I've been out of the scene for so long that I'll allow you to talk back like that?"

"No, Sir," she said, but in reality, she knew there was a part of her that wanted to see how far she could push him. She had the feeling the answer was, not far.

"Back to what I was saying," he said. "If you do come without permission, I'm going to punish that naughty pussy first with my hand and then with my belt. Understand?"

"Yes, Sir." She knew she wouldn't come without permission now. No way. She wasn't going to have him use a belt on her most private parts.

"Good girl." He teased her inner thighs with both hands and she had no problem being still, but when he took his thumbs and started rubbing her slit, she had to fist her hands.

Holy fuck. His hands.

He may not have been in a scene for years, but his hands definitely remembered how to touch a woman *just so* in order to have her dancing on the edge of orgasm. She'd thought since it'd been so long and because he'd indicated how badly he needed to take the edge off, that he'd make quick work of foreplay.

In fact, she'd been betting on it.

But she'd have lost that bet and, to be completely fair, it made sense that he would show the same intensity with sex that he showed with everything else. His fingers somehow knew just how to stroke her and she bit the inside of her cheek to keep from moaning.

Finally, she heard the rustle of foil.

"Look at me, Marie."

She hadn't known she'd closed her eyes, but she opened them to find his intense stare upon her. Though there was a slight softness she hadn't ever seen before.

"I've been fantasizing about this for years," he said, and his voice was rougher than it'd been moments before. "I want you to know exactly who's entering you."

She wanted to tell him that there was no way she wouldn't know, but he'd told her to be quiet, so she obeyed. It was almost too much, looking into his eyes as he started the careful push into her body. He was completely unguarded, or at least more unguarded than she'd ever seen him. His gaze was so intense and yet it held the emotion she'd always suspected he buried under his normal dour expression.

She couldn't help the tiny gasp that escaped her as he thrust completely inside her. It was more than sex, more than the joining of their two bodies into one. This was Lennox, the man she'd wanted for more years than she could count and what they were doing transcended anything she'd ever done before. Somehow she knew that she would never experience anything similar with anyone else.

"Jesus, Marie," he said, and he broke eye contact first, throwing his head back as he began a slow pumping rhythm. "So good."

He lifted her hips and on his next thrust, he went even deeper, hitting a different spot inside her. Gradually, he picked up speed, still going as deep, but the speed had her rushing toward release, until she remembered that she wasn't allowed.

She tried to count by threes, then she did multiplication tables in her head, until she couldn't remember six times seven. Finally, she settled on running through ballet moves, over and over.

"I'm going to come so hard," he said. "Hold yours back and I'll reward you."

It was damn near the hardest thing she'd ever done. But she called upon all her strength and even when he thrust deeper inside her than he'd been before and released into the condom, she held back.

He leaned over her, placing his hands on either side of her, breathing heavily. She wanted his weight on her, wanted to feel him pushing her down, holding her under him. He ran his hands up and over her body, and since she hadn't climaxed, she quickly found herself on the edge again.

"So good, Marie," he murmured. "Everything about you is good."

She loved how strong she felt being able to make a man like Lennox let go of his control. Knowing she was the one who'd finally broken through his defenses and touched the Dominant inside him was heady. She wondered if what she felt was something similar to how a Dom felt when a submissive yielded to their control.

If so, she understood the appeal.

He pushed back up from the bed. "Everything was good, but if you think I'm finished with you, you are sorely mistaken. I'm just getting started."

She shivered under his smoldering gaze that promised so much. Wanting to please him, she remained still and waited for instructions. Besides, he might've had some relief, but she was still on the edge.

"Go to the bathroom and clean up," he said. "You have five minutes. Then meet me in the living room."

She took her time getting out of bed, wanting to see what he was going to do, but he gave her ass a quick slap and told her to get to it. Not wanting to provoke him further, she waited until she had twenty seconds remaining and hurried into the living room.

She tried to take in everything he'd set out, but as soon as she stepped into the room, he said, "Eyes on me. None of that concerns you right now."

She didn't want him to find any fault in her—she wanted to be the best damn submissive he'd ever been with. She pushed everything from her mind and focused on him. His eyes were dark and held a hint of wicked pleasure as she walked toward him. Without being told, she went to her knees before him and bowed her head.

He dug his fingers into her hair. "Someone's being a good girl now."

She remained silent, looking at the floor.

He chuckled. "Someone must really want to come soon."

Again she didn't say anything because one, it wasn't a question and two, duh.

He didn't say anything else, but she heard him step away, and then came the rustling of a cloth. It was several more seconds before he spoke again.

"When you stand up, you'll see I have a sheet on the floor. I want you on your back on top of it."

She almost moved, but remembered in time that he hadn't told her to stand, he said *when you stand*. She waited.

"Good girl," he said. "You may stand now."

Obeying his earlier command not to look around, she only looked at the floor to find the sheet. It was plaid, and she didn't recognize it. He must've brought it out of his car. Somehow that made her feel better, knowing that she wasn't using Winnie's things.

She situated herself on the sheet, and waited.

"Hands above your head, and knees spread." His voice was rough again, gravelly, and filled with desire.

She moved into the position he wanted, feeling horribly exposed as she did so. But this was Lennox, and she knew him; more than that she trusted him. And, holy hell, did she want him.

"Lovely," he said. "You are beautiful in your submission."

And when he said things like that, she wanted him forever.

He started whistling, *whistling*. She had never heard him do that before. Was it something he always did in a scene? Or was it just her? Either way, it made her happy. She couldn't remember the last time she had seen or heard him be so carefree. Surely now he would see how he needed his Dominant nature, and he wouldn't repress anymore.

She watched as he walked to the blanket and sat beside her.

"I like you spread out for me like this. So trusting and giving. Seeing you like this is a feast for my soul." He brushed a wayward piece of hair from her forehead. "Now, I did promise that if you held off on coming that I would make it worth it, didn't I?"

"Yes, Sir," she whispered.

"You should know I always keep my promises. Here's what we're going to do: I'm going to spend time learning everything I can about your body." He rose to his knees. "Close your eyes and just feel. Don't move."

Her heart pounded and her mouth was so dry. She still couldn't believe they were together like this. She took one more glance at him, just to make sure it was real, and closed her eyes. Almost immediately, his hands were on her.

First, he stroked her collarbone. "Your skin is so pale and delicate. I'm almost afraid to touch you. But from that spanking I gave you earlier I know there's nothing fragile about you. You are a strong and determined woman and you turn me on so much."

Heaven help her if he decided to talk the entire time he touched her. There was no way she could remain still.

Light as a feather and so soft she thought she imagined it, his fingers brushed down her arms. "I wonder if you like light touches." His fingertips danced along her ribs, stroked the inside of her elbow, and gently canvassed her belly.

Yes, she wanted to shout, she liked light touches.

"Hmm," he hummed. "I'll take those goose bumps to be a positive sign. But I wonder . . ." His hands left for a brief second and when they came back, he pinched her nipple.

It was so unexpected, she couldn't hold back her gasp of surprise.

"Yes," he said, his voice a combination of humor and lust. "You like it harder, too. Don't you?"

"Yes, Sir." She answered him quickly, hoping that in doing so, he'd give her more.

He didn't disappoint—almost immediately, he pinched her other nipple, but this time when he let go, his mouth replaced his fingers. When he sucked her deep into his mouth, the pleasure was so intense, she saw stars for a few seconds. When he let go, she was torn between not wanting him to repeat his action on the other side for fear of pleasure overload and desperately wanting him to continue.

But when he nibbled at her other breast, she realized she was in more trouble than she had ever imagined, and for the first time in all her years as a submissive, she understood why Doms were called "Master." Because the way Lennox worked her body and drew out feeling after feeling and sensation after sensation was nothing short of masterful.

He continued playing with her breasts for several minutes, or maybe it was an hour, she had no frame of reference and couldn't really tell how much time had passed. Nor did she care. He did exactly what he said he was going to do.

He explored every inch of her, testing different touches and teasing relentlessly. She had no doubt he was cataloging every response and would never forget a reaction. Though she did nothing but remain still under his scrutiny, when he pulled back, she felt like she had run a marathon.

"What are you thinking?" he asked, and it wasn't until he smoothed his fingers over her brow, that she realized she'd had it wrinkled.

Tonight she vowed there would be nothing other than honesty between them. "That I've never experienced anything more incredible in my life."

"You looked as if you were thinking very hard."

"I was trying to decide if you were real, Sir."

He brushed her cheekbone with his knuckles. "Does this feel fake?"

"Not so much fake, Sir. More like too good to be true."

"On the contrary." His hand brushed lower, sweeping down her side and coming to rest on her hip. "What's too good to be true is you here, spread out like this for me. Why do you think I want to spend so much time exploring you?"

"I don't know, Sir."

"Because the more details I can learn about you, the more I can convince myself you're really here."

She wanted to reach out and touch him, but told herself that there would be time for that later. Instead, she simply said, "I'm not going anywhere, Sir."

"Not for tonight, anyway," he said, and before she could answer, he lowered his head and his lips were on hers in a kiss that left no doubt as to what his plans were for the rest of the night. His exploration of her continued with his kiss. He was equal parts soft and demanding, but she knew he was being just as thorough in his study of how she liked to kiss as he'd been in determining how she liked her breasts touched.

He tilted his head and she parted her lips under his because in this, this kiss, she could explore and study him as well. She nibbled on his lower lip, smiling to herself at the groan of pleasure he couldn't suppress when she nipped it harder.

"Looks as though I'm not the only one who likes soft and hard in equal measure, Sir," she whispered against his lips when he pulled back a bit.

"Not by a long shot." He moved so he was holding himself over her, stationed between her legs. She shifted her hips slightly, brushing his erection as she did. He let out a low growl.

"I think I could spend hours kissing you, Sir."

He gave her a brief kiss. "Yes, but then we might not have time for other things."

"Other things, Sir? That's a bit vague. Perhaps you better explain."

His eyes grew even darker and his voice was much lower when he replied. "Other things. Like me pushing your knees apart and telling you to hold yourself wide open for me so I can feast on your pussy. Or maybe telling you to get on your hands and knees with your ass in the air and your sex exposed for my viewing pleasure. With you in that position, I could take my cock in my hand, stroke it lightly, and imagine how good it's going to feel when I sink it deep and hard inside you."

He thrust his hips forward just a touch, just enough to where she got the briefest hint of his erection. "Do you feel me? Feel how ready I am to slide into you deep and fuck you hard?"

"Yes, Sir. Please."

He gave a short laugh. "Oh, it's *please* now, is it?"

Damn him, damn him, damn him for teasing her. It was cruel and unusual. Especially when he'd told her to be still. She'd like for him to try to be still with someone whispering naughty things to him while at the same time teasing his cock. She'd bet he couldn't do it.

She gave her hips a slight wiggle. Which, of course, he noticed.

"If you want this cock again and if you want to come sometime in the next few hours, I suggest you remain still the way I asked you to," he said, and the tone of his voice made it clear he was completely serious. "Is that clear?"

"Yes, Sir," she said, pleased she didn't whine.

"Are you going to be good and stay still?"

Was he serious with all the questions? "Yes, Sir."

His grin went from merely evil to totally diabolical. "Excellent, because now I'm going to do exactly what I said. Hold your knees wide open for me so I can taste your pussy."

She wanted to groan and tell him that he was the devil incarnate, but at the last minute she decided she'd much rather have his mouth on her.

"Good girl," he said when she closed her eyes and obeyed. "I'm impressed. You gave serious thought to talking back, didn't you?"

Her eyes flew open. How did he know?

"It surprises you that I know you so well, doesn't it?" he asked, getting into position between her legs. "I'm not sure why. I've known you for years. You work for me. I pay attention and I know how your mind works."

She swallowed. Someone had been paying attention. A lot more attention than she'd thought possible. She wasn't quite sure what to do with that information.

But it wasn't the appropriate time to think about such things right now. Not with him settled between her legs, his breath hot against the skin of her inner thighs. His lips so close, she could almost feel them. She'd think about it later.

He peppered kisses along her upper leg, from her knee to just below the juncture of her thighs. His fingers circled dangerously close to her clit.

Much, much later.

In the same way he'd shown mastery of her breasts, he did the same below her waist. Except this time, there was no rough, no hard. Only soft, achingly tender kisses and caresses. She had no doubt he would be just as knowledgeable and devastating while being rougher, but the way he tasted her, the method he used to please her, worked in such a way that every wall she'd ever put up was shattered. With his reverent touch, he slowly peeled away any remaining mask, so that even though she'd been naked before him for quite some time, now she was completely exposed in a way that left her feeling even more vulnerable.

His tongue delved into her and her arms shook with the effort it took to be still. Her breath came out in pants, because his mouth on her was the most incredible experience.

Just when she thought she couldn't hold out any longer, he pulled back. "I could do that for hours," he said with a grin that told her he knew exactly how wild she felt and how close to the edge he'd brought her. "And I might be tempted to do just that if I didn't need to be inside you so badly."

Thank goodness he felt the same, because there was no way she'd last hours with him doing that.

"You remember how I said I wanted to fuck you?" he asked, rising to his knees.

She tried not get her hopes up that he was finally going to take her again. "Yes, Sir."

"Get that way." He stroked his cock, almost lazily.

She scurried to get up on her hands and knees facing away

from him. Though she expected it, she jerked when he ran a hand across her backside.

"Much as I'd like to fuck this ass, I can't seem to get enough of your pussy tonight." He dipped a finger inside her. "You're so wet for me, aren't you?"

"Yes, Sir."

He hummed in acknowledgment and she gave a silent cheer when she heard a foil packet crinkle. "I should have let you do this, but I'm afraid I'd come the second your hand touched my cock and what would be the fun in that?"

He pressed against her opening and she struggled not to push back to get him inside quicker.

"Be still until I say differently and I'll let you come."

Thank goodness. She decided to focus all her attention on remaining still. A plan that worked right up until he started the slow push into her. A throaty moan escaped because somehow he felt even bigger than before, especially positioned the way they were.

"That's okay," he said when she tried to stifle her moan. "Let me hear you. Just don't move."

Free to voice her pleasure, she made sure he heard exactly how much she liked what he was doing. "Yes. Ugh. Yes. Harder."

He grabbed her hair and pulled back. "Who's fucking you, Marie?"

"You are, Sir."

He gave her hair a jerk. "Say my name, damn it."

"Lennox," she said, the latter part of his name coming out in a moan as he adjusted his next thrust. "Yes, like that."

He smacked her ass. "Are you telling me how to fuck you?" he asked, never breaking stride.

"Sorry, Sir." She had to stop talking, she was getting dangerously close to babbling. "It just feels so good."

"Show me. Move those hips. Fucking take me. Come whenever you can."

She could have wept with relief. Finally. She moved her hips in time with his, angling to take him deeper and loving every second that he was inside her. This was what she'd been waiting for all those years. What she'd wanted. She'd always envisioned Lennox being like no one else, but had wondered if that was just wishful thinking on her part. Now she knew she'd been right.

His grip on her hair tightened, and he started moving faster and harder. She didn't think anything else had ever felt as good. Her orgasm was approaching quickly and she did everything she could to hold it at bay, simply because she didn't want this moment to pass.

He slipped his other hand between them and circled her clit. "I'm not coming first. Get there."

She knew with his hand working her clit and the angle he was hitting with his thrusts, there was no hope of her stopping anything. She relaxed her body and let it crash over her.

Lennox kept driving into her and as soon as her first orgasm passed, another prepared to take its place.

"Yes," he grunted. "Again."

This time when she came, he followed, pushing deep inside her and holding still as he released into the condom.

Exhausted, she collapsed on the floor, stunned when he followed. But unlike every other man she'd ever been with, he didn't stay beside her. He held himself over her back, peppering kisses up and down her spine.

"My god, you're perfect," he whispered along her skin in a low voice she wasn't sure was meant for her ears. He dropped his head and trailed more kisses along her shoulder blades; his face was prickly and gooseflesh popped up along where he kissed.

She'd thought they would go to bed now, turn in, call it a night. But when he trailed a hand between her legs, she realized she was mistaken. Again?

He chuckled, telling her she'd spoken out loud. "Yes, again. Being with you does something to me. Give me a few minutes and I'll be ready."

It should be impossible for a man of his age to get hard again so fast, but after only a few minutes of caresses and dirty talk, he was ready again. Heaven help her, he was going to make her overdose on orgasms.

But then she felt the cold trickle of lube and tensed. No way, no fucking way.

"Relax, Marie." He never slowed or stopped in his preparations. "I know it's been awhile, but I'm getting inside that ass of yours. I promise I'll go slow."

Slow or not, her last experience with anal had been with a newbie Dom and she'd ended up safewording. "My last time was painful, Sir. I said *red* before it finished."

He paused momentarily. "If I do anything you don't like, safeword. But I have a feeling you'll enjoy it."

She wasn't sure if it was because it was Lennox, or if he was really that good, but by the time he started fucking her there, she was well on her way to her fourth orgasm. And when he pulled out and drew her close after another earth-shattering release, she knew she'd never doubt him again.

* * *

"I'LL BE BACK," he whispered with a light caress to her arm.

The bed dipped slightly as he got up. She should probably get up herself and go to the bathroom, but she was too tired to move. She needed a shower, too. But it had been so long since she'd had must-shower-after sex that she couldn't work up the energy to do that either.

Nope, she wasn't going anywhere. She was going to stay right where she was, in this bed that had now become her happy place, and remember every moment with him. God, she was sore all over. Sore in the most amazing, wonderful, can-we-do-it-again way possible. She didn't think there was an inch of her flesh that he hadn't touched, licked, bit, or kissed in the last few hours.

She let out a happy sigh just thinking about it. Or maybe it was an exhausted-in-the-most-blissed-out-way sigh.

Her eyelids grew heavy. She'd think about it tomorrow.

"Marie," Lennox said from beside her. "Come on. Let's get you cleaned up."

"Not moving," she said into the pillow. She didn't even lift her head.

"You don't have to move," he said, and then he picked her up and carried her into the bathroom.

She'd been mistaken when she thought he'd gone to the bathroom to take care of himself. He'd been preparing the space for her. Lit candles were everywhere. She was thankful for the soft lighting because if he'd turned on the overhead light, it would have been too much.

He'd also filled up the bathtub, which looked so inviting with the steam rising from the water filled with lavender-scented bubbles.

"Think you can stay upright long enough for a bath?" he asked, his breath tickling her ear.

"I'll do my best, Sir." Because now that she was in the bathroom looking at the tub, she really wanted to get in.

He placed her gently into the tub, a huge freestanding and clawed showpiece, and knelt beside it.

"You aren't getting in?" she asked. He was still naked, so there was no reason he shouldn't join her. She scooted up, but doing so pulled her already sore muscles and she groaned.

"No." He pushed the hair back from out of her eyes. "Now is when I get to take care of you."

Aftercare. In her mind, she'd always seen aftercare as something a Dom had to do, not necessarily something they enjoyed.

She scooted away from him as best she could in the tub. "I can bathe myself. You don't have to."

"I never said you couldn't, but I want to do this." He picked up a washcloth and let warm water dribble down her shoulder.

She hummed in pleasure because it felt so good, but she still didn't move to relax. "You're naked, you're probably as tired as I am, and there's no reason for you to be on the floor giving me a bath."

His hand with the washcloth stilled. "Marie. Doing this calms me. It allows me to touch you in a way that will bring you comfort and to ensure you're okay. It helps me with my own drop and I'm probably going to have a steep one since it's been so long since I've been in a scene."

131

Well, damn. She hadn't considered it like that.

"So," he continued. "Unless you use your safe word, you're going to sit in that tub and let me do this. And I'll go ahead and warn you now that when you get out, I'm drying you off, putting you to bed, and then I'm going to give you a massage, and finally, we're going to cuddle."

She would have laughed, but his expression was so serious. Then she thought about curling up in bed, wrapped in Lennox's arms, and she nodded in acceptance, moving back so he could reach her better. So far, she'd refused to think beyond tonight as to what the future might hold for them. Yet she knew she might not get this chance again and she wanted nothing more than to spend a night in his arms.

"Yes," she said simply.

When he began to bathe her, she marveled at his hands. His hands that had brought her so many different sensations in the past few hours held one more surprise for her. They were achingly tender.

He washed her as if she was a delicate vessel he feared would shatter at the slightest touch. As he cared for every part of her body, she felt his touch become reverent. Even as he helped her out of the tub and carefully dried her off, he was still caring and gentle.

Next he wrapped her in warm towels and carried her over to the bed where he rubbed the soreness out of her body. She was left feeling warm and cherished, and as he climbed in beside her then gently curled himself around her, she realized she didn't know him at all.

* * *

MARIE WAS CURLED up on her side, snoring softly. He held her, trying to name the emotion he was feeling, when it hit him. He was jealous. Jealous of sleep.

If that wasn't the craziest thing he'd experienced, he wasn't sure what was. Whoever heard of being jealous of sleep? But he was. Right now, sleep possessed her and he wanted to be the one to do that. Not to just hold her body, but to hold her mind, her soul. All of her.

He supposed he should draw some comfort from the fact that he was the one who'd worn her out so thoroughly that she slept so deeply. But damn it, he wasn't near finished with her yet.

She needed sleep though. No doubt she was exhausted from all the heavy emotions of the day, not even counting the crazy sex they'd recently had. He sighed and tightened his arms around her. It'd been too long since he held a sleeping woman.

He buried his nose in her hair and sniffed. She smelled like sex and sunshine, with a hint of lavender still lingering.

"Mmm," she mumbled, her voice heavy with drowsiness. "Are you smelling me?"

He chuckled. "I thought you were asleep?"

"I asked you first."

"Yes." He smiled.

"In that case, to answer your question, I was asleep. I'm a light sleeper."

"I didn't mean to wake you up." He wouldn't say he was sorry, because he wasn't.

She rolled over to face him. "It's okay. I don't mind." She reached up to run her fingers through his hair. Her actions were hesitant and that shocked him. He'd never seen her unsure before. Always, she was confident and secure.

"Your hands feel good," he said, hoping to reassure her in case she was afraid of how he'd react to her touch.

"Yeah?" she asked, bringing her other hand up to join the first one.

"Mmm, so good."

"I'm glad."

He was, too. Though he was also afraid that he was experiencing a dream and would wake up any minute to find himself alone. He lowered his head to brush her lips in a gentle kiss.

"Talk about feeling good," she whispered. "I like kissing you."

He kissed her again and once more it struck him that he was in bed, kissing Marie. Marie. The woman he'd wanted for so long was here, in his arms. He smiled against her lips.

"I like doing a whole lot more than kissing you," he told her. He knew she had to be sore, so he wasn't going to take it beyond kissing.

"I like that, too." She dropped her hand to brush his erection and he groaned.

"Fuck, Marie. I'm trying to let you rest. But if you keep that up . . ."

She wrapped her hand around his length. "I don't need to rest."

"Aren't you sore?"

"Yes, but since I've wanted this for years, do you really think I'm going to let a little soreness stop me?"

He was so tempted and, though he tried to resist, his resolve fell away with each stroke she gave him.

"You want it, too," she taunted, knowing the truth of her words because she held the evidence of his desire for her in her hand. "Don't deny us. Give it to me. Give me this cock again."

He groaned because he knew he was facing a losing battle. "Marie."

"Please, Lennox."

She had shattered his walls—he no longer had any defenses when it came to her. "I don't have the strength to turn you down anymore."

"That's not a bad thing in my opinion."

"Maybe not," he said. "But we're going slow and easy this time."

"Blah. I've never been a fan of slow and easy." She rolled away from him. "I think I'll go back to sleep."

He took her words as a personal challenge and to start, he ran his hand down her back to the crack of her ass. "Roll back over and I promise you'll never say 'blah' to my suggestion of slow and easy again."

"Pretty sure of yourself, aren't you, Sir?" she asked, but still didn't roll over.

No, he wasn't. He was anything but sure. That was the problem when it came to Marie. He cared about her too much, and as a result, he felt like he was always second-guessing everything he did with her. He didn't remember things being so challenging with Winnie.

But he wasn't going to think about Winnie right now. He wanted to focus on Marie.

Since she hadn't rolled over, he peppered kisses along her shoulder blades. He tickled the nape of her neck with his breath and made sure she felt his erection as he pressed himself against her back. He was going to feel like the world's biggest fool if she didn't roll over and look at him.

That's when he noticed her hands gripping the sheets and how white her knuckles were. Her breath was once more becoming choppy and he knew if he slipped a finger between her legs, she'd be wet.

"I've decided I don't want you to turn over, after all," he whispered in her ear, and he knew she heard the rustling of a condom packet. "I'm going to take you from behind. Lift your leg for me, Marie. Let me make us both feel good."

She moved her upper leg, barely giving him access.

"That's the way," he continued. "Going to fuck that pussy slow, but I'm going to be buried in you so damn deep. Do you want my cock inside you? Fucking you long and slow and hard?"

"Yes," she whispered so low he could barely hear her.

"Say it louder," he said. "Tell me you want it, or you get nothing."

"Yes. I want it," she spoke louder this time.

He slipped a hand between her legs to make sure she was ready for him. Finding her wet, he lined himself up and slid into her slowly. She moaned in pleasure.

"You like that," he said. "Like me sliding into you. Filling you up."

He held still, just to enjoy the moment of being inside her. She pressed her hips back toward him, he took them in his hands and, holding her still, thrust into her completely.

"So deep." He pulled out and flexed his hips forward, going

slow, but knowing he'd hit the spot inside her that drove her wild. He continued, even when she tried to get him to go faster.

He let go of her hips and took her hands in his. "Slow and easy, remember?"

She gave a grunt of displeasure but held still for him. He took her surrender for the gift it was and on his next thrust, he stilled himself within her, then pushed forward, going deeper than ever before.

His reward was her softly muttered cursing, which made him smile. He had her exactly where he wanted her now. He repeated the action several times; each time she reacted the same way.

He bit the back of her neck. "Changing your mind about slow and easy?"

She mewled as he pumped into her again, rocking his hips for maximum penetration. She gasped. "It may be slow, but there's nothing easy about it. You're sending my body to critical levels of pleasure."

He held still. "I can stop."

"No!" She let go of his hands, reached behind her, and held him to her.

He kissed the spot he'd bitten earlier and picked up where he'd left off.

"Lennox," she moaned as he lightly brushed her nipple.

"Mmm?" he asked, once more moving lazily within her.

"Don't ever stop."

She sounded so lost in bliss, and so sincere, it hurt his heart. "Oh, Marie. You cut me to my very soul."

When she brought his hands up and kissed them, the tender touch made his chest constrict even more. Somehow they'd gone from Dominant and sub to Lennox and Marie. Somehow their BDSM kink scene turned into making love. He'd lost all control of everything and that should have bothered him. When he took time to think about it later, much, much later, it would bother him.

But for now, this moment, with Marie soft and pliable in his arms, arching against him, wanting and taking whatever he'd give her, he didn't care. He'd always known it'd be different with Marie, that was part of why he'd stayed away from her so long. One touch, one kiss, one night and it'd be over. He now knew exactly what he wanted and how and who to get it from.

It was a knowledge that saddened him even as he drove them both to the release they craved. A release he wished he could hold back forever, because as she stiffened in his arms and clenched around him in climax, it was bittersweet.

It had been the best night of his life, he knew that, without question. And he also knew it could never, ever happen again. Not with anyone, but especially not with Marie. As much as he hated to do so, the Dominant within him needed to be buried once more.

He inwardly cursed the night that would all too soon turn to day, holding her close as if by doing so, he could keep the sun from rising.

MARIELA WOKE UP alone the next morning. She told herself she shouldn't be surprised. In reality, it was what she had expected. But she couldn't help but feel disappointed that she wasn't proven wrong. She sighed and wondered if the Lennox waiting for her downstairs would be the same one who had shared a bed with her last night.

She took her time getting dressed and in the bathroom, afraid of what she would find and wanting to postpone it as long as possible. She heard him talking in a low murmur downstairs. He would've heard her walking around, so he knew she was up. Unable to postpone the inevitable any longer, she took a deep breath and descended the stairs.

He was talking to someone on the phone. She walked past him and went to the kitchen, surprised to see that he had cooked. There were pancakes and eggs warming on the stove. She felt a brief glimmer of hope—maybe he would be the same man who'd shared a bed with her last night. She fixed her plate and allowed herself to think it.

"Marie."

And with that one word, said in that distant tone, all her hopes came crashing down. She closed her eyes, took a deep breath, and turned to face him. "Good morning, Lennox. I didn't know you cooked."

"I've been known to do so on occasion."

She risked a glance at him. He didn't look as if he had slept at all, with dark circles under his eyes and his shoulders slumped. No, she decided. It was not going to end well.

"Listen," he said.

She held up her hand. "Sit down. I'm not going to hear this with you standing up looming over me."

He pulled out a chair from the kitchen table and sat down. She braced herself for what was to come.

"Last night," he started.

"Was pretty damn amazing," she finished.

He sighed as if dealing with a petulant child. "Marie," he said.

139

"No," she insisted. "If you're getting ready to say what I think you are going to say, you first have to admit the truth about last night."

"Last night was amazing," he said.

"Last night was pretty *damn* amazing," she corrected.

"It was pretty damn amazing." A small smile tickled his lips, but did not spread to the rest of his face. She wondered if she had the strength to hear what he was getting ready to say. "However," he continued, "it cannot happen again."

"Because I work for you?"

"Among other reasons."

She wasn't hungry anymore. She wasn't feeling much of anything anymore. Except angry. "What are the other reasons?"

"I can't be a Dom again, Marie."

"You say that like it's something you can turn off. You and I both know that's not the case. And whether you want to admit it or not, you are a Dom. Which you proved last night, no matter what you're saying now."

"Let me restate, I can't live as a Dom anymore. I accept that I will always be one."

She gave a sad laugh. "As much as I expected this morning to go like this, I really wish you would have proved me wrong."

He shrugged. Obviously not caring that he was stomping all over her heart.

"Tell me this," she said. "Do you really think you being a Dom forced Winnie into that car?"

"No. I don't think it forced her to the car, but I believe if I were vanilla she would still be here today."

"That is the most absurd thing I've ever heard."

"That doesn't make it untrue."

She took a deep breath. "Are you really so egotistical that you think you hold the power over life and death?"

His head shot up. "I don't think that."

"Don't you?" She stood up and scraped her dish into the trash. If this was the way he was going to be, she was going back to the island. Maybe there she could pretend like last night didn't happen.

But even as she thought it, she knew it wouldn't work. The night before had been the most incredible one of her life. There was no way to pretend it didn't happen. Maybe, though, the memories wouldn't be so raw on the island. God, she hated the mainland.

She turned to walk out of the kitchen.

"Where are you going?" Lennox asked.

"Not that it's any of your concern, but I'm going back to the island."

"In this?" he pointed to the window. It was raining. Hard, but nothing she couldn't handle.

"It's a little bit of rain. It's no big deal."

"It's coming down hard and it's forecasted to get worse."

"Then I'd better get going so I can still call for a boat."

Lennox pushed back from the table and stood up. "No academy boat is going out in weather like this and you know it."

Yes, she knew that. She also knew she had to get out of the cabin. "I'll drive to the dock and wait for the rain to let up."

"I don't think that's a good idea."

"And I really don't care what you think."

He reached out to her, but she jerked away. "Marie."

"Don't Marie me. All you had to do today was show a little bit of kindness and affection. Just a little. Prove to me that the man

I was with last night is buried under those layers of horseshit you pass off as feelings. But you can't do it, can you? Maybe you don't have feelings after all."

She had to calm down or she was going to start crying, and the one thing she did not want to do was to cry in front of him.

"Let me go, Lennox. If you feel anything for me, let me leave."

He didn't stand in her way this time. She walked past him and grabbed her purse and her keys from the foyer table. She didn't have anything else with her. He followed her to the front door, looking as though he wanted to say something but was unable to get the words out.

She pushed the front door open and was hit in the face by a gust of wind. The rain had picked up a bit, too. It didn't matter, it wouldn't take too long to make it to the docks. There was a café nearby where she could sit until the rain slacked off. Anything was better than sitting in the cabin with him.

She jogged through the rain to get to her car and shivered when she made it inside. She sat for a few minutes, rubbing her hands together as the heater warmed up. Finally, she inched her car forward. Driving in the rain was not her favorite thing to do, but it was part of life in the Pacific Northwest.

Thankfully, traffic was light and it took her no time to get on 101. She had just started to relax when the car in front of her slammed on the brakes and swerved off the road. Too late, she saw the wooden pallets in the middle of her lane. She jerked the steering wheel to avoid hitting them and hydroplaned.

Brakes squealed.

Someone screamed.

Then nothing.

* * *

LENNOX GAVE HER a fifteen-minute head start, then he grabbed his keys to go after her. Damn foolish woman. Driving in this mess. He'd catch up with her at the docks and hopefully talk some sense into her.

Her comment that all she needed this morning was a bit of kindness and affection struck him deeply. He shouldn't be cold to her. She deserved better. He knew he could never be who she needed him to be, but that didn't mean he had to be cruel to her. Especially after last night. In one night, she'd torn down every wall, every barrier, every mask he'd created, and she'd shown him how much he was missing.

Their night together had been glorious. She'd been the embodiment of every fantasy he'd ever had. Better than any fantasy, actually. The way she'd submitted to him? He now knew what he was giving up by denying his true self. He was only hopeful that the memories would be able to sustain him.

He'd not been on the highway long when sirens sounded and he saw an ambulance approaching in his rearview mirror. An overwhelming sense of dread filled him, even though he told himself it was ridiculous and uncalled for. The emergency vehicle could be going anywhere, for any number of reasons.

The cars in front of him started to slow down and the feeling of dread grew worse. Obviously, there had been a car accident. He told himself it didn't mean anything and that his imagination was running away from him.

The traffic slowed further, eventually coming to a complete stop. In the distance, he saw the ambulance pull to the side of the road. He took his phone and called Marie. Just to see if she was stuck in the same traffic, that was all. Or at least that's what he told himself as the traffic began to move slowly. And just because she didn't pick up didn't mean anything serious. There were a number of reasons why she wouldn't answer her phone and none of them involved her being the person who needed the ambulance.

The crash site grew closer and traffic inched slowly around the twisted car in the road. Which looked exactly like Marie's car.

He pulled off the road and stumbled out of his car. His hands trembled so badly he dropped his keys. Leaving them in the dirt, he nearly tripped in his haste to get to the car. "Marie!"

A uniformed officer held him back. "Give them space to work, sir."

Lennox watched in horror as the first responders worked before him and his whole world collapsed when they moved out of the way and he caught a glimpse of the unresponsive driver.

WINNIE'S JOURNAL

Lennox has been training me for a few weeks now. He says I'm doing really well. I think I'm doing excellent seeing as how I'm not really a sub. Of course, I can't tell him that. I'll admit, some parts of it are really hot and as it turns out, Lennox likes to talk dirty. Who knew?

Sometimes I think I'll come just from hearing him talk. I can't, though. He has this silly rule that I can't have an orgasm without his permission. He has to grant me permission before I'm allowed to climax and the worst part is, he says it's not just while we're together in bed or wherever. I'm not allowed to climax anytime without his permission. Even alone in my bed at home.

That's beyond fucked up if you ask me. But sometimes, okay a lot of the time if I'm being honest, I think it's worth it. I just wonder if I can keep this up long term?

CHAPTER
Eight

Mariela was walking through the woods and it made her feel sick because she knew she was on the mainland and not the island. She turned around, trying to find a way out, but the trees were so thick and tall, they made everything look the same. Her chest grew tight and she felt a bit panicky because the light was fading and it would grow dark soon.

She searched frantically for a path or anything that would lead her out of the woods and to the water. It was close, she felt it. Now all she had to do was find it. The first thing she had to do was calm down, she told herself, so she stopped, closed her eyes, and took several deep breaths.

"You won't find your way out with your eyes closed."

It sounded like . . . but it couldn't be. Mariela spun around.

"Surprise." Winnie sat on a rock, her legs crossed and a big smile on her face.

147

Mariela screamed.

Winnie's smile disappeared and in a flash too quick to see, she moved from the rock to stand directly in front of Mariela.

"Stop it," Winnie said. "Don't do that."

Mariela nodded and forced herself to stop screaming, but it took several tries before she could get any words out. "You're . . . here and now I'm here . . . am I . . . oh shit." Everything grew fuzzy and she felt the earth tilt.

Winnie slapped her. "Don't pass out on me. And no, you're not dead. You can say it, you know. I'm well aware of what I am."

"Why am I here?" Mariela wasn't sure she believed her. After all, she'd always thought if you saw dead people, you were also dead. That's the way it should work anyway.

"I'm guessing you did something stupid and now you need advice."

"You're going to give me advice?" Mariela laughed. "That's funny. You were always the one asking me for advice."

"I know, right? Isn't it funny how the universe works? It took dying for me to get smart."

Mariela sobered up. She was standing with her best friend, the woman who was like a sister to her. She'd never thought to see her again and suddenly her eyes prickled with tears. "It is you. I've missed you so much. Can I hug you?"

"Better not. Now come over here and sit down. We've got a lot to go over and not much time. You have to find your way out before dark."

"What happens at dark?"

"Don't ask."

"I just did."

Winnie sighed. "I turn into a pumpkin, okay? Now sit."

Mariela sat on the rock Winnie had recently vacated.

"First of all," Winnie said. "You have got to cut Lennox some slack."

"What?"

"He's grieving. I'm hard to get over."

"I don't mean any disrespect, but seriously? You've been gone for three years."

Winnie laughed. "You still have it, I see. He hasn't killed your spirit yet. That's good, because he's a hardheaded one."

"What are you talking about?"

"The way you tell it like it is. He needs someone like you, he just hasn't accepted it yet."

Mariela knew she should feel uncomfortable talking to her dead best friend about her old lover. However, she figured it was completely ludicrous to be talking to her dead best friend anyway, so the topic of conversation really didn't matter.

"If you're talking about Lennox," Mariela said, "it's never going to happen with us. I've tried. We don't work."

"And here I thought you'd have a little bit more spunk."

"Pining after Lennox zapped the spunk right out of me."

"I'm sorry I took him away from you," Winnie whispered. "I shouldn't have gone after him. You were better suited for him. Still are."

"But he loved you. And you were right, he's still grieving. I don't think he'll ever get over you."

"He's not grieving me. He's grieving who he thought I was."

"What do you mean?"

Winnie looked at her in shock. "You don't know? I can't believe he hasn't told you."

"Told me what?"

"I should probably let him tell you, but I guess I can at least tell you my side."

None of this made any sense to Mariela. Not why she was dreaming about this—at least she thought it was a dream—not why Winnie was here. And especially not what she was talking about.

"You were always the submissive. Remember that night we met Lennox? You knew who and what he was, but you'd never talked with him. I, on the other hand, took one look at him and I said, "He's mine," and I didn't care that you wanted him, too, or that you could actually offer what he needed. I was young and so damn sure of myself. I thought I could make myself a submissive."

Mariela found it hard to breathe. Winnie wasn't submissive? What?

"Lennox knew right away that I didn't know what I was doing, but I begged him to train me and I eventually wore him down."

"I had no idea."

"Of course you didn't. Did you think I was going to confess to you that I was only pretending to be kinky so I could have Lennox? I'm not proud of the way I treated him. I was awful. Especially toward the end. And especially on . . . that day."

Things started to fall into place for Mariela. All the things he'd said or done suddenly took on new meaning. Why he didn't want to scene. Why he pushed her away. Why he carried the guilt of Winnie's death.

"That's why he opened the academy," Mariela said with a gasp. "That's what he meant when he said it was his penitence."

"Yes, and he's done a fantastic job with it, but it's time for him to move on. And he should do it with you."

"By move on, you mean leave the academy?"

"Whatever it takes. I'll leave that up to you."

Mariela snorted. "Right, because he's going to listen to anything I say. I'm the very last person he'll listen to. He's not the man he was."

"You'll be surprised. He values you and your opinion more than he lets on. And who he is hasn't changed, he's still the same, just with a new perspective on things."

Mariela decided it wouldn't be polite to tell Winnie she was batshit crazy. In fact, the only thing that was more ludicrous was the possibility of Lennox leaving the academy.

"He needs to put the past away and you're the only one who can help, because you know what he's gone through. If that means he needs to work somewhere else, help him find something. He's too good of a man to wither away into nothing and he's too much of a Dominant to live without a strong submissive." She stood up. "Be kind to him, Marie, and you two will have the life you both deserve. I love you both and always will."

Mariela hopped down. "Wait! That's it? Where are you going?"

"It's almost dark, you have to go. We can't have you see me turn into a pumpkin, now can we?" She made a scoot motion with her hands. "Go on now."

Mariela looked around. "But I still don't know where the water is."

"Listen to your heart, it won't steer you wrong." She smiled. "And listen to that Andie woman, she's pretty smart, too. I would have liked to have spent time with her."

Mariela knew she wouldn't see Winnie again and suddenly her heart ached like when she'd lost her first time. "I'll miss you."

"I know, sweetie. Like I said, I'm a hard woman to get over."

Mariela laughed and flipped her the bird.

Winnie blew her a kiss. "Go take care of your man."

SHE HURT EVERYWHERE.

Mariela refused to open her eyes. If she kept them closed, maybe she'd find her way back into the forest. It had been cool there and peaceful. But most of all, nothing had hurt.

"I think she's waking up," a voice she didn't recognize said.

A warm hand touched her forehead. "Marie?"

Lennox. What was he doing? Hadn't she left him at the cottage?

"Are you awake?"

"No," she tried to say, but it came out as a moan.

"Don't try to talk," Lennox said.

But why? If she didn't talk, how would she know where she was? Or why everything hurt so fucking much? And what Lennox was doing here?

She opened her eyes just enough to make him out. He looked horrible, but he tried to smile when he saw her open her eyes.

"You scared me," he said.

She licked her lips. "Hurts," she managed to get out. "Why?"

His smile disappeared. "You're in the hospital. You were in a car accident. Do you remember?"

She tried to think back, but she could only remember the forest. "Winnie."

A look of shock mixed with grief crossed his face. "Like Winnie, but you're here."

She shook her head. He didn't understand. "I saw her."

His mouth opened but nothing came out. Her eyelids were growing heavy, and she didn't have the strength to keep them open.

"Stay," she mumbled before the darkness swept her away.

THE NEXT TIME she woke up, someone was holding her hand. She took a quick assessment of her body. She still hurt, but the pain was localized to her legs now. Her mind seemed clearer and though she could remember Winnie and the forest, they both seemed further away than before.

She opened her eyes and discovered it was Lennox holding her hand. His head was down.

"Hey," she said to get his attention.

He jerked his head up and her heart caught in her throat because his eyes were red, like he'd been crying.

"You're awake," he said with a weak smile that did nothing to erase the sadness in his eyes.

"Yes," she said. "Why were you crying?" She was in a hospital, was something wrong with her? "Tell me."

"It's nothing," he said, confirming her fear. Something was wrong with her.

"Liar. Tell me." She struggled to sit up, but found she couldn't because her right leg was too heavy. Why would her leg be heavy? She looked down, but her legs were covered. "Is it my leg? Is that why it hurts so much?"

"Marie," he said. "Calm down."

She saw it in his eyes. Something was wrong. "Lennox, please."

He took a deep breath and looked toward the door as if hoping someone would come in and rescue him. No one came, and when he turned back to her, there was no emotion in his expression.

"You broke your leg," he said. "In the car accident."

A broken leg? Well, that wasn't the end of the world, unless there was more he wasn't telling her.

"I had a broken leg before," she said. "It's a pain, but not a big deal."

He shook his head. "Perhaps *break* isn't the right word. Your right leg was crushed. You were in surgery for hours."

She blinked, shocked by his words. "But I'll be okay, right?"

He didn't say anything.

"Lennox?" She couldn't keep the panic from her voice.

"The doctors said you should be able to walk after therapy. You'll probably always have a limp. . . ."

She couldn't catch her breath. *She should be able to walk?* Did that mean there was a chance she *wouldn't* walk again?

"Dance." It was only one word, but at this point, it was all she had.

Lennox took her hand.

Oh my god.

"In time, Marie," he said, looking her in the eyes. "But I know you and I know you can do it. You can push through this and I bet you'll be twirling around us before you know it."

She couldn't speak. What would she do if she couldn't dance? Dance was her entire life and without it, she was nothing.

"I'm sorry," he said.

As she watched, he dropped his head again and stroked her hand. She knew exactly what he was doing and she could hit him.

"Don't you dare blame yourself," she said.

154

"Why shouldn't I?" he asked. "It's my fault you left the cottage all upset. If I hadn't said those things I did, you never would have gotten in the car angry and the accident wouldn't have happened."

"Do you ever get tired, Lennox?" she asked.

He cocked an eyebrow. "Tired of what?"

"Being responsible for every damn thing that happens in the universe." He started to say something, but she spoke before he could. "Don't even try to deny it. To listen to you, it's your fault Winnie died and your fault I got into a car accident."

"Isn't it?"

"No, it's not." She sighed. "Believe it or not, you could not have stopped me from getting in that car. I doubt you could have stopped Winnie either. And you sure as hell can't take responsibility for my car accident or the telephone pole Winnie wrapped her car around."

She hadn't convinced him of anything. The weight he'd carried after Winnie's death was back, and from the looks of it, he'd doubled that weight. Because of her. He now blamed himself for her accident and whatever lasting effects it will have on her.

"You were never meant to carry that much guilt, Lennox. At least let me carry my share. I shouldn't have gotten into the car in the mood I was in. But I was hell-bent on getting out of that cottage and nothing short of a war would have stopped me. Certainly not you."

"Then we shouldn't have argued."

Was he fucking serious? That was the most asinine statement she'd ever heard. What were they supposed to do, agree on everything? Never disagree? That didn't make any sense.

She was getting ready to tell him as much when someone

knocked on the door. Thankful for the diversion, she looked that way expectantly to see who it was and grinned as Andie and Fulton walked in.

"Hey," Andie said. "Look who's up."

"Hi, Mariela." Fulton set down a vase of light pink roses. "We picked these up for you."

"They're gorgeous. Aren't they gorgeous, Lennox?" Mariela waved to the couple. "Come on in. Fulton, give those to Lennox so he can find a spot for them. It'll be the first useful thing he's done all day."

Andie and Fulton exchanged a look, obviously picking up on the tension between the two of them.

"Um," Fulton said. "We can come back later if now's not a good time."

"That might be for the best," Lennox said.

"Absolutely not," Mariela insisted. "Now is perfectly fine. Don't listen to him. In fact, Fulton, why don't you take Lennox out for coffee or something, so Andie and I can have some time for girl talk."

Lennox looked none too pleased with her suggestion and that was just fine by her. She was the patient, and if he didn't go with Fulton, she'd kick him out or have a nurse do it for her. She was tired of his attitude. Tired of his self-imposed martyrdom.

Andie glanced at Fulton, obviously searching for some guidance.

He nodded. "Come on, boss. Let's go find some coffee."

Lennox stood to leave. "I'll be back, Marie, and we'll finish this conversation."

You bet your ass we will. But she didn't say that. Instead she smiled and told the men to take their time. It wasn't until they'd both left the room that she felt she could relax.

Andie sat down in the seat Lennox had recently vacated. "Whew. What was that about?"

Mariela waved as if shooing a bothersome fly. "Nothing. Just Lennox being himself."

"It sure didn't look like nothing."

"I'm just tired of his shit. The way he acts like everything's his fault." She took a deep breath, needing to calm down. The last thing she wanted was to get herself worked up. The hospital would probably kick out all her visitors.

"He blames himself for your accident, doesn't he?"

"Yes, and it's completely ridiculous."

"Do you want to talk about it?"

Not really. But she had to talk to someone about what happened. "I went to the cottage, I knew he'd go there when he left the island. And we . . ." She closed her eyes. She hadn't yet had the time to process last night and everything about it still felt raw and tender. She sighed and Andie placed a hand on top of hers. "It was wonderful. Incredible. It was everything I'd imagined and fantasized about and so much more."

And then they'd woken up the next morning and it was back to the same old treatment from him. She looked away from Andie, not wanting to see the pity she knew would be there when she told her what happened next.

"This morning, he acted like it was nothing. Nothing." Mariela swallowed. "I should have known and expected it, but it surprised me and we had a horrible argument."

"Just like Winnie."

Mariela nodded. "Very much like Winnie. You know about my leg."

Andie nodded.

"He thinks it's his fault because we argued."

"What does he think? That no one should ever argue?"

"I guess. Or at least he shouldn't."

Andie didn't say anything.

"Seems as if no matter what, plan or no plan, Lennox and I are doomed for failure," Mariela said.

"I wouldn't look at it like that," Andie said. "You're not a failure."

"I don't see how you can call it anything else. I mean, seriously, he's acting like it never happened and I have a busted leg? It doesn't get much more of a failure than that."

Andie shook her head. "I think you're looking at it the wrong way."

Mariela just gave her an *are you kidding me with this* look. Because, really?

But Andie was determined she was correct. "You and Lennox had an amazing night, right?"

Mariela nodded.

"That in and of itself is progress."

"I would be more likely to agree with you if he didn't act as though the whole thing never happened."

"That's what I mean," Andie said. "He's acting like that because he hasn't processed the new development yet, and until he does, it's safer for him to shove it in the 'not yet' box in his brain."

Mariela decided Andie had lost it. "And you think once he's processed it, he's going to profess his undying love?"

"Nope, I still think he's going to shove it to the 'not yet' part of his brain."

"What good does that do me?"

"It's up to you to get that night out of the 'not yet' box and in the 'I can't live without this' box."

"I'm not even sure he has an 'I can't live without this' box."

"Trust me. He does."

Mariela yawned. "I'll have to try to locate it."

"I should let you rest. All this talking and planning can't be calming you down. And I promised the charge nurse that I wouldn't overexcite you."

"Trust me, if being in the same room with Lennox didn't overexcite me and send my bp through the roof, talking to you won't either."

"I believe you, but just to be safe, let's talk about something else." Andie reached into her bag. "I brought you some of my homemade granola and some superfood powder you can add to water. Hospital food is pathetically devoid of necessary nutrition."

"Thank you," Mariela said as Andie placed the items on a free shelf in the tiny hospital room closet.

"When do you start PT?"

"I'm not sure, I haven't even spoken to a doctor yet."

"I heard Lennox tell Fulton they were going to stop by the nurses' station on the way to get coffee. Maybe they'll ask for your doctor to come by."

With all that had been going on with Lennox and then Fulton and Andie coming by, Mariela had pushed anything having to do with her leg to the side. But she couldn't get rid of it completely, and every time she thought about it, a chill took over her body. What if the injury was worse than they thought and she never walked again? How could she live if she didn't dance?

Dance was such a big part of her life. It was like breathing. She couldn't separate herself from breathing, she doubted she could remove herself from dance either. She was a dancer. Without dance, who was she? Would she even recognize herself?

Unbidden, hot tears ran down her cheeks.

"Mariela?" Andie asked.

"What if I never walk again? And can't dance?" Mariela asked. "How can I go on?"

"First of all," Andie said. "Don't get all negative and pessimistic on me. Of course you'll be able to walk again, because you're going to have the best medical team known to man working with you. Not to mention me."

Mariela gave a small snort.

"You may laugh, but I can be a little stubborn. Just ask Fulton."

Mariela knew that for a fact.

"And since I'm so stubborn, I'm going to do everything in my power to get you up and walking. In fact," Andie's eyes sparkled and Mariela knew she was in trouble then. "I'm going to bet you'll be up walking and dancing at the Holiday Ball."

Mariela did laugh then. "Now I know you've lost it. Lennox said they're not sure when I'll be able to walk and you're saying I'll be dancing by the end of the year?"

"Crazier things have happened."

"Not many."

There was a knock on the door and Fulton stuck his head in. "Ready, Andie?" He glanced over to Mariela. "Nurse said we needed to let you rest, so we're going to go for now. We booked a room in the city for tonight, so we'll be back tomorrow."

"You guys don't have to do that." Mariela hated the thought of her friends going out of their way for her. Especially since they would be staying on the mainland. Granted, not everyone felt the way she did about that.

"It's okay, really," Andie said with a knowing glance at Fulton. "This is like a little mini escape for us."

"We don't need to hear the details." Lennox came up behind Fulton and slapped him on the shoulder. He passed him and stepped into the room. "You two go on and get out of here. I've got things covered."

Mariela waited until the couple left before she talked to Lennox. "I thought the nurse wanted me to rest?"

"She does."

"Then why are you staying?"

He settled into the chair and closed his eyes. "Because I am."

Damn stubborn man. She huffed and pulled the covers up, willing herself to sleep and surprised when it came so quickly.

WINNIE'S JOURNAL

Oh god, what have I gotten myself into?

CHAPTER
Nine

Lennox was there when Mariela was released from the hospital a few days later. She frowned when she saw him.

"I thought Fulton and Andie were coming," she said.

"Change of plans."

The look she gave him suggested she thought there was more to it than that. "I would have thought Andie would have called me in that case."

He shrugged. He sure as hell wasn't going to mention that he'd told Fulton to forbid Andie from calling Marie. Lennox feared that if Andie had told her he was picking her up, Marie would have found some excuse not to be released. She'd never said it in so many words, but he couldn't help but think she'd blame him for the accident. It was for the best she didn't know that he had manipulated things in order to be the one who took her home. Whether she liked him or not had no bearing on the fact that he was the reason she was in the shape she was in.

"I'll get you to the island and get you settled." He didn't want to bring up how they needed to talk about her rehabilitation. There was time for that conversation later, after she rested.

He found, once they got in the car and headed out on the highway, that he wasn't sure what to talk about. Small talk seemed too light. Silence would be preferable. Anything heavy he didn't feel ready to discuss with her. He wasn't going to talk about them, the crazy wonderful night at the cottage, or her future at the academy.

He decided he might try his hand at gossip. There were rumors floating around the school about Master Nader and his supposed new girlfriend. Marie would want to know. But when he glanced to his side, he discovered she was snoring softly.

He couldn't help but smile at the sight. She was such a firecracker. He needed to remember that no matter what front she put on, she'd been in the hospital and needed to take it easy.

Unbidden, the scene came back to him.

"But we're going slow and easy this time."

"Blah. I've never been a fan of slow and easy. I think I'll go back to sleep."

"Roll back over and I promise you'll never say 'blah' to slow and easy again."

Forget that. He wasn't going to mention any kind of easy anytime soon.

She was still sleeping when they made it to the docks. If it hadn't been for how sheepish she looked when he woke her, he would have thought she did it on purpose.

"Sorry I'm such rotten company." She yawned. "Who would have thought sitting in a wheelchair would be so tiring?"

Once they were on the boat, she stayed inside while he piloted them to the island. He'd asked that no one be at the docks when they pulled up. Marie only liked to be the center of attention while doing a scene. Outside of that, she preferred to disappear into the crowds.

So unlike Winnie. He'd found himself comparing them more and more lately. Since they were so close, some might have assumed them to be similar in many ways. But what struck him lately was how different they were.

Although he'd never admit it, the comparison started with sex. Marie had been free in her submission—she owned her submissive nature, and she made no excuses for it. Winnie, after the first few years anyway, saw it as degrading and said it made her feel weak. She didn't understand that hearing that made him feel weak, too.

Because what kind of Dominant makes his submissive feel worse?

"Thank goodness there's no one here," Marie said, when they arrived at the empty dock. "I was so afraid everyone was going to be out to greet us."

Thank goodness, he'd finally gotten something right. About damn time. "By order of the headmaster," he said. "I know you well enough to know you only want to be the center of attention when you're naked."

She laughed and he smiled. He didn't think he'd heard her laugh the entire time she was in the hospital. Maybe being back on the island would be good for her and allow her jovial personality to come back.

"God, that sounds awful, doesn't it?" she asked, still giggling. "But how very, very true."

He helped her out of the boat and into the waiting golf cart. But if he thought the return to the island would lighten her mood, he was wrong. She grew more and more somber the closer they got to her residence. By the time they arrived at her door, she was completely pale.

"Marie?" he asked.

"I can't do this," she said, and for the first time since he'd known her, she looked scared.

"Can't do what?"

"Any of it. I can't be here like this. I can't teach. And . . ."

"Marie?"

She looked down at her hands in her lap. "I can't be here with you and act like that night never happened."

That was the crux of it. The lack of mobility and the teaching were ancillary. It was the fact that they'd dropped all their boundaries and had sex. Though even he knew it went much deeper than mere sex. Somewhere deep inside, he'd known that night if he didn't stop and send her back to the island before things progressed any further that they would end up like this.

As many times as he'd told himself it was only one night, that one night didn't mean anything and nothing had changed, he had known. Deep down, he'd known that he'd never be satisfied with only one night with Marie. It meant a hell of a lot, and it'd changed everything.

But now, sitting outside her place in a golf cart, on the day she got released from the hospital, was not the time to have the needed conversation.

He took her hand and she looked at him in surprise. "I know we need to talk, but I think we both can agree that now is not the best time. You've gone through a very rough ordeal and you have a hard road ahead of you. Let's take it one step at a time."

He hated to admit it, but that was probably the most honest he'd been with her and it shamed him to no end. Somehow, she must have heard and understood the truth in what he said because she simply nodded.

He gave her hand a squeeze before letting it go. "Thank you. I think the one step we'll do today is get you settled. How does that sound?"

A single tear ran down her cheek. "Like a really, really good idea."

He wiped away the tear. "Two *really*s? Are pigs flying?"

"Get me inside before your ego blows up anymore," she said, and he was glad to hear a hint of laughter in her voice.

He pushed her inside to where Andie and Fulton waited. Andie had volunteered to stay with Marie while she settled into a routine. She'd told Lennox at the hospital that she'd helped care for her grandmother while she was in high school. Marie had balked at first, but eventually agreed. Lennox had wanted to be the one to stay with her, but he knew she'd never allow that.

It was probably for the best. At least until they were able to discuss what had happened and how they were going to move forward.

* * *

TWO WEEKS AFTER her release from the hospital, Marie was going batshit crazy. She was able to get around her apartment with crutches. Andie came by every afternoon to see her if she hadn't already stopped by the main building. Even Lennox dropped in a time or two, but his visits were awkward and tension filled.

Her problem was she didn't have enough to do. Lennox sent over paperwork she could work on, but those tasks were mainly administrative and she finished them quickly. She had already taken care of everything she could do for the Holiday Ball, and she was seriously thinking about taking up knitting or something. Absolutely anything to keep herself occupied.

Lennox came by the Sunday afternoon she was going through her books, trying to find one she hadn't read three times already and kicking herself for not placing her online order sooner.

"You know," he said from the doorway. "They do have electronic e-readers now, or you can download a book straight to your phone. Wonderful thing, technology."

She glared at him. "I know that. I just don't want to read an electronic book. I like the feel of paper on my fingers, the smell of a book."

"Just saying, you could get so many more if you'd—"

"Succumb to the dark side?"

He eyed the pile of books. "It'd be easier to carry, too."

She sighed. "Why are you here, Lennox?"

"And a good day to you, as well."

Damn it, why did he have to be in a good mood? Why couldn't he be pissy and dour like he'd always been in the past?

"Look, I'm glad everything is great and wonderful in Lennox land, but here in my reality, I'm losing my mind."

He nodded and that's when it hit her that he was up to something. He had that look in his eyes. God help her.

"I've been thinking about that because I know the last few weeks have been rough on you." He motioned her into the kitchen. "Let's go sit and talk."

"I'm tired of sitting," she said under her breath and, if he heard, he didn't give any indication of it.

He sat down and looked at her with such excitement for whatever his plan was, she sincerely hoped she liked it. Looks such as the one he wore now were rare and she'd hate to disappoint him.

"You remember the plans I had made for the cottage?" he asked.

"Yes."

"I've decided to move forward with the renovations."

She couldn't help it, she smiled. The changes he'd proposed for the cottage were wonderful and she was so happy he was moving forward with them. More importantly, she knew Winnie would have loved them.

"That's great," she said. "I think your idea is absolutely perfect for the cottage."

"I'm glad to hear you say that, because I actually would like for you to be involved."

She nodded. "Oh, sure. Anything you need, just let me know. I have tons of time."

He winced at that. She felt a little bad, simply because she knew he already blamed himself for the accident and now he'd probably feel like it was his duty to keep her occupied.

"This should definitely keep you busy," he said.

"Do tell."

"I'd like for you to be in charge of the renovations. I can't take care of everything that needs to be done and run the academy, too." His eyes pleaded with her. "And truthfully, I don't trust anyone else to oversee this other than you. Because you loved her, too."

She couldn't speak for several seconds. He wanted her to be in charge?

"Are you sure you want me?" she asked.

"Yes, like I said, I trust you and you were like a sister to her. You knew her better than anyone and I don't want the cottage merely renovated, I want it to have her touch. Only you can do that. Probably better than I can."

"Can I stay here or do I have to move to the mainland?"

"You can work from here. No need to move off the island."

"Okay. I'll do it."

Just saying the words made her feel better. She had a purpose again; she felt better than she had since before the accident.

WINNIE'S JOURNAL

What do you do when your entire relationship is built on a lie? I don't know. I'm not who he thinks I am and I'm reminded of that every time I look in the mirror. Hell, every time I look at him.

He doesn't know. It's so strange to me that he wouldn't know. He for damn sure knows everything else. It baffles me how he doesn't know this one thing that's the most fundamental and important of all things. How is it he knows what I'm thinking, but he doesn't know who I really am?

Ten

I t didn't take long for Mariela to see that Lennox wasn't lying about the renovations keeping her busy. Between the red tape involved with getting the permits and near daily chats with the contractor, she felt like pulling her hair out.

"Seriously," she complained to Andie one afternoon a few weeks into the project. "Do you know how much time I spend following up with people who never get back to me? I mean, really? Who's working for whom?"

"I agree, it's crazy." Andie walked into Mariela's living room, carrying a cup of coffee for each of them. "I recently fired a few distributors for the kitchen because they lacked any semblance of customer service."

Mariela's phone rang, but she ignored it.

"Do you need to get that?" Andie asked.

"No, it was Lennox. He's calling for his daily update."

175

"How are things going with him?"

Mariela sighed. "It's not. We talk about the cottage, but that's it. Every time I try to change the subject or talk about us or what happened, he either has to leave or says we'll talk later. And later never comes."

"He has to talk about it sometime."

"You would think." Mariela took a sip of coffee. "When I told him I'd do this, I thought working on the cottage would give us time to talk and work things out. But it hasn't. It's the same as it's always been."

"Hang in there. Men just need time. They're not as smart as we are. It takes them longer to grasp things." Andie nodded toward her leg. "How's your leg?"

Mariela forced her expression to remain neutral. "Good. I'm hoping I'll be able to move to a boot instead of crutches before too long."

What she didn't say was that with each day that passed, dancing seemed more and more out of reach. She hadn't been dancing before the accident, why would after it be any different?

Andie looked like she was going to say more, but a knock on the door interrupted her and she cocked an eyebrow instead. "You expecting someone?"

"No."

"I'll get it." Andie walked to the front door and Mariela heard her. "What are you doing here, handsome?" Which told her it was Fulton.

She didn't hear his reply, but several seconds later, he appeared in the doorway to the living room, carrying a large box.

"This came for you at the main building. I decided to bring it

176

by since I knew I'd run into Andie." Fulton looked around and Mariela suddenly realized what a mess her place was. Thanks to the cottage project, her workspace extended far beyond her desk. Papers were strewn across the coffee table and piles lined the wall.

"You can just leave it there," she said.

"What is it?" Andie asked, peering over her shoulder.

"Some notebooks and stuff that the cottage crew found when they were working. I told them to ship it here."

She actually wanted to get her hands on the items before Lennox saw them. She wasn't sure exactly what was in the box, but the last thing she wanted was for him to come across something and regress back into his dour funk again. She planned to look through them and get a feel for what they contained. Only then would she consider showing them to Lennox.

Andie waited, clearly expecting Mariela to open the box. But for some reason she didn't want to open it with people around. The things in the box belonged to Winnie and she didn't want to share those things with anyone. At least not yet.

"I'll open it later," Mariela said. "I need to see if I can get the contractor on the phone. I've been told there's a small leak, but a leak is a leak and I'm learning *small* is relative."

Fulton set it down. "Do you need me to carry anything down to the main building?"

"No, I'm good, thank you." What she wanted was for both of them to leave so she could open it without curious eyes watching.

Andie must have sensed her mood. She stood up and took Fulton's hand with a smile. "Walk back with me? I have to get dinner started."

Mariela waited until the sound of their voices disappeared

before turning around. The men at the cottage had placed everything in a cardboard moving box. With trembling fingers, she cut through the tape and lifted the top. Inside was a gray plastic storage bin. She lifted it out carefully, took a deep breath, and raised the lid.

She thought it was a bit anticlimactic, because all she saw inside were papers and notebooks. Then she laughed at herself, because seriously, what had she expected to find?

Shaking her head, she started taking out the papers. They didn't appear to be anything of importance; most looked like old credit card statements. She couldn't imagine the need for them so many years after Winnie's death, and she put them in a pile to discard.

Under the papers, she found notebook after notebook. She leaned back in her chair with a smile, flipping through them. Notebooks filled with sketches and drawings and ideas for paintings. She would put these aside for Lennox, he'd want to see them.

She pulled a pad out of the bin and gasped. It was filled with sketches of Lennox. Mariela never knew Winnie to draw or paint people. She flipped the pages one by one, in awe of this unknown talent her friend had. The images captured his likeness to a fault. The slight tilt of his head and the tiny smirk on his lips.

She wondered why Winnie never told her she did portraits and if Lennox knew. She ran her finger over one of them with a rare smile. Somehow, Winnie had captured the lightness and joy of the moment in his eyes. It was stunning. She wanted so badly to keep the pad to herself, but she didn't want to withhold anything from Lennox.

She set the pad aside and reached for the next item in the tub. This wasn't a notebook or a pad, but a thick leather-bound journal. It was held closed by a leather band, and she debated whether or not to open it. It had a different feel about it. When she brushed her fingers across the cover, it was as if the secrets inside whispered to her.

She looked over her shoulder and told herself she was being ridiculous. She was in her home. Alone. So why did she feel like someone was standing behind her?

Guilt, she told herself. Survivor's guilt. Guilt that Winnie had died when she crashed her car and Mariela had lived through her accident. Guilt that even after all these years, she still wanted Lennox.

It was time to move on, though, and that meant letting go of everything. She untied the book and almost dropped it when she saw that it was indeed a journal. Winnie's flowing script filled the pages, each one of them dated.

She wouldn't read it. It was personal and private. Mariela closed the journal, but didn't set it aside. On second thought, why shouldn't she read it? It couldn't hurt Winnie.

Maybe she'd just read one. Make sure it was what she thought it was.

She flipped to a random page and started reading.

I shouldn't be doing this. Someone should stop me before I start something I can't stop. But god help me, I don't want to. I want him too much and I'll do anything, not just to get him, but to keep him.

I shouldn't even argue with myself, I know I'll do it. I've already told Marie that I wanted to talk to her. She doesn't know what it's about yet and won't she be surprised when she finds out what I want.

I wish I could see her face. . . .

Mariela slammed the journal closed. She was not going to read this. She was not.

She lasted three more minutes before she opened it to a different page, this time near the back.

It's getting worse. I can't keep living this lie. I'm going to have to tell Lennox. I don't know what he'll do. And I'll have to tell Marie. She'll be so disappointed.

Then I think, maybe it won't be so bad for her. I can tell she likes Lennox. I should have let her have him in the first place. It was so selfish of me to insist on being something I'm not. But I love him and to this day when he calls me his Winnie girl, I still go mushy inside.

If I could just go back and do it over. I'd do it all so differently.

But I didn't. And now I'm left with a mess.

She closed the journal again, not understanding what she was reading. What was Winnie hiding? And what did she mean that Mariela would be disappointed? She didn't want to read anymore, it was too private and it hurt too much.

Maybe she'd give the journal to Lennox and let him decide

what to do with it. She should ask him exactly what happened between him and Winnie.

God, that had been a horrible day.

SHE HEADED HOME *early from the ballet academy. The owner had a family emergency so she'd closed at noon. Mariela didn't know what to do with the unexpected free hours. What she should do was clean her apartment, but where was the fun in that?*

What she wanted to do was shop, but until she got her paycheck, she was too strapped to spend any extra money. Maybe she should call and see if Winnie wanted to meet for coffee. It had been months since they'd had serious girl talk and lately Winnie had seemed a bit depressed.

Honestly, she didn't know what could be bringing her down. As far as Mariela could see, Winnie had it made. She was a successful artist, she was in the prime of her life, and she had Lennox as a Dom. Seriously? What more could she want?

Mariela parked at a nearby café and reached for her phone to call Winnie when it rang with her ringtone. She couldn't help but smile. Winnie must have read her mind. They were always doing stuff like that.

"Hey, girl," Mariela said, answering the phone. "I was just getting ready to call you. What's up?"

The sniffles on the other end told her something was wrong.

"Winnie? Are you okay? What's wrong?"

"I can't . . . I can't . . ." Her voice broke up as the sniffles grew into sobs.

"Where are you? Where's Lennox?"

But her questions only made her friend cry harder.

"Winnie?"

A horn sounded from the other end of the line.

"Tell me you aren't driving." Mariela's heart pounded. "Winnie, you better not be driving. You pull over right now or I'll personally ask Lennox to spank your ass."

Tires squealed. Winnie screamed. Metal collided with metal.

Silence.

THE RINGING OF her phone jerked her awake. Damn. Did she fall asleep? What time was it?

She reached for her phone and squinted at the screen. Lennox.

"Hey," she said.

"Are you okay? Did I wake you?" he asked.

"No, I wasn't sleeping, and yes, I'm okay." She didn't want to tell him she'd been napping. He'd probably send her to the doctor or worse, bring a doctor to her. "Just didn't have my phone with me."

"That's not safe, Marie. You know better."

"Yeah, yeah, yeah. Spare me the lecture."

"Are you sure you're okay?" he asked. "You sound a bit off."

How did he always manage to know her so well? That he could tell just by her voice that something was off?

All she had to do was go back to that night and she knew the truth. It had been so obvious then, how well they fit together, how they completed each other.

"There is something I want you to see. Can you come by?" she asked.

"Sure, give me about fifteen minutes, I need to wrap something up here."

She nodded before realizing he couldn't see. "Sounds great." But he had called her. "Was there something you needed to talk to me about?"

"No, I was just calling to check on you."

He did that every few days. Called her out of the blue, just to see how she was doing. She'd like to think it meant something, but deep inside, she knew what it was. He felt guilty because of the accident, and since he felt like it was his fault, he would call to check on her to ease his conscience.

That was it. Nothing more.

But she really wanted it to be more.

While she waited for his arrival, she straightened the papers and notebooks, putting the journal at the bottom of the pile. She stopped by the bathroom, briefly, to make sure she looked decent, and chided herself the entire time, telling herself she was being silly. This was only Lennox. She'd known him forever.

Yes, her inner voice whispered, *but it wasn't that long ago when you knelt before him and offered your whole self to him.*

He showed up at her door looking devastatingly handsome moments later. Even with the slight frown he wore on his face.

"What?"

"I just wanted to put my eyes on you. Make sure you were okay."

"Damn," she said, as they made their way to the living room. "Do I look that bad?" She'd just checked herself in the bathroom.

"It's not so much how you look. There's something about you, I can't put my finger on it."

183

Crazy talk, she decided, but didn't tell him that because deep down, she had a feeling he was right.

He sat down on her couch and nodded toward the box. "You aren't moving, are you?"

"No. Fulton brought that by earlier. It's actually what I wanted to show you."

He looked at the box with considerably more interest, but didn't make a move toward it. He was waiting for her, she realized. For her to say something else.

"The workmen found it in one of the cottage's downstairs closets." When he didn't say anything, she continued. "It had mostly papers, I threw some of them away and kept a few for you to look through. There were also several sketchbooks."

He sucked in a breath. "That were used?"

"Yes, I laid those aside for you." She knew how proud he'd always been of Winnie and her work. "And there's a journal."

"She kept a journal?"

"It appears so," Mariela said, and she rushed to add, "I flipped through it and read about two pages, but I had to stop because it felt invasive to me."

Mariela picked up the journal from the table beside her and passed it to Lennox. He took it hesitatingly, as if it would bite him.

"I had no idea she kept a journal," he said, flipping it over and running his fingers over the leather. "I don't know if I want to read it either."

"Why?"

"Not sure I want to read what she really thought about me."

His answer didn't make any sense. Whenever he and Winnie had been together, they seemed like the most perfect couple. But

184

his words when paired with the snippets she'd read in the journal left her thinking there were a lot of things she didn't know about the two people who were so important to her.

She leveled her gaze at him. "What exactly happened that day?" She knew they'd argued about something, that Winnie had gotten in her car and driven away. Minutes later, Winnie called her and lost control of her car, which ultimately led to her death.

He stood up and walked to a window. "I don't like to talk about it and I don't very often. But in light of everything, I think you should know and, afterward, you can decide if you want to read the journal or not."

"Would you like something to drink?" she asked. He certainly looked as if he needed something.

"Yes, I actually would, but I think I should do this sober." Turning from the window, he looked relieved, for lack of a better word. "And maybe in telling you what happened with Winnie and me, you can see why I feel the way I do about you and me."

Of course, she knew those two things would be related in his mind. Suddenly, though, she wasn't sure she was ready for the truth.

You are, the air around her seemed to whisper.

She didn't believe that tiny voice, but regardless, it didn't appear to matter to Lennox one way or the other. He was ready to share his story, and if he was strong enough to tell it, she was strong enough to listen.

And maybe, just maybe, he was right, and understanding what happened with him and Winnie would shed light on their own relationship. Deep inside, she knew that was what she wanted. To move forward with Lennox. And if that meant listening to him talk about Winnie's last days or reading the journal? Hell, Lennox could talk all night and she'd read every last page in that leather book.

She nodded and he took a seat beside her. She hadn't been expecting that; she'd thought he'd keep his distance. Instead, he was so close, she felt the heat from his body. Had her couch shrunk?

"You know, of course, that when we met, she had no experience with BDSM. She never hid that fact. But she told me she knew about the lifestyle because her best friend lived it. And she convinced me it was what she wanted. Looking back, I should have known something was up." He closed his eyes as if remembering. "The signs were there, but I was either too blinded by her or too sure of myself to question anything. So, after we went out a few times, I agreed to train her to be my submissive."

So far, he hadn't said anything she didn't know. She remembered having conversations with Winnie around that same time. Mariela had actually been the one to encourage her to talk to Lennox about being trained. It had been one of the hardest things she'd ever done, but both of them looked so happy together. Had she been wrong in pushing Winnie?

"We were fine for a time. She showed no signs of disliking being my submissive. I've searched my mind so often since her death, to see if I missed something. A significant look. Anything. I can't find anything."

Her eyes widened as he spoke. It seemed to mesh with what Winnie had written in her journal. Had her friend not been a submissive, or was it Lennox she had a problem with?

"But little by little, the cracks started to form in our relationship. She spent hours in her studio and would stay up late, into the early hours of the morning. I felt her slipping further and further away from me, and I was clueless as to how to get her back."

Mariela clenched her fists. Why hadn't Winnie told her anything about this? Winnie was closer than a sister to her. She didn't think they had any secrets from each other. And yet, to hear Lennox tell it, their problems had started not too long into their relationship. Had Mariela been that blind?

Suddenly, she remembered bits and pieces from a dream she had in the hospital. Or at least she thought it was a dream. She frowned. Had it really been Winnie?

"Don't get me wrong," Lennox continued. "I know I wasn't blameless. I could have done a lot more, and what I did do, I could have done much better. A relationship between two people can only be as good as the effort they both put into it, so don't think I'm blaming Winnie, because I'm not."

"I don't think that," she said. "I have to say, though, that I'm very surprised there were issues between the two of you. I never got even a hint of discord." She still couldn't get over that. She had been so close to Winnie, how did she miss it?

"That's not so unusual, though, is it? Doesn't everyone put on a mask in public?"

"I didn't think of myself as public." And the fact that either one or both of them thought she was, hurt.

"I didn't mean to hurt you by saying that."

"I know you didn't."

He placed a hand on her knee. "But I did anyway and I'm sorry."

"It's just . . ." She searched for the words. "I'm beginning to feel as if there's this whole side of Winnie I didn't know about, and it's a bit disturbing."

She couldn't keep her eyes off his hand and the way it rested so casually on her knee. She wasn't sure, but she thought it might be the first time he'd touched her since she'd been released from the hospital.

He squeezed her knee. "I can't imagine she purposely hid anything from you. I think she was more afraid that you'd judge her."

Her forehead wrinkled. "Judge her about what?"

"Winnie wasn't truly a submissive."

The truth hit her square in the chest, because so much made sense now. And as it did, an entirely new feeling swept over her: guilt. Guilt that she hadn't seen the truth. Guilt that she didn't push harder when Winnie said everything was "fine." And there was something else. She was angry. Angry at Winnie for lying to both her and Lennox. Lying about who she was and what she needed.

"So, that day . . ." she started, looking at him.

He'd gone pale and looked even more so because of the stark contrast to his black hair.

"I confronted her. I'd told her to be waiting for me and she wasn't. I expected it, of course, but it felt so final when she disregarded my instructions. I knew then the relationship was over. I couldn't do vanilla and she wasn't made for kink. I'd been so proud of the submissive I'd trained, and then I found out that I'd made one of the worst mistakes a Dom can make."

"She told you she wanted to be trained, you had to take her at her word." If he blamed himself, it only made sense that Mariela took some of the blame as well.

"That's not the worst part. I told her I wanted to separate. I couldn't cut it off with her completely. I loved her too much. But I wasn't sure how to not be a Dom and I needed space to think." He blew out a deep breath and looked at the ceiling. "She lost it. She called me every rotten name she could think of and stormed out of the cottage."

Mariela filled in the rest. "And she got in her car and crashed."

"Yes." He hung his head. "I should have stopped her. She wasn't in the right frame of mind to drive."

Right frame of mind to drive. All at once, all the air left Mariela's body. "Oh my god."

Pure horror washed over her as she replayed the last phone call she'd had with Winnie. Her vision started to fade and she dropped her head between her knees so she wouldn't pass out.

"Marie?" He placed a hand on her back and she heard the fear in his voice.

"Oh my god," she repeated.

"What?"

She didn't straighten up. She couldn't. To do so would mean she'd have to look at him and she couldn't do it. Not when she told him what she had to tell him.

"All this time," she said, forcing herself to stay calm and not to cry. Not yet. Not just yet. "All this time, you've been blaming yourself and it was me. It was me."

The hand that had been rubbing her back stilled. "What do you mean?"

He knew Mariela had been on the phone with Winnie when the accident happened, but they'd never discussed anything other than his sorrow at her having to hear everything as it occurred.

Her stomach soured as she remembered him saying once that as hard as it was for Mariela, he felt peace that Winnie had been in touch with someone when she died. Even if it was by phone.

"On the phone with her. I could tell she was upset. I told her she better not be driving when she was that upset and that if she didn't pull the car over I was going to have you spank her ass." She took a deep breath and closed her eyes as she forced the rest of the words out. "It was seconds after that when the crash happened."

Lennox was silent from his place beside her. He started rubbing her back again. "You can't blame yourself, Marie. You didn't know."

Now the sobs started. Because how the hell was it okay for him to blame himself for Winnie's death but she shouldn't do the same? God, they were both so fucked up. Both of them, and she doubted there was anything, anywhere that could make either of them normal again.

"So what?" She sniffled and sat back up, but still refused to look at him. "You get to corner the market on guilt? Isn't there enough to spread around?"

"I won't have you blaming yourself for what happened."

"But you can? Well, then fuck you."

Her guilt and grief were rapidly turning into anger. But seriously, who did he think he was anyway?

"Marie," he said, and he didn't sound upset or angry. Just tired. So very tired. "Don't."

He placed a hand on her shoulder, but she jerked away. "Don't touch me."

He sighed, clearly displeased with her response. "Believe it or not, I know how you feel."

"Right." She snorted. "Because you've been carrying guilt for years. You'll have to excuse me, it's a new feeling for me."

"I don't blame you."

For some reason, that really pissed her off. She wasn't sure if it was his Dom nature coming out or what. "You always do that, you know."

"Do what?"

"Act like you're the judge, jury, and executioner. Guess what? You're not. And your feelings of guilt aren't any more valid than mine."

"I didn't mean to imply they were."

She didn't answer. She crossed her arms and waited. For what, she wasn't sure. But she somehow knew if she said anything, it would be something she'd regret. As much as she disliked him at the moment, she didn't want to say anything to permanently damage their relationship.

"I also wanted to tell you that I was going to be away for a bit," he said.

It was the very last thing she expected him to say. "Where are you going?"

His face had regained that stonelike expression she knew so well. She hated that expression. "Someone Terrence Knight knows is wanting to start a BDSM school on the east coast. He's going to be in Portland for a few weeks, and Terrence invited me to spend some time with him."

"Andie's Terrence Knight? The actor?"

"Yes."

"How long will you be gone?"

"A week or so." He closed his eyes as if in pain. "I have to get away for a little while. For my sanity."

She wasn't sure what that meant, but he sounded sincere and she knew exactly how he felt. "I hope the time away does you good."

She hoped it did both of them some good.

CHAPTER
Eleven

Marie's hands shook only a little as she filled out the paperwork that would allow her into the club. Not for the first time, she was thankful Fulton had ties to the club and had taken care of the needed recommendation to help her gain entrance.

Lennox had been gone for two weeks. Two. After he'd said he'd be gone for a week or so. She supposed two weeks technically fit into the definition of "a week or so" but still. . . .

She had never gone so long without hearing from him or talking to him, and though she'd known she'd miss him, she'd not anticipated how much or how intently. Maybe it was foolish, but she'd feel better if she could just see him.

The young woman working the front desk took her paperwork and started entering Mariela's information. "Fulton Matthews is your recommending member?" she asked with a lift of her perfectly sculpted eyebrow.

"Yes," Mariela answered, finding the woman's renewed interest in her humorous.

She stopped typing and picked up a pen. "Any chance he'll show up tonight?" She started twisting the pen. "To, you know, play or something?"

Mariela shook her head. "No, he's not in town."

"Shame. Even if I had to watch him play with someone else, it'd still be nice to see him. Last of the great single Masters."

"Not so single anymore. He collared a friend of mine not too long ago."

"Seriously? Damn. Never thought that would happen."

Mariela had never thought it would either. But Andie was exactly what Fulton needed. And likewise, Fulton was perfect for her.

"I actually know another guest here, too." Mariela hadn't planned on bringing up Lennox, but the woman behind the desk seemed so friendly. "Tall, dark hair. Doesn't smile a lot."

The other lady's eyes widened. "Master Mac? Right?"

Master Mac? What the hell?

"The guy I'm talking about has never gone by that name before."

The lady in front of her shrugged. "He said it was new for him, but that he liked it. One of the club submissives picked it out for him."

Mariela was unprepared for the overwhelming rush of possessive jealousy that swept through her so hot she felt as if it would burn her alive. Maybe it had been childish of her, but she'd thought their night together meant something to him. That perhaps he might not be able to bring himself to play with anyone else afterward.

She wasn't even totally convinced it was the same man, but on the off chance it was, at least she had advance warning. Taking a deep breath, she worked up the courage to proceed inside. After all, she hadn't come all this way to sit in the shadows.

"If that's all I need to do, can I go change?" Mariela asked.

"Sure. The ladies' dressing room is through those double doors and to your right. There's an entrance to the club from there."

Someone else entered the main doorway behind her and the woman's attention shifted to them. Mariela picked up her bag and headed to change.

There were only a few other women in the dressing room. Mariela couldn't help looking at them and wondering if any of them was the submissive who gave Lennox his new nickname.

Two of the women present smiled and said hello, but no one attempted to start up a conversation. She hurriedly changed into her chosen fetish wear: a nearly see-through lace corset and micro miniskirt. As far as footwear, she undid the boot that had replaced her cast. Technically, she wasn't supposed to take it off except to shower, but what would a few minutes hurt? To compensate, she put a brace on and wrapped her right ankle. Then did the same to her left, so she wouldn't appear injured. Would Lennox be surprised to see her walking?

As soon as she stepped out into the club, she was hit with the smell of sex, sweat, and leather. That, along with the deep pounding bass of whatever music was being played, served to remind her why she didn't frequent clubs. There was nothing about this intense public environment that turned her on.

Her eyes scanned the crowd, taking in the scene as well as

looking for Lennox. The decor was mostly dark: deep reds and black. A bar was set up along the far wall and a dance floor separated an area filled with couches and a public play space.

Her eyes drifted upward to the balcony. Fulton had told her a lot of people went up there because it was quieter. If she knew Lennox, that's where he'd be. Sure enough, it didn't take long for her to spy him in one of the corners talking to someone who looked a lot like Terrence Knight.

She was almost ready to head up the nearby stairs when a tall, redheaded woman approached the two men. The woman all but ignored Terrence and only spoke with Lennox. He wore an expression of surprise, like he wasn't expecting her, and her heart sank because she had the strangest feeling she was looking at one of the women he used to spend his Friday nights with.

The woman looked over her shoulder as if she was talking to somebody, or waiting for a signal. Lennox looked in the same direction and she saw his mouth move, talking to somebody out of her line of sight. She gasped because the next second, he gave the redhead a big hug. And that hurt. He had never hugged her like that. Never.

She should leave before she did something stupid like burst into tears. But as she took a step to spin around, she ran into a massive man. He reached out to steady her.

"Whoa, hold up. Are you okay?"

Ow. Fuck!

She had nearly twisted her bad ankle in her haste to flee, it hurt like the devil. She tried to ignore the pain and instead looked up to see who she'd run into. Obviously, she didn't know him, but everything about him exuded Dominant. He was rather nice-looking, rugged, more blue-collar than white. The hand on her shoulder confirmed that. It was rough, a working man's hand. The complete opposite of Lennox.

She smiled. "Yes, sorry, I was thinking about leaving. But now I think I'll stay."

The look of pure delight covered his expression. "Really? Because I was about to ask if you'd like to get a drink?"

"I'd like that very much." And without a backward glance to Lennox, she followed him to the bar.

His name was Matt. He worked in the lumber industry. And he had been a Dom for eight years. She told him she was a dancer, but didn't mention the fact that she taught at the RACK Academy. She told him she was new in the area, which wasn't a bold-faced lie, but it was stretching the truth a little bit. She also added that she was looking for a new club.

He was sweet, commanding, and charming. He was everything a woman would want in a Dom, except for the fact that he wasn't Lennox.

Yet when he asked her if she'd like to play, she accepted.

"Any hard limits?" he asked.

"Blood play, body fluids, sex, fisting, breath play."

He nodded. "Safe word?"

"Red." The butterflies in her belly were having a party. Holy hell, what was she getting ready to do? Play with a man she didn't know, in a club she'd never been in, all to make a man who didn't even know she was there jealous?

She was one thousand percent out of her mind.

"You mentioned sex as a hard limit," he said, his blue eyes steady. "Can you elaborate?"

She'd intentionally been vague to see if he'd pick up on it. He rose a few notches in her book. "I don't want any sort of penetrative sex."

"Got it. Are you opposed to orgasms?"

"I don't know a woman alive who is," she said as dryly as possible.

He laughed. "Just making sure." He looked around the club, probably trying to find an open space. "Go wait for me by the wooden bench, and from here on out, I expect to be addressed as Sir."

She thought it was more than likely her imagination that she was being watched by Lennox as she made her way to the bench. Yet with each step, she couldn't shake the feeling that someone was drilling holes in her back with the force of their gaze.

Probably just curious club members, she decided. She was new, after all.

It wasn't surprising that no one approached her as she walked to the bench. What was surprising was the redhead who'd been talking with Lennox—scratch that, who'd hugged him—stood at the edge of a crowd gathered near the bench.

Mariela was proud that she didn't look around to see if Lennox was also nearby. He shouldn't even be a thought in her head at the moment. She was playing as Matt's sub and he deserved to have the focus of her attention.

With downcast eyes, she knelt by the bench, wincing just a little when her ankle protested the position. Damn, she probably should have mentioned her ankle to Matt.

"Very nice, Mary," Matt said, suddenly appearing before her.

Mary? Why the hell was he calling her Mary? Had he already forgotten her name? She gave serious thought to correcting him, but decided not to. What did it matter anyway? She wouldn't see this guy after tonight.

"You may stand, strip, and lean over the bench. Keep your head down. Your eyes are for me only, not the rest of the club. As far as you're concerned, we're the only ones here. Understood?"

"Yes, Sir." That was an odd request, to keep her head down, but she really didn't want to know if Lennox was nearby, so she didn't mind too much.

In her rush to get to her feet, she moved too quickly and a sharp pain radiated up her leg. Hot tears sprang to her eyes, but she blinked them back, thankful that her head was down and no one saw.

She worked quickly to undress. Her ankle hurt when she moved it, but she didn't say anything because her ankle had nothing to do with the scene she was playing with Matt. She couldn't help but wonder what he had planned. If she had to guess, from the setup, she'd go with an impact scene. Maybe a paddle or flogger.

Though she wasn't with the Dom she wanted to be with, she was strangely looking forward to whatever Matt had in store. Outside of that one night with Lennox, it'd been way too long since she'd played with a knowledgeable Dom. Especially one who was a stranger. Excitement pulsed through her body.

Oh yes, she'd forgotten the rush that preceded a scene.

With her head still down, she turned and walked the few short steps to the bench and leaned over it. Matt moved behind her and pushed down on her upper body.

"All the way, grab the holds at the bottom," he said.

She had to stand on her toes to reach them and she hoped she was able to hide her wince of pain. She decided she must have, because Matt didn't comment on it. She took a deep breath and waited for further instruction.

He shifted behind her, and gently stroked her backside. Though she didn't mean to, she compared his touch to Lennox's. She'd been right in her assessment—Matt's hands were far rougher. And though his touch was nice, that was really all she could say about it. It didn't make her ache with longing or burn throughout her body like Lennox's touch.

He spanked her a few times in warm up and she counted the lines of woodgrain on the hardwood floor. The first stroke of a flogger caught her a bit off guard and she jerked, putting more pressure on her bad ankle. She sucked in a breath at the pain.

Matt didn't stop or slow down, and truthfully, she didn't want him to. She wanted him to flog her, to take her away momentarily from all her problems and to leave her mind so transfixed she didn't feel the urge to count woodgrain.

He gradually picked up speed and it was a decent flogging. He was perfectly adequate as a Dom, but that was it. She wondered if Lennox had ruined her for other Doms? But how could that be when he'd never flogged her?

"I get the distinct impression you're not with me, Mary."

Hell, there he went with the Mary again. She rolled her eyes. This was a mistake. She shouldn't have agreed to do this. Lennox was probably still upstairs and all she'd have to show for the club visit was a sore ankle.

The next strikes of the flogger were low on her body. He struck the back of her calves, the tips hitting just above the brace, and she yelped. Finally, she let go of the handhold and fell hard to her feet. Pain shot up her leg.

"Damn it. Red," she exclaimed as she slid to the floor.

"Mary?"

"Her fucking name is not Mary."

Mariela groaned at the sound of his voice. Of course. Now he'd show up. Now, when she was on her ass in front of god and everyone in a new club.

"Who are you?" she heard Matt ask.

"I'm her employer."

"Man, that's fucked up." Matt had certainly nailed that one. "But this is my scene and you need to leave."

Except she didn't want Lennox to leave. She was embarrassed as hell and felt like shit, but she didn't want him to leave. "Lennox. Stay."

She glanced up in time to see the look of triumph on his face. And a polar opposite look on Matt's.

"Are you with him?" Matt asked, and to Lennox, he added, "I asked her if she wanted to play. She didn't say she was with anyone."

"No, I'm not with him." Mariela tried to stand, but her ankle hurt too much. "He's a friend is all."

"Where's your boot?" Lennox asked with a bit of anger in his tone.

"In the dressing room," she mumbled.

Lennox gave a signal to someone behind her.

"You didn't tell me you were injured," Matt said.

She reached her hand up to Lennox. "Help, please."

Lennox scooped her up while glaring at Matt. "You didn't ask if she had any medical issues?"

As Lennox's words sank in, his face paled and he saw his error. "No. But she should have told me."

"Agreed," Lennox said. "And I'll be having that conversation with her privately. But for now, I want you to see your mistake as a Dom."

"Who are you?" Matt asked.

But instead of answering him, Lennox turned to the group of men he'd been standing with upstairs. "This lack of communication between players is exactly what I was telling you that you needed to watch out for. Both parties were in error here, but it is imperative that you ensure your Doms know what to ask when negotiating a scene."

Lennox was here consulting? Mariela looked at him in shock. What the hell?

"Marie, the submissive here, hurt her leg in a car accident and it would appear that she is supposed to be wearing a boot. Is that right, Marie?"

She felt her face heat. "Yes, Sir."

"And you didn't feel it necessary to let the Dom you were playing with know about the injury?"

Damn him for doing this in public. "I didn't think he'd do anything that would put stress on my leg or ankle."

"And as a sub in the scene are you supposed to know everything he has planned?"

"No, Sir."

"Exactly. Which is why Doms rely on the submissive to not withhold important information. Wouldn't you agree?"

Oh, she was going to let him have it when they were alone. "Yes, Sir. I royally fucked up. Not telling the Dom I was playing with about my ankle was fuckup number three. Playing with someone was fuckup number two. But my number one fuckup was giving a shit about you and coming here in the first place."

Several of the surrounding people gasped at her words, several others snickered. Lennox glared at her.

"Are you trying to earn a spanking?" he asked.

"I don't know. Can you do anything other than run your mouth? Sir?"

She didn't know what she was doing. The words simply left her mouth without any communication with her brain. Perhaps, deep inside, she was hoping he'd punish her. But one look at the expression on his face told her that he was onto her.

"I happen to recall a very similar situation involving another submissive who was trying to goad me into punishing her." Lennox spoke very calmly. "You gave me some excellent advice. Do you remember?"

Oh, hell.

Lennox laughed, and she realized she'd spoken out loud. "Exactly."

The tall redhead approached them carrying her boot and no one said anything as she buckled it in place.

When she finished, Lennox motioned toward the Dom in the front of the group he'd been addressing. "Eric, please cane Marie for me. When you finish, bring her to me in room C. Be sure to be mindful of her injured leg and ankle."

She cursed under her breath, but Lennox simply nodded at her and turned away, heading toward the aftercare rooms along the back wall.

Eric cleared his throat. "Back over the bench, Marie. Flat on your feet this time."

Fuck. Fuck. Fuck a duck.

LENNOX FORCED HIMSELF not to look back, even after he heard Eric tell Marie to bend over the bench. He told himself he had to keep going to prove to her that she could not control him. Nor could she goad him into getting her own way.

He made it to the aftercare room, but just as he was getting ready to open the door, a manicured hand stopped him.

"Wait a minute," Rachel said. "Not so fast."

It had shocked the hell out of him when he saw Rachel and her new fiancé at the club. From the look on her expression, she had been just as shocked as he was. He had assumed, incorrectly, that because her husband-to-be didn't want her operating her house of submissives, that he wasn't into kink. On the contrary, Lennox had learned that he was a well-known Dominant.

"Rachel," he said.

She stood with her head tilted and her arms crossed. "Who was that?"

"I'm sure you heard. She's my employee."

"You might have fooled some of the people here with that line—I doubt it, but it's possible. But you sure as hell didn't fool me."

He sighed. He really didn't want to discuss Marie with her. He really didn't. "Our relationship is . . . complicated."

She laughed softly, and it pissed him off a bit. "Why is that funny?" he asked.

"You want complicated? I'll give you complicated. My fiancé?" At his nod, she continued. "Is also my brother-in-law."

Lennox wasn't sure if she had any siblings or she meant that . . . holy hell.

"Yes," she said with a smile. "You guessed correctly. He's my husband's older brother."

"I bet that makes Thanksgiving interesting," he said dryly.

She, of course, didn't back down from the conversation. "It was strange at first, but everyone's actually been really nice about it. I mean, we obviously never would have gotten together if Steven hadn't died. But he did and through that pain and grief, Dean and I found each other and fell in love."

He wasn't able to formulate a response or any sort of question before she asked, "Marie is somehow connected to the woman you lost, isn't she?"

He was so shocked, all he could do was nod.

"Sister?" she asked.

"No." He coughed. "But she may as well have been. They were best friends."

"I think in some ways that's worse than a sibling."

He thought about that. "Perhaps, but in a lot of ways it's better."

She reached out, as if to touch him, but at the last minute stopped. Probably she remembered where she was and that her Dom would not want her touching other men without his permission, and though he'd agreed to the hug earlier, that didn't mean she could touch Lennox whenever she wanted. After all, this was a BDSM club, not her place of business.

"Either way you look at it, your shared past, the grief, all of it, it can either make you stronger together or it can drive you apart. I saw the way you looked at each other. More than that, I saw her watching you before we all went downstairs. It's probably why she agreed to scene with Matt in the first place."

Marie had been watching him? That meant she probably saw him hug Rachel. Hell.

Rachel nodded. "Eric's bringing her this way. Be kind." She hesitated and then added, "I'm inviting you to the wedding. Bring her as your plus one."

She left right as Eric brought Marie to him. From her expression, she'd witnessed his exchange with Rachel. Lennox opened the door and thanked Eric.

"I'll take it from here," he said before turning to Marie. "Come on inside."

She desperately wanted to ask about Rachel, he could see it in her eyes. But she'd just been caned, so she probably didn't want to speak out of turn.

"Rachel is an old friend," he said, deciding not to share exactly how he knew her. What would it do other than to bring her more heartache? "She's here with her fiancé. I was unaware they'd be here tonight." He chuckled. "Of course, I wasn't expecting you either."

She didn't say anything. He took her hand and led her to a nearby couch and pulled her into his lap. He buried his face in her hair.

"I'll take care of the cane marks in a minute. Right now, I just want to hold you," he whispered.

She sobbed lightly, holding him tightly while she cried. And while he hated her tears, he knew she needed to let them out and that they couldn't move on until she did.

He lost track of time as he sat there, holding her. He breathed her in like she was the air he needed to survive and, at the same time, marveled that he never felt that way about Winnie. He wasn't sure how long it was before she stopped crying, but in that time, he had categorized every detail he could about her—the various colors in her hair, the shape of her ear and the adorable swirl it had that he wanted to run his tongue around. So many small details he'd never taken notice of, even on their one night together.

Had he ever studied Winnie's ear? He didn't think so. Of course, Winnie was never one who could stand to be held for any length of time. Odds were, he never had the chance to study her ear.

Marie had stilled in his arms. Worse, she'd become tense, as if she was putting up with him holding her only because she had to.

"Marie?" he asked. "Are you okay?"

"Yes, Sir," she said, but her voice didn't sound at all convincing. "I think I'm ready for you to take care of the marks now."

He wasn't sure if that was what she really wanted or if she just wanted off his lap. Whichever it was, he did need to care for the welts. He shifted her and told her to bend over his lap.

She shot him a look that told him in no uncertain terms what she thought about his request, but she did it anyway.

Eric had only given her six strokes, a bit lighter than what he would have administered, but understandable since the other Dom was a stand-in. Besides, he'd much rather Eric have erred on the side of caution than to have gone in the other direction and given her too many.

She was quiet as he applied cream to the welts. She didn't move a single part of her body. In fact, she was so compliant, he wondered what she was thinking. He wanted to ask her, but he realized he had not earned either her complete trust or the right to her thoughts.

Since he had no right to her thoughts, he felt it appropriate to include her in his. Even though he couldn't predict how she would react to the information he was getting ready to share. Was it cowardly to tell her while she was bent over his lap? He wouldn't be able to see her face. While she might not always voice her thoughts, he was typically able to get a feel for them by her expression.

He would wait then until he finished her aftercare before he told her. Not only would he be able to see her face, but it would prevent her from taking off immediately after he finished caring for her.

She tried, though. As soon as he indicated she could get up, she tried to leave the room.

"Thank you," she said. "I'll be going."

He held out a hand to stop her. "Don't leave just yet."

The indecision on what to do played across her face. "I need to get back." She glanced around the room. "It's late. . . . I . . ."

He reached out a hand to stop her. "Marie, wait."

She hesitated and bit her bottom lip. Still undecided.

"Please," he added.

It was the *please* that did it. Maybe it was a cheap and dirty trick, but he would have done a lot more and played a lot dirtier to keep her from leaving.

She nodded and gingerly took her seat, folding her hands and placing them in her lap, as if sitting down to a formal dinner. He admired the fact that she did so; he knew it was difficult for her to sit down at the moment.

"Thank you," he said. "I'm making some changes in my life, and I wanted you to hear about them from me."

That was enough of a shock to capture her entire attention.

He saw no reason to drag out the decisions he'd made. He contemplated taking her hands, but thought that might be a bit melodramatic.

"I've found I've enjoyed my time away from the academy. So much so, that it's made me wonder if it's the academy holding me back and keeping me from moving forward. In my professional life, sure, but more importantly, in my personal life."

Her forehead wrinkled. "I'm not sure I understand, Sir."

He sighed and this time he did take her hands, running his thumbs over the top of her knuckles in what he hoped was a soothing manner. He didn't care if it was melodramatic or not, he wanted the connection with her when he told her what he needed her to know. She looked momentarily shocked, but didn't pull away. Perhaps understanding on some level that he needed to touch her.

"I'm going to take a leave of absence from the academy," he said. Her jaw dropped open in surprise, so he quickly added, "Just for the rest of the term. I'll be back before the new year."

"I don't . . . I can't . . ." She shook her head.

"It really won't be a change for you, since you're staying at the cottage." It sounded like he was trying to explain or get her approval and he didn't want to come across as unsure in any way about his plans.

"It just doesn't seem right, the academy without you."

He wasn't sure, but he thought there might be tears in her eyes. "It's just a month or so. I've been running the academy for years and do you know how much time I've taken off?"

"Not any that I remember," she admitted.

"So wouldn't you think I'm due a few weeks?" he asked softly.

She bent her head and took a deep breath. When she looked up again, her eyes were definitely wet. "I don't know why it's bothering me so much. I guess I just take for granted that you're always going to be on the island. And it won't seem right without you there." She sniffled. "I'll be moving back next week."

It wasn't like her to be so emotional, and it struck him almost immediately what was behind it. Subdrop. Damn it all. And he hadn't anticipated it. If he'd been thinking more clearly, about anything other than his own purpose, he'd have expected it.

What kind of an ass was he that he brought up his plans for a leave right when she was going through subdrop?

"Marie." He gently took her in his arms. "I'm sorry. I know exactly why it's bothering you."

"You do?" She took the tissue he handed her and wiped her nose.

"Subdrop."

"Oh," she said. "It's been forever since I've had subdrop. I forgot how awful it feels."

"And I should have known better. I'm a headmaster of a BDSM academy and I didn't even think about the impact of the scene on you."

She started to say something, but he stopped her. "Don't even think about telling me it's okay. Because it's not. It was selfish of me."

"But," she said, "if you hadn't told me now, when would you have told me?"

He shrugged. He really hadn't thought about not telling her tonight. As soon as he'd seen her in the club, he knew it had to be tonight. "I don't know," he confessed.

"Wouldn't it make sense then that if you didn't tell me tonight, I might hear it from someone else?"

He stroked her knuckles again, amazed at her clarity of thinking. "That is most certainly the truth, but it doesn't erase the fact that I could have gone about it differently."

"I think." She took a deep breath. "I think we need to talk, but I'm afraid I'm not in the right frame of mind at the moment."

She was right, of course. "I have a hotel room booked. You're more than welcome to stay with me if you don't want to go back to the cottage tonight. We can talk tomorrow, after your emotions have leveled out and you've had some sleep."

He could see her struggle: the part of her that wanted to stay with him warring with the part that wanted to prove she didn't need his company. "I promise to keep my hands to myself."

His words sparked something in her because some of her old spunk returned when she answered, "And if I don't want you to keep your hands to yourself?"

He wasn't about to make a promise he couldn't keep and he knew if she wanted him, he wouldn't be able to refuse her. "I promise nothing will happen that you don't want."

She tilted her head. "Okay. I'll stay with you tonight. But I'm not sure where I want your hands right now."

If he knew her at all—and he was certain he did—it wasn't that she wasn't sure where she wanted his hands. Rather, it was that she was unsure how she felt about where she wanted his hands.

Her uncertainty was probably for the best anyway. They needed to sit down and have a serious talk before they did anything physical again. "It's not something you have to decide right now." He stood up and held out his hand. "Come with me back to my hotel. You can take a hot shower and I'll order us a good bottle of wine."

"Make it aged whisky and you have yourself a deal."

Her insistence on whisky made him smile, because it was so Marie. "Deal," he said. "I'd rather have whisky over wine any day."

With that settled, she took his hand and rose to her feet.

MARIELA HAD A feeling that agreeing to spend the night with Lennox in his hotel room wasn't going to go down as one of her better decisions. She knew agreeing to spend the night with Lennox in his hotel room along with a bottle of aged whisky surely wouldn't.

But, hell, she was still in shock over his cool and calm statement that he was taking a leave of absence from the academy. Where in the world had that come from? It didn't even seem like him. The academy without Lennox was like her not dancing.

Which, when she stopped to think about it, actually had happened. How long had it been since she'd danced? Just her? For her?

Long enough that it was going to take more than whisky to make her feel better.

Tonight, though, she knew feeling blue was more than not being able to dance. She was still experiencing the effects of subdrop, and though it'd been awhile since she'd dealt with it, she'd dealt with it enough in the past to know that she would get through it. In fact, if the patterns of the past held up, she'd feel better as early as the next morning.

Of course, that didn't make her feel any better *now*. No, now she just wanted the promised shower and whisky. And a naked Lennox.

No.

She could not let anything happen between them tonight. Nothing. No way. No how.

Out of the corner of her eye, she watched him as he drove them to his hotel. He wasn't saying anything. Was it possible he was already regretting his offer for her to spend the night? His jaw wasn't tight, though, and usually she could tell when he was upset about something because it would be obvious in his jawline.

He wasn't regretting asking her, she decided. He was allowing her to come to terms with the fact that she accepted the offer. She was also willing to bet he knew her lie for what it was when she told him earlier that she wasn't sure she knew where she wanted his hands. The truth was, she knew exactly where she wanted his hands. What she didn't know was did she want them before, during, or after her shower?

I'll take D, all of the above, please.

She didn't realize she'd giggled until he looked at her with a smile on his face. It struck her then how relaxed he looked. She didn't want to examine him in great detail because he'd get a kick out of that, but he actually looked more like the Lennox she'd first met several years ago as opposed to the haunted man who had lived such a hollow existence the last few years.

Could it be possible that running the academy for so long was part of what had him living in the past? The more she thought about it, the more sense it made. He hadn't started the academy out of some burning desire to train Doms and subs. It hadn't been a lifelong dream. In fact, on more than one occasion, he'd called the academy his penance for what happened to Winnie.

It was selfish of her, she was willing to admit that, but she couldn't stop wondering what would happen to her if he left. Would she stay at the academy? Did she want to remain on the island without him there? She didn't think she did. And she didn't even want to think about what it meant that she'd spent nearly three years at a job simply because she wanted to be near the boss.

Damn it. She was an idiot.

"We're here," he said.

The car had already come to a stop, and she wondered exactly how long they'd been parked at the hotel. From the amused expression on his face, it had been more than a few minutes.

"I was thinking about something," she said. Which might possibly be the lamest statement that had ever been uttered.

"Obviously," he said, not even trying to hide his amusement.

She almost snapped at him. She had the right to do so, she thought. If you looked at the last few hours, she'd put up with the shock of seeing him, hurting her ankle, getting caned, finding out Lennox was taking a leave of absence, and then being asked to accompany him to his hotel room—hell that was enough for her to be lost in concentration.

But she was tired of snapping at him. She wanted to go back to the easygoing person she was even a few short months ago. So she bit back her sarcastic remark.

If Lennox could do it—and hell, the last time she'd seen him as easygoing as he seemed to be today, had been years ago—then she could, too. Part of her grew giddy as her mind tried to comprehend the possibilities of both of them putting aside the sarcasm and being kind and carefree and maybe even, god forbid, having a laugh every once and awhile.

She flashed a smile at him. "Yes, I was thinking about how nice a hot shower would feel, followed by some whisky."

"Far be it from me to stand between a woman and her creature comforts." He hopped out of the car, and before she could unbuckle her seat belt, he'd opened her door to help her out.

Her heart was light as they walked into the hotel, and his hand on the small of her back? It felt like it belonged there.

By the time they'd made it to his room, though, some of the *What the hell am I doing?* had kicked back in. She shoved that voice to the back of her mind, and told herself the only thing she'd agreed to was a shower and a drink, she held her head high and crossed the threshold into his room.

"Point me to your bathroom," she said, keeping her focus away from the bed. *Look anywhere except the bed. Anywhere at all will be fine. Doesn't matter where.*

"Just to the left of the bed." He pointed.

She scurried into the room he indicated, but not before her eyes caught sight of the bed. Huge. King-sized. Fluffy pillows. Thick downy comforter. The sort of bed you crawled into when you didn't have plans to leave for days. The sort of bed you took your lover to when you wanted to keep them there. The sort of bed that you would sink into after hours of two entwined bodies and too many kisses to count to get a bit of sleep before waking up and doing it all again.

She closed the bathroom door behind her and leaned back against it, taking a deep breath. She could do this. Shower and whisky. Shower and whisky. That was all. Shower and whisky.

The more she said it, the less she believed it. Lennox had probably known that from the start. He expected her to just take a shower. She looked through the items that the high-end hotel had left on the counter and giggled. Poor Lennox. He had no idea what he was in for.

She was going to make sure there was no doubt where she wanted his hands.

MARIE WAS TAKING too damn long in the shower and to Lennox that meant one thing: she was planning something. Probably a seduction scene. But he'd been serious when he'd decided they needed to discuss things before doing anything physical again.

Damn it, though, if she came out the way he expected her to, he couldn't just turn her down. Heaven knew he'd hurt her enough the last few years and he'd do anything in his power going forward not to cause her emotional pain again.

Which meant he had to revise his plans.

He kicked his shoes off and poured them both a shot of whisky. Then he thought better of it and poured them both a double. He held off drinking any until she could join him.

Finally, after what seemed like hours, the bathroom door opened. Marie stepped out in a sweet, lavender-smelling, steam-filled mist. Wearing only a towel. He couldn't keep his eyes off her.

She saw exactly what she did to him and, judging by the slight grin she wore, she liked it. Because she walked toward him in a manner that focused his attention on the towel wrapped precariously around her petite body. He couldn't help but think about how little it would take to remove it completely.

"I didn't have anything clean to put on after my shower," she said.

She stood close enough to him that he could smell the bath soap and shampoo she'd used. Lavender. It was like the hotel knew exactly how to drive him crazy.

"Here," he said, spinning around. "I have an extra shirt you can wear."

He expected her to go back to the bathroom to change. But when she dropped the towel, right there next to the bed, and held out her hand for the shirt, he could have smacked himself. Of course she'd drop the towel in front of him. That had been her plan since deciding to step out of the bathroom in a towel in the first place.

"You act as if you've never seen me naked before." She lifted the shirt over her head and slipped her arms through. "You have, many times."

Of course he had, but only once before with a bed in such close proximity. And they both knew how that night went.

"I poured us some drinks." He walked over to the minibar where he'd left the glasses and carried them both to her.

She took hers and headed out to the balcony. He wanted to

tell her that it was cold out there and she should stay inside. Before he could, she pushed back the curtains, exposing an outdoor heater.

"Fancy place you're staying at." She opened the glass door and stepped outside to turn the heater on.

He joined her, looking over the city. "I haven't been out on the balcony."

She raised an eyebrow. "You? Who insisted on a balcony in your apartment on the island?"

He hated repeating what he'd said earlier; it had pained her when he said it, but it was the only explanation he could give. "I think it goes back to the island being a large part of what's holding me back."

She didn't say anything, but turned away and took a sip of her whisky. "God, that's good." She took another sip.

"I learned about whisky from the best."

"I taught you well."

"You did." Wanting to change the subject, he asked, "How are you feeling?"

She stretched in what had to be one of the most erotic things he'd ever seen and took another sip. "The shower made me feel better. The whisky makes me feel human."

"Trust me." He spoke without thinking. "There's nothing even vaguely human about you. You're one hundred ten percent goddess."

She chuckled and turned back to look out over the balcony. "What are we going to do, Lennox?"

"I don't know," he answered honestly. "I'm not sure I want or need to go back to being on the island all the time. I have to see if I can find who I was before . . . before Winnie died." He felt the familiar ache in his chest at the thought of her, but somehow, maybe because he'd finally voiced exactly what happened, it didn't feel as intense and didn't last as long as it normally did.

Marie knew, of course, what those words cost him. She tenderly placed a soft hand over his death grip on the railing. "Then you should go see if you can find him."

"But I want to be near you. I want to see if what we have can become something and I can't drag you away from the island." She wasn't living at the academy while she was overseeing work on the cottage, but she'd be heading back to the island soon. Besides, he'd spoken with Andie a few times about how Marie was doing, and according to her, the strain of being away seemed to be taking its toll.

"Maybe I need you to be away from the island, so I can tell if it's the island or something else keeping me there."

By *something else*, did she mean him? The faint wetness growing in her eyes seemed to indicate that was the case.

"But," she continued, "I think no matter what we decide or where either one of us goes after the first of the year, we should both agree to complete honesty between us."

"I hate that I've acted in such a way that you even have to say that." How deeply had he hurt her? And yet she still stood steadfast in her feelings for him. The depth of her loyalty and the strength of her character humbled him.

"I think the blame lies with both of us, but truly that's neither here nor there. Let's not look to the past." She lifted her hand from his, only to place it on his upper arm. "I'm looking to the future."

"I want to be the type of man you deserve," he whispered.

"You always have been," she said.

He knew that wasn't the case, not even close, but he wasn't about to argue with her. Not when she closed her eyes and leaned toward him. Before, he would have pulled away. Even before they'd walked out onto the balcony, he probably would have stopped her.

But she had asked for honesty from him and he would not have been honest to pull away from her. Her lips and her kiss were gifts he didn't deserve, but if she was going to offer them to him, he'd be a fool to turn them away. He'd been a fool for years and he refused to go backward.

He lowered his head to meet her halfway. The freedom of being honest filled his soul near to bursting. He eased her lips open with his own and could have kicked himself for letting so many years pass while he denied who she was to him and what she meant.

His fingers tangled in her hair and she moaned, moving even closer.

"God, Marie," he said against her lips. "I want you so bad, but I can't allow myself to take you. Not tonight. Not when I'm going to be going away."

"I don't care."

"But I do and it wouldn't be fair." It was the hardest thing he'd ever done, but he took a step back. "When I take you again, and I plan to, there will be nothing to hold us back."

She yawned and then blushed at his grin. The whisky had

already had an effect on her. "Okay," she said. "But will you hold me while I sleep?"

It would not be a comfortable night if he did. With her nipples evident through the material of his shirt and how its hem barely grazed her upper thigh, he was guaranteed to fight an erection. Yet, he considered it a small price to pay.

"I would be honored."

CHAPTER
Twelve

Six Weeks Later

It wasn't raining. Lennox took the nice weather as a sign he was doing the right thing. He made one stop on his way to where he was going and was in and out of the store in five minutes.

It had been six weeks since he'd promised Marie total honesty and held her all night while she'd slept. In those weeks apart, he'd grown stronger. Part of that came from admitting and accepting his Dominant nature would always be an essential part of who he was. Part of that came from carrying a burden that was not meant for him. It wasn't meant for anyone, actually. Today, he planned to put it down and not pick it back up.

The garden cemetery was located outside of town, by the sea. He'd selected it because Winnie loved the ocean so much. His heart hurt as he remembered having to decide where she'd be buried. At twenty-nine, she hadn't given death a second thought. And why should she have?

He started walking along the well-maintained stone walkway to the headstone he'd had to pick out that same day so many years ago. He clutched the flowers in his hand, remembering and waiting for the overwhelming grief and guilt to hit him.

It didn't come. Instead he felt happy at the good memories he had shared with her.

Her headstone was plain. Anything too ornate would have been out of place at the seaside location. He ran his fingers across the engraving of her name.

WINIFRED LOUISE PRICE
BELOVED

He couldn't hold back the half snort, half laugh because it hit him how much she'd have hated that tombstone.

"I'm sorry," he said. "Hell, it seems like all I ever did was apologize to you for some reason or another. I guess this is just one more. But if you could see this, well, you'd know I had to apologize for it. All I can say is I was in a daze after you died and I wasn't thinking straight."

He placed the bouquet of pink and white roses at the base of the tombstone.

"I actually haven't been thinking straight for a good number of years and I'm going to correct that today. I spent so much time since you've been gone blaming myself, but I've come to realize that there were two of us in that relationship and I have to share the blame with you. That sounds crazy, doesn't it? But it's true, I've tried to keep the blame all to myself and I can't anymore."

He took a deep breath and looked out over the ocean.

"I won't say our relationship was wrong, because I loved you and love is never wrong. But you know as well as I do that we were never going to be truly compatible. And if it wasn't for you, for us, I never would have met the one person I'm most compatible with.

"Part of me was buried with you, but I can see now that it doesn't have to stay that way. I'm not dead. And I'm sorry you are. I'm so sorry and if there was anything I could do to bring you back, you know I would. Because a part of me will always love you. And I know now that it's okay for me to love someone else. It doesn't take anything away from what we had.

"Marie didn't come with me and that's okay. I think it's better this way." He wrinkled his forehead. He hadn't seen Marie since the night she'd stayed in his hotel room, and they'd only spoken on the phone a few times. She knew where he was, though, and she'd told him he needed to be here alone. He saw now that she had been right. "She said she told you good-bye in the hospital. I don't know about all that. But we've made your cottage into something you'd be proud of and your legacy lives on. You won't be forgotten." He kissed his hand and gently touched the cold stone. "I love you, my Winnie girl."

As he turned to leave, a soft gust of wind blew gently across his face. Surprising only because of how warm it was.

MARIELA STOOD AT the doorway of the academy's ballroom welcoming guests as they arrived. For some reason there was a touch of melancholy in the air. Or at least it felt that way to her. Maybe it was because Lennox hadn't arrived yet, and without him the academy and, as a result, the Holiday Ball weren't as lively as they had been in the past.

"I just had a call from Lennox," Fulton said, walking by her from inside the ballroom.

"Oh." Mariela gave what she hoped was a *why are you telling me* grunt.

"You can't fool me, you know." Fulton smiled at her less-than-believable performance.

"That obvious?" she asked.

"I'm afraid so."

Realizing there was no point in trying to fool him, she asked, "How is he? Is he coming? What did he say?"

Fulton laughed and held up a hand. "One at a time."

A couple from the mainland who knew Lennox and who came to the ball every year picked that time to approach her and make small talk. She did her best to be polite and to act interested in what they were saying, but it was hard. She shot Fulton a look that she hoped conveyed how much she wanted him to stay and continue their conversation.

The couple finally left and she grabbed Fulton by the elbow and dragged him to a less traveled area of the room.

She crossed her arms. "Spill."

Fulton was known as being one to tease and kid, but he must have picked up on how desperate she was to hear news about Lennox, because he answered her directly. "He's doing well. Yes, he's coming. Should probably arrive within the next thirty minutes. He also said he tried to call you, but it went straight to voicemail."

She gasped and dug in her purse for her phone. It was off. She muttered a few choice words and turned it on. Would he call again? Or would he simply show?

"Mariela?" Fulton put his hand over hers and she saw that her fingers had been trembling. She looked up at him. "It's going to be okay. I can honestly tell you that he feels the same way you do."

She nodded, not sure she believed him.

"Whenever he's called me in the time he's been gone, he always asks how you're doing."

"Really?" she couldn't help but ask.

"Yes, really." Fulton had a huge smile on his face, and she knew if she didn't change the subject or find someone else to chat with, he'd start to tease her in earnest.

"Excuse me," she told him. "I think I'm going to hit the ladies room before he gets here."

Fulton caught sight of Andie across the room. Mariela could've probably told him she was going to take her spaceship to provide assistance in repopulating Planet X and he'd only nod and say "okay." She slipped away while he moved toward Andie.

Inside the bathroom, several people stopped her to comment on the decorations, how great the band sounded, and how awesome the food was. All Mariela could think about was whether Lennox would be there thirty minutes from when Fulton talked to her or from when he spoke to Fulton. Because she really didn't know what time he'd called Fulton.

He could possibly be here any second!

"I'm sorry," she said to the woman currently chewing her ear off about where she bought the Christmas tree. "I just remembered I'm supposed to meet someone."

She didn't wait for a reply, but nearly ran from the bathroom.

She looked around the room for Fulton. She had to know what time he'd talked to Lennox.

Damn it. Why didn't she see him? He couldn't have gone that far. She spun around to look for him outside the ballroom and ran smack into someone's chest.

A familiar pair of arms came around her at the same time she looked up and into the eyes she'd been fantasizing about the last few weeks.

"Where's the fire?" Lennox asked, and his smile was so genuine, it made her ache with happiness.

And his lips. She needed his lips.

Not even bothering to answer his question, she snaked her arms around him and pulled him toward her. She wasn't sure what came over her as she pressed her lips against his.

Lennox seemed momentarily taken aback, but it was mere seconds before his arms tightened around her. God, the feeling of being in his embrace again was the best feeling in the world. She held him to her tightly, never wanting to be parted from him again.

Lennox must have felt the same because it wasn't until several nearby people discreetly coughed that he pulled away.

"Welcome home," she said, once she managed to catch her breath. "I missed you."

"I missed you, too." He dropped his head to whisper so no one other than her heard him say, "And later tonight I'll show you exactly how much."

Her heart raced. "I'm going to hold you to that."

He took her hand. "But first we must be social."

She groaned, but knew he was right and walked alongside him.

"The decorations are beautiful," Lennox said, looking around the ballroom. "Not that I would have expected anything else."

"Thanks, but you know, after a few years, you get it down pat pretty quickly." She tilted her head, wondering if he'd made peace with his demons or if they still haunted him.

"What?" he asked. "What's the look for?"

"How was your time away?" But that really wasn't the question she wanted to ask.

"You mean have I found peace with myself and Winnie for what happened?" At her nod, he continued, "Yes, I think I finally have."

She smiled. "I'm glad." And she was. He could move on now. Maybe they both could.

"I went by her grave today," he said. "And, for the first time, I didn't walk away feeling guilty."

He truly had found what he'd been searching for. She didn't want to say she was glad again, so she simply nodded.

"I talked to her for a while. Explained a few things." He got a faraway look in his eyes and they looked misty, but just for a second. "It's funny. I had the strangest feeling she was standing there, that she was nearby. Watching and listening."

The skin on the back of her neck tingled and she reached up to rub the sensitive spot.

"I bet she was," she said.

"Makes sense." He nodded. "That she would come by one last time when I was finally ready to say good-bye."

"You really told her good-bye?" Something that felt a lot like hope started to swell within her chest. "For good?"

"Being away from everything helped me to realize I'm not dead and I need to stop acting like I am. And I realized how foolish I was in denying my Dom nature. Don't you find it to be slightly ironic that I planned to end my relationship with Winnie because I couldn't give up being a Dom and yet that's exactly what I did when she died?"

"I'd say that's a bit more than slightly ironic."

He reached out a tentative hand and brushed her cheek. "It's what you've been trying to tell me all along, isn't it?"

She tried to concentrate on what he was saying, but it was too hard with the gentle way he touched her. The light stroke of his fingers against her skin brought to mind memories of the night they'd spent together in the cottage. Her body remembered his touch and longed for more of it. She felt herself lean into his hand.

"Oh, Marie," he whispered. "Look at me."

She lifted her eyes to capture his gaze and her heart nearly beat out of her chest. The look he had for her was so different than any expression she'd ever seen on his face before, even with Winnie. It was a look of determination, love, and promise, but more than that, it was a look of new beginnings.

He ran his thumb across her bottom lip. "Dance with me?"

She nodded mutely and allowed him to lead her into the main section of the ballroom. As they passed the guests, everyone grew quiet. Her cheeks heated.

Lennox bent down to whisper in her ear, "Sorry, looks like you're the center of attention and I know you only like that when you're naked."

"That's okay," she whispered back. "The only other option is to strip down to nothing and I don't think that would fit with the holiday-party spirit."

He gave a low chuckle but didn't speak again until they'd made it to the dance floor. She expected him to take her in his arms, but instead, he simply kept hold of her hand and turned to face her.

"You and I have worked together for how many years?" he asked.

She wrinkled her forehead, both because for one, she couldn't remember exactly how long it'd been and two, for the life of her, she couldn't fathom why he was asking her that now. "Umm, almost three years?"

"That's what I thought. It doesn't seem possible, but I don't think we've ever danced together."

They hadn't. She couldn't believe he hadn't realized it sooner. "No, we haven't. In fact, one of the things I remember from all our previous balls is how upset I'd get watching you dance with damn near every woman in the room, except me."

"I was too afraid before," he said.

"And you're not anymore?"

Instead of answering, he swept her into his arms and began leading her around the room. There were a few other couples dancing, but Mariela felt as if every eye in the place was on them. Had she been able to tear herself away from Lennox's gaze, she would have looked.

"We may not have danced before tonight, but you're the only woman I'm dancing with tonight," he said.

"That hardly seems fair to all the other women here."

"Too bad."

He pulled her close then and she wasn't able to think about other women, the decorations, or who was watching. As they danced, everything around them disappeared into a low hum and, for those few precious moments, even the other people seemed to fade away until it was only the two of them and a thousand white lights.

He was an accomplished dancer; she knew as much from observing him in the past. Yet her observation fell far short of experiencing his hard body pressed against her. Or the way his hand settled along the small of her back as if it belonged there. It most certainly hadn't left her with any indication of how it'd feel to have his warm breath tickling her ear.

"You're like magic in my arms," he said. "It's as if I've never danced before."

She almost told him he was being corny but decided not to. The newly exposed tender side was such an interesting contrast to his old self. She could put up with a bit of corniness if she had to.

From the corner of her eye, she saw Fulton and Andie take to the dance floor. No doubt they were hoping for a song to play for a swing dance. Andie caught her eye and gave her a not-so-subtle thumbs-up that made several people nearby laugh.

"Those two," Lennox said, shaking his head. "They're nothing but trouble."

"Agreed," she said. "But it's the good kind of trouble, so we'll let it slide."

He looked down at her, his voice serious, though his eyes were filled with laughter. "And what kind of trouble am I?"

Oh yes, she thought she could definitely get used to this new side of Lennox. She pretended to be thinking. "Mmm," she hummed. "Depends."

He pulled her to a stop and covered his heart with his hand. "Depends? Marie, you wound me."

They were drawing the attention of the crowd again. Marie felt her face heat and she pulled him to her, trying to get him to dance again. "Stop it. Everyone's looking at us."

"You could get naked." Lennox waggled his eyebrows.

Who was this man? After the night in the hotel, she'd tried to hope his easygoing nature would remain. She didn't want to be disappointed again, even though that's exactly what usually wound up happening. But now, she allowed that hope to bloom. He was actually smiling and teasing.

She pushed his chest. "You wish."

"Damn straight."

"You want to know what kind of trouble you are?" she asked. "The absolute worst kind."

"That's a good thing, right?"

"You're also incorrigible."

He didn't say anything, but pulled her into his arms for another spin around the room. "Admit it," he said while she tried to ignore all the stares they were getting. "You like me incorrigible."

"Honestly." She made sure he was looking at her before she continued. "I don't know what to think about this side of you. I've never seen it before."

He grew serious. "I think this is the real me. The me I was . . . before everything happened."

She tilted her head. Was that true? She wasn't sure she truly remembered a Lennox before Winnie. "Really?" she couldn't help but ask.

"Yes. It's just been so long." He took a deep breath. "But I feel free finally. Normal."

She had to admit, she really liked the return of the old him. "How do I know you'll stay like this? That you won't revert to the Lennox I've known all these years?"

"I can't promise I won't have days when the darkness comes

back, but I think those days will be few and far between." He smiled. "If I have you with me."

Her heart began to pound. Was this really happening?

"Tell me I haven't lost you, Marie." He must have misread her silence. "I'm not going to live in the past anymore. There's a part of me that still feels guilty over Winnie's death, but I'm not going to let it rule my life for a second longer. And if I have you, I think with time, that part of me will slowly fade away into nothing."

Yes. She felt her body warm with his words and the promise they represented. This was really happening. He must have seen the realization dawn in her eyes, because she saw hope begin to flicker in his expression.

"Tell me yes, Marie," he begged. "Tell me I haven't lost you. That you'll be with me and stand by me as I rejoin the life of the living."

Tears made her eyesight blurry. She reached up and brushed his cheek. "Yes," she whispered. "A million times yes."

"I love you," he said.

"And I've always loved you."

She didn't notice they'd stopped dancing again until he leaned forward and kissed her soundly. She was further shocked by the applause that seemed to burst from the crowd as soon as his lips touched hers.

He held her tight, though, and wouldn't let her pull away. He broke the kiss long enough to whisper against her lips, "Deal with the attention, just this once. Let them all be happy for us."

"Only for you," was all she got out before his lips were once more on hers for a long, deep kiss. She wondered if the people clapping had any idea what she and Lennox had gone through to get to this point.

When he let her go and she risked a look at the gathered crowd, there were several people in attendance who were wiping their eyes. They did. They knew. And they were celebrating with them.

Lennox noticed, too. He lowered his head. "I say we get out of here while we still can and answer questions later."

And there would definitely be questions. She estimated they had about five minutes before the crowd descended upon them. How could there not be questions? The headmaster who had been alone for so long and the best friend of his dead girlfriend?

"I agree," she whispered. "Let's get out of here."

It was almost too late. As they started off the dance floor, a subtle shift in the crowd seemed to drift toward them. But just before they were surrounded, someone tapped silverware on a glass.

"Ladies and gentlemen, if I may have your attention." Fulton stood at the front of the room and gave them a wink. "RACK Academy has decided to start a new tradition this year. . . ."

"Now," Lennox grabbed her hand, and they all but ran from the ballroom.

It wasn't until they were outside and well on their way to his place that Mariela asked, "What new tradition?"

She'd been in charge of the ball for years and this was the first she'd heard about a new tradition. Lennox squeezed her hand. "A silent auction. To benefit the children's home Fulton grew up in. It was his idea and he asked me a week or so ago." He laughed. "I thought it was a good idea, but I'll admit, I had no idea it'd be such a lifesaver."

"I love it. What a perfect way to give back to the community. Kids at Christmas, there's nothing better." It was absolutely perfect.

"You don't mind I didn't bring it up to you first? I know the ball is yours to plan."

They were almost to his door. "Not in the least. I like a good surprise every now and then. Besides, it offered us a chance to escape. I like it so much, I'm going to write a big check."

He unlocked his door, but hesitated. "I want you to know, you're the first woman I've ever brought here."

She wasn't sure why he felt the need to admit that, but for whatever reason, it seemed important to him. "Thank you for telling me."

He opened the door and let her in first. She didn't even take the time to look around, but turned and faced him instead. "Know what I want?"

His gaze turned predatory. "I certainly hope so. I hope it's the same thing I want."

"I want you. I want you to dominate me."

"And here I thought I'd won you over to slow and easy."

She slipped out of her coat. "Do you really want slow and easy?"

His eyes never left her body as she toed her shoes off. "Hell no. I want you under me and I want it hard and rough and long and dirty, and when we finish, I want to do it all again. I want to touch every inch of you and just when you think you can't live without me inside your body for one more second, I want to thrust inside you so deep, you'll think I've become a permanent part of you. I want to fuck you for hours, and when we're exhausted and can't move anymore, I want to pull you into my arms and hold you while we both fall asleep."

A shiver ran through her at his words.

"How does that sound to you?" he asked.

"Like the best idea you've ever had, Sir."

"In that case, there's a black bag in the coat closet. Go get it and carry it into the bedroom and wait for me there."

A black bag? Did that mean what she thought it did?

She gave him a quick, "Yes, Sir," and hurried to the closet to retrieve the bag. It was heavy and confirmed what she hoped. At least, she thought it did.

She placed it just inside the door and took the few steps necessary to make it to the middle of the room. Dropping to her knees, she took a deep breath. Though it felt similar to when she'd knelt for him in the cottage, it was vastly different. This time, there were no more secrets between them. More importantly, there was no guilt.

He walked into the room and she actually felt giddy. After all they'd been through, fought through, and come to terms with, they were finally here.

"You look incredible, Marie," Lennox said, a touch of awe and wonder in his voice.

Her chest swelled with pride. He wanted her and he thought she looked incredible. Though it was a natural reaction to thank him, she decided to do so with her actions and obedience instead of with words.

Though her head was down, she could still see his feet just inside the door. He reached down to pick up the black bag.

"You probably guessed what this was and you're partially right. The submissive you saw me talking with weeks ago before I exited the club, Rachel? Her fiancé told me about this local lady who makes all her toys by hand, and after he showed me the work she'd done for him, I called her. I can't tell you how much fun I had picking out new toys to use on you."

She knew he already had toys in his possession. Old ones. Ones he'd used on Winnie. She hadn't considered how it would feel if he used those on her, but now that she did, she realized how thankful she was that he'd wanted to purchase new toys. Further proof he was putting the past behind him and facing the future.

He dropped the bag beside her, his body in front of her. "But right now, I'm not going to use toys on you."

He wasn't? She frowned.

"While I think you look lovely in that gown, I want you to stand and take it off for me."

Maybe he was going to play without toys. That would be fine by her. She liked the idea of him only using his hands. And other body parts. She quickly rose to her feet, smiled, and within seconds had the gown off. Lennox took it from her and hung it in a nearby closet.

"I'm going to ask you to do something," he said, his voice low and calm but filled with authority all the same. "I know it's going to be extremely difficult for you, but I'm going to ask you to at least try. For me."

Her mind raced, trying to imagine what he could possibly have in mind. Their hard limits were almost identical.

"Don't frown," he said. "At least not before you've heard what it is."

She forced herself to relax her expression.

"Very good." He walked backward to the bed and sat down.

Why was he sitting down? It made no sense. "To begin, I'm going to ask you a few questions. What do you do for a living?"

This was hands down the oddest way to start a BDSM scene that she had ever heard of. If he hadn't been acting as a consultant for the last few weeks, she'd have thought maybe he'd been out of the lifestyle too long.

"I'm a dance instructor, Sir," she answered, deciding to go along with it. She trusted him. But why had he said this would be difficult?

"You told me once that you didn't have any trouble dancing for work. Is this still the case?"

"Yes, Sir."

"When was the last time you danced outside of work?"

She could be bratty and say of course she had danced outside of work, after all, she'd done it when she danced with him. But that wasn't the type of dancing he was talking about and she'd been the one to tell him that, if nothing else, they should have honesty between them.

Her belly began to ache as she slowly started to understand where this conversation was going. God help her.

"It was before the fall students arrived, Sir," she said in a voice barely above a whisper.

"When was the last time you tried to dance outside of work?"

"The last time I tried was probably sometime in September, Sir."

"Do you want to dance again? Stop and think before you answer."

She allowed the question to sink into her soul, down into the depths of who she was. And when it made it there, the answer was clear. She was a dancer. She danced.

"Yes, Sir. Please," she whispered as if he held the key to her ability to dance.

"Dance for me, Marie," he spoke in his low and commanding Dom voice. "Don't think. Close your eyes and let your body move."

Tears filled her eyes, because he thought it was just that easy. Close her eyes and move. Like she hadn't done that a thousand times. Now it would be one thousand and one. Worse still, she would disappoint him and she hated that because they hadn't even done anything yet.

But she wanted to do everything she could to please him, so she closed her eyes and took a deep breath. She heard him move from the bed and seconds later, the familiar sound of Mozart filled the air.

Her breathing was choppy because she knew she was going to fail. The tears she'd tried to hold back ran down her cheeks anyway and she sniffled. She sensed more than felt him move behind her.

"What's my job as a Dominant?" he asked, the heat from his breath on the nape of her neck sending shivers down her spine. "Tell me."

"To ensure my needs are met, Sir."

"Do you need to dance?"

"Yes."

"Why can't you?"

The answer came to her so quickly, she couldn't believe she hadn't realized it before. "I've lost my song, Sir."

The pain of that admission pierced her heart and she inhaled deeply, as if forcing air into her lungs would lessen the realization. More tears swelled behind her eyes, because she somehow knew he'd understand.

He oh-so-tenderly ran his hands down her arms and entwined their fingers. "Let me help you find it."

He stretched their arms out and then wrapped them around her. She felt his strength pour into her and for the first time in too many months, her feet moved in a pattern of ballet steps she'd known forever and so well, she could recite them in her sleep. But it'd been months since her body had answered the call of dance, until today.

Lennox kept her hands firmly clutched in his, even as he let her feet move. Little by little, her confidence grew and she twirled in his arms. Even then, he only let go of her for a second before she was safe and protected, back in his embrace.

He continued to hold her while her feet grew accustomed to the once-familiar feeling of her beloved ballet. How he kept up with her, she wasn't sure, but he was always there, ready to hold her or her hands, and to whisper that she was strong and beautiful.

"Keep your eyes closed," he commanded after some time. "And dance for me."

She felt a brief moment of panic as he let go of her and stepped away, but she focused on keeping her feet moving. They knew what to do, she didn't even have to think about it. The slight soreness in her right ankle barely registered with her.

Eyes closed, and no longer holding onto Lennox, she allowed the music to infuse her body. It was almost like being in subspace, she realized. She could shut her mind down, and instead of giving control to a Dom, she yielded to the power of the music. Yet even so, she knew that in reality she was yielding to Lennox, because he held power over the music.

The most overwhelming sense of freedom swept over her and she felt as light as a feather. As she danced, the burdens of the last few months slipped away, soon followed by the weight of the last few years. She was free. Finally free. Before she knew it, she was laughing as she danced.

The song continued, coming to its inevitable end. The last few notes played out, drifting through the air. By the time silence filled the room once more, she was kneeling on the floor, breathing heavily.

She'd done it! She'd danced!

The tears that came this time were tears of joy. She hadn't realized how empty she'd been without dance in her life. Now that she had it back, she was overwhelmed by peace and happiness. It was as if the joy inside her was too much to contain and it had to spill out some way.

Lennox was behind her almost immediately, pulling her into his embrace. She sighed as his arms came around her. Being in his arms, sated and exhausted by the emotional intensity of what she'd done, this was heaven. And she didn't ever want to leave.

She nestled deeper into his arms. "I love you."

The words were out before she could even think about them. They came so easily this time. He tightened his arms around her.

"I'll never get tired of hearing those words." He kissed her cheek and helped her to stand. "Come to bed."

"Bed?" She didn't understand. What about the toy bag? What about his plans?

He gently turned her so she faced him. His eyes were wet, too. "I don't think there's anything we can do tonight that will mean more or touch me the way watching you find your song and love of dance again did." He gave her a tentative smile. "I need time to process it and recuperate."

She yawned and he chuckled. "You may have a point," she admitted sheepishly.

He climbed into bed first and held the sheet up so she could join him. His arms were warm and though she'd slept in them once before, tonight they felt like a safe haven in a new way.

"Promise me," she said and then yawned.

"Anything."

"That tomorrow you'll open your toy bag."

His laughter warmed her even more and she didn't think he was going to answer, but right before sleep claimed her, she heard him murmur, "I promise."

WINNIE'S JOURNAL

I had the strangest dream last night.

I dreamed of a dark and deep forest where there was no night, only day. It was by the sea, but I couldn't cross the ocean. (I don't know why and I didn't try to cross. It was just something I knew and accepted.) It was peaceful and I was happy. Looking back now, that's funny because I'm so not the camping type.

Anyway, I was walking through the forest and in the distance, I saw Lennox and Marie. They were far away, but I knew it was them and I knew they couldn't see or hear me. It was sort of like they were on TV, except they didn't know they were being filmed.

They were a bit older in my dream. Odd, because I hadn't aged. And it's not like they were old old. I mean, they didn't have gray hair. Well maybe now that

I think about it, Lennox might have had a few strands around his temple, but honestly? It just made him hotter.

So they were walking by the sea and somehow I knew they could cross it and yet, even knowing that, I wasn't jealous. I was content in the forest. Again, funny as hell, right? Because, me? In the forest? Dreams are strange. But that wasn't even the strangest part. What happened next was.

Lennox and Marie were holding hands while they walked and, again, I wasn't jealous. I actually felt happy. I could tell they were talking, but I couldn't hear them. Lennox must have said something funny, because Marie laughed. One of those belly-deep laughs that I haven't heard from her in ages. They stopped and Lennox smiled and touched her cheek. She turned her head and kissed his palm, bringing her hand up to hold his.

That's when I noticed it.

Marie had a tattoo on her wrist. Totally out of place on her. Marie has never expressed any desire to get a tattoo and Marie with a tattoo makes about as much sense as me finding contentment in a forest. But there's more.

Lennox knelt down on one knee and held something out to her. The sun bounced off of it and I could tell it was an engagement ring. Marie started to cry, but she nodded her head. Lennox stood up and put the ring on her finger and they kissed. One of those kisses. You know the type. The go-get-a-room type.

The whole time I was smiling and cheering for them and I realized I was crying, but they were tears of happiness.

Then I woke up and I felt sad because part of me wanted to be in the forest.

CHAPTER
Thirteen

"That's the last entry," Lennox said as he closed the journal.

They were eating breakfast in his room the next morning. He'd read Winnie's journal a little at a time while he'd been away from the academy and he'd wanted to share the last thing Winnie wrote with Marie, since it was both odd and mentioned her.

She'd been silent while he read the entry out loud, and he hadn't thought anything about it, but looking at her now, he realized she'd gone completely pale.

"Marie?" he asked.

She blinked. "It really says that about a tattoo?"

He'd had no idea reading the entry would get such a shocked reaction from her. Not the tattoo bit anyway.

"Winnie had a dream about me proposing and you're hung up on a nonexistent tattoo?" He cocked his head to the side. "What am I missing here?"

She opened her mouth, but nothing came out.

"Marie? Are you okay?"

She nodded.

"Take a deep breath and tell me what has you upset."

"I'm not upset so much as I'm shocked." She took a deep breath. "The tattoo thing. I've never told anyone that. Not even Winnie."

He waited while she took a sip of coffee.

"I feel as though I need something stronger than coffee." She was trying to tease, but it didn't carry over to her expression or tone of voice.

"Maybe later," he said.

She closed her eyes. "I've always had this idea, this thought, that if I found a Dom and he offered me his collar and I wanted it, that I wouldn't wear a literal collar. Too cumbersome while dancing." She opened her eyes and met his gaze. "Instead, I'd ask for him to pick out a tattoo to go around my wrist."

It was as if something sucked all the air right out of the room with her words. His chest grew tight even as a shiver ran down his spine because something in the back of his mind whispered, *Yes*.

"There's more," she said.

There couldn't be, he wanted to say, but she spoke with a conviction that left no room for doubt. He didn't say anything; rather he nodded for her to go on.

He sat in amazement as she told him of the dream she'd had while in the hospital. At least she'd thought it was a dream. Now, after hearing Winnie's final journal entry, she wasn't sure. Neither was he.

She finished and they both sat in a stunned silence for several long minutes.

"Wow," Lennox finally said.

"Exactly."

"I wonder." He thought about it some more and changed his mind. "Nah, forget it."

"You were wondering why she's never come to you." She didn't ask it as a question, she stated it like the fact it was.

"Actually, yes." He wasn't surprised Marie knew him so well, and in a way, it was a bit comforting.

"She only appeared to me and Andie when we were in the hospital, and she had that dream days before she died." Marie tilted her head. "So unless you're seriously injured or near death, I don't think she would."

"In that case, I don't want to see her." He remembered his visit to her grave. "I've already said my final good-byes anyway."

Silence fell back over the room and Lennox felt the air between them shift into something that bordered on melancholy. He only had himself to blame; he was the one who brought up the journal. Now it was up to him to change the dynamic of the room back.

He pushed away from the table. "Since I've said my final good-byes, I'm going to focus my time and energy on the future." He held out his hand. "I would like for you to join me."

The smile that instantly came over her face told him he'd done the right thing. And any lingering traces of gloom fell away when she asked, "Might the future involve your toy bag?"

"Definitely," he said. "In fact, if you'd like to experience it, go kneel beside the bed. Naked."

He'd been slightly unsure that she'd want to do anything physical after reading the journal entry together, but the way she hopped out of her chair and tore her clothes off as she scampered to the side of the bed alleviated that worry.

Moving slower, but with no less enthusiasm, he headed toward his future.

MARIELA SMILED AT the floor at the sound of him unbuckling his belt and unzipping his pants.

"Before we do anything else, I want that sweet mouth on my dick. Since that last night in the cottage, I can't tell you how many times I've jerked off to that memory."

She raised her head and licked her lips. He chuckled at her open mouth.

"The thing is, Marie, you're not going to give me a blow job. I'm going to fuck your mouth."

The thought of having him in her mouth while she sucked him off had made her hot. But hearing him correct her assumption and tell her what it was really going to be like? Hotter than hell.

She nodded.

He grabbed her hair. "Nice that you approve, but even if you didn't, you'd still open that mouth wide for my dick. I'm in charge right now and there's only one way to stop me."

And, she said to herself, there was no way she was safewording today.

Before, he'd let her take him in her mouth. Not today. Today, he tipped her head back and thrust his cock inside, holding her head still while he used her.

"You have the sweetest mouth. So hot and wet around my cock.

I could fuck it for hours." He pumped himself in and out several times. "Now I want you to open your throat for me. I want all the way in."

It'd been ages since she'd deep-throated anyone, but she wasn't going to let that stop her. She nodded around his cock even though she had a feeling he wasn't looking for her agreement. She took a deep breath. She could do this.

He went slower this time and she forced herself not to gag even as her eyes watered. Deeper and deeper he went, until he finally sighed and pulled out.

"So damn good," he said, while she caught her breath. "Again."

He repeated his actions several more times and each time it got a little easier. Finally, he pulled all the way out.

"Such a good cocksucker. That mouth is all mine, isn't it?"

"Yes, Sir."

"And who does that throat belong to? Who gets to fuck it?"

"You, Sir." A wave of excitement washed over her as he declared ownership over her body. It seemed like a dream, her best dream ever. She was his. She belonged to Lennox. She wanted to jump up and tell the world, but for the moment, she'd settle for simply basking in his ownership. Even if it was only for this moment in time.

"That's right." He stroked her hair and just that simple touch sent electric tingles throughout her body. "Now, stand up and finish undressing me."

She rose gracefully to her feet. This wasn't anything she'd been asked to do before and she found it rather hot. She stood before him, loving how his eyes were dark with desire for her. For her.

She was going to take her time and enjoy this because he hadn't said she had to do it quickly. Starting with the top button she undid his shirt. Whenever her hands would touch his skin, he'd suck in a breath.

She made her way down the length of his chest, one button at a time, and after reaching the bottom, she slid her hands in between the cotton of his shirt and the warmth of his skin. Her fingertips brushed across the span of his chest, learning the landscape of his body with her touch.

"God, Marie, your hands feel so good."

"I'm glad, Sir."

He fisted his hands in her hair and pulled her head back. "Everything about you feels good." She couldn't respond because he lowered his head to her throat and nipped her. "Mmm," he hummed. "You taste good, too."

He lowered his head for another nibble and she whimpered.

"Now finish," he said with a smile in his voice.

She wasn't sure her legs would continue to hold her the way he was talking, and especially when he added in those little bites with his teeth. It made her shiver.

"Cold?" he asked, running a hand down her arm.

"Anything but, Sir." To prove it, she moved to her knees in what she'd decided was the best and easiest position to take off his pants. Since she was on the floor, she couldn't tell from her current position if he was looking and watching her or if his attention was focused on something else.

In her mind, she had his complete attention. Judging by the way his fists were balled at his side, he wasn't able to concentrate on anything but her.

She slid his belt out of his pants. She contemplated handing it to him in offering, but instead rolled it into a tight circle and put it on the floor. If he wanted her to do something else with it, he'd let her know.

He didn't say anything, so she started pushing his pants down, making sure to accidentally on purpose brush his erection a time or two or five. By the time she had his pants completely off, his knuckles were white from balling his fists so tightly.

She only felt slightly bad about it. Scratch that. She didn't feel bad at all. Feeling powerful, she sat back on her heels and waited for him to give her further instruction.

Above her, she heard Lennox take several deep breaths.

"Spread your knees," he said, and she couldn't help but notice that his voice was rough around the edges. "Put your hands on your knees. Palms up."

She moved into position quickly, not wanting to give him any reason to stop what he was doing. What he asked for was a common position, but it had been awhile since she had been in it. She forgot how exposed it felt. She forced herself to take several deep breaths to calm her racing heart.

"Marie?" he asked. "Are you okay?"

How well he could read her. It was another thing she had not experienced with the newbie Doms, that almost freaky ability to read her.

"Yes, Sir," she said. "It's just been awhile since I've been in this position. I'm a little excited."

"Only a little?" he teased.

A nervous giggle escaped her. "Slightly more than a little, I guess."

"Hmmm." He ran his fingers through her hair, pulling slightly.

"I've dreamed of having you in this position for so long and for so many years, now that it's here it seems almost like a dream."

Anticipation hummed through her. "I know exactly what you mean, Sir. I feel the same way."

For the next few minutes, he simply stood there with his hands in her hair, allowing them both the time to enjoy the sensation. As she knelt before him, she felt herself grow strong with his presence. Almost as if her submission was the key to her power. In some ways maybe it was. And she believed the same was true for him. For as they stood there, his hands seemed to grow stronger. With each breath he took, he dropped deeper and deeper into his Dom headspace. By the time he took a step back, she felt she was well into subspace.

"Forehead to the floor. Ass in the air." Even his voice sounded more powerful, and she shifted into the requested position immediately.

He walked around her. "Other than that night at the cottage, it's been years since I've been in a scene. While I'm nearly positive I could make it work with whatever I decide to use, I'll be the first to admit I should reacquaint myself with my toys before I use them on you."

He moved so his feet were on either side of her head. "There will be nothing used on you other than my hands. Your only bonds will be my commands and your desire to obey them. Understood?"

"Yes, Sir." She nearly panted in excitement.

"Move onto the bed, on your back. Keep your legs spread."

"One request, Sir."

"What would that be?"

She licked her lips. She'd never done to anyone what she was going to ask permission to do. In fact, she was pretty sure she'd safeword if anyone had asked her before now, but with the way he stood, she couldn't think of anything else.

"I'd like permission to kiss your feet, Sir."

She couldn't tell if her request unnerved him or not. The only indication it might have was the sharp intake of breath he gave. He slowly answered, "Yes, you may."

She didn't dare look up at him, but instead kept her head low to the ground. She brought her lips to hover above his right foot before she slowly pressed them down onto his skin. She kept her position as she moved to the left and repeated the action on that foot.

"Thank you, Sir."

"Thank *you*, Marie. That's not something that I've ever had done before."

"It was a first for me, too."

"In that case, we'll talk about it later. For now, go ahead and get in position on the bed."

She was somewhat shocked no one had kissed his feet before and she looked forward to discussing it with him. Later. At the moment, she wanted to play. She stood and kept her head down while she moved to get on top of the bed.

Within seconds, he was above her. "You aren't to move. If I want you positioned differently, either I'll move you or I'll tell you to move. Understood?"

"Yes, Sir."

"Let's see how wet you already are." He ran his hand between her legs, chuckling as he drew back from her. "Damn, Marie. Already soaking. It'd be so easy to slip my cock into you and ride you hard. Give you the fucking I know you want so badly."

She pleaded with him with her eyes.

"But we both know it's not going to be that easy, don't we?"

She took a deep breath. Part of her wanted him to follow through on his words. If she thought about it too much, she could probably come from the words alone. And if she imagined it . . .

His cock nudging her open, parting her as he prepared to claim her. He'd hold still and then—

A sharp slap landed on her right inner thigh.

"Where were you drifting off to?" he asked with another hard slap, but this one to her left thigh.

"To where you fucked me."

"Not just yet, my impatient sub." More slaps rained down on her exposed thighs. "Have you ever been spanked on your thighs before?"

He was inching closer and closer to where she throbbed with need. Just a little higher. "Only by you, Sir."

"What do you think?" he asked as he spanked her harder.

She thought she was going to come, that's what she thought, but when she opened her mouth to tell him, all that came out was, "Mmph, good, yes."

He gave her an evil smile. "Hold your knees to your chest. I'm going to work on the backs of your thighs. This way, no matter what you do for the next twenty-four hours, you'll be sure to remember me."

As if she could possibly think about anything else. She almost let out a snort, but at that exact moment, he spanked the back of her thighs and it stung with that delightful sensation of pain edged with pleasure. She could only moan in bliss as her body accepted what he was doing.

"I love how you submit to me." He didn't pause what he was doing, he kept right on spanking her. "It's like the highest of highs."

Just as she grew used to his spankings, he slipped a finger inside her. "Someone liked what I was doing. You're even wetter now."

She begged him with pleading eyes to take her, to make her his completely. He put his finger to her lips. "Clean it."

If a finger was all he was going to give her, she'd take it and be happy. She sucked his finger into her mouth, in much the same way as she had his cock before. This time, though, she kept her eyes on his and she saw his need and desire matched her own.

"Good," he said. "You're so good."

She let out a sigh of relief as he climbed onto the bed. He drew himself up to his knees and put her legs on his shoulders. Her eyes widened at the thought of what he was getting ready to do.

"I like that look in your eyes," he said. "You know exactly what I'm about to do and what position I'll be in."

She nearly whimpered as he lined himself up. Just the thought of it nearly made her come.

"You'll be so tight like this. So tight and hot around me."

She closed her eyes. God help her, if she didn't come from the thoughts of what he was going to do, she'd come from his words.

But he wasn't finished playing. He took his time, dragging his tip through her wetness. Almost slipping inside, but not quite. One pass. Two.

On the third she did whimper.

"Are you ready for me to claim you, Marie?" His voice was rough. "If so, then open your eyes and watch."

Her eyes flew open and only then, with her eyes on his, did he finally press inside her. Then he stopped.

"You've held my heart for too many years," he said, holding himself still. "For far longer than I ever allowed myself to admit. But I can't call those wasted years, because I don't think they were. They were growing years for me and they were necessary so that I could become worthy of you."

She wasn't allowed to talk, and she realized he'd planned it that way on purpose. There was no need for her to speak, though, for she knew he saw her love for him in her eyes. She knew when he reached down and gently wiped away the tears that had gathered there.

"Oh, Marie. I have no idea what I've done to deserve you, but it must have been phenomenal."

Then there was no need for him to speak as he slowly pushed his way inside her. She realized as he began moving that though it had been painful at the time, their journey had progressed as it should. Even one year ago, they would not have been in the right place for each other.

Only now, after walking through the fire, alone, could they face the future united.

Fourteen

Six Months Later

He'd made them wait six months. Lennox said he was being reasonable. Marie told him he was a closet sadist.

But today was the day and her belly was filled with butterflies, even though she had no reason to be nervous. Maybe, she pondered, she wasn't nervous, maybe she was overly excited. After all, this was the day she'd been longing for for years.

Today she would officially become his.

She resisted the urge to pinch herself.

They weren't going to have a traditional collaring ceremony, but they had planned a reception at Winnie's cottage. Although now it was known as the Winnie Price Community Art Studio.

Andie had asked her if she felt strange having the reception at the place Lennox had shared with another woman. Marie answered honestly that she didn't. She was secure in Lennox's feelings for her, and she'd promised herself she was no longer going to have any jealousy toward a dead woman.

"Why are you pinching yourself?" Lennox asked, and she felt her cheeks flush. They were in his car on the way to the tattoo parlor.

"I didn't know I was," she answered with a grin. "I guess I'm making sure I'm awake and this isn't a dream."

They had stopped at a red light. He reached for her hand and brought it to his lips for a quick kiss. "It's not a dream."

"Does that mean you're going to tell me what you've designed?" He'd been working on her wrist tattoo for months and he'd refused to let her see.

He laughed. "I don't see how one relates to the other, but regardless, no."

She faked a huffing noise and crossed her arms.

"You'll see it soon enough."

Yes, she knew that, but it was so much fun to tease him. In reality, she loved that he wouldn't show her ahead of time. It was like Christmas in June.

"I know it'll be beautiful," she said.

"Thank you," he said.

She also knew he'd stressed about it, wanting it to be perfect. Andie hadn't seen it, but she said Fulton told her Lennox had shown him five different sketches before deciding on the one he wanted. She smiled inwardly at that, rubbing her right wrist where his design would go.

They pulled into the parking lot of the Portland storefront. It was a one-man shop, so only the artist's car was parked out front. Marie waited in the car after it came to a stop. Lennox always insisted on opening her door for her. It took months for her to get used to, but she thought she finally had.

Holding hands, they walked into the studio and she noticed he held a folder in his opposite hand. They greeted the artist and a few minutes later they were both seated at a table. Lennox tapped the folder.

"I'm going to show you the design before he starts," he said.

She guessed it was probably so if she hated it, he could change it. She came close to telling him that there was no need, that she'd love anything he drew for her. But he wanted to show her, she decided. She wasn't going to argue. Especially since she wanted to see it so badly.

"Thank you, Sir," she said.

He opened the folder, and she held her breath as he slowly slid the sheet of paper out. He kept his eyes on her while he flipped it over so she could finally see.

Marie was speechless and covered her mouth in surprise. She couldn't keep her eyes off the drawing.

"It's beautiful," she whispered.

"You like it?"

She tore her gaze away from the drawing so he could see the sincerity in her eyes. "I love it."

It was a delicate drawing, made to look like a fragile bracelet, and consisted of two lines twisted together. On the inside of her wrist, there would be a charm with *LM* inside.

"I didn't want anything too outrageous." Lennox traced the drawing with his finger. "But I wanted it to be seen. And with your comment about dancing, I didn't want it too in-your-face either."

She took his hand and entwined their fingers. "It's absolutely perfect. I can't imagine anything any better."

He picked up her hand and kissed her there. "I love you."

"Are you ready?" The tattoo artist asked.

Marie had never felt more ready for anything in her life. She gave him a big smile. "Yes," she said so enthusiastically, even Lennox laughed in amusement.

The artist waited, though, and instead of moving forward, he gave Lennox a nod.

Lennox took both her hands. "Marie, I know we've discussed this at length, but now that we're here, I want to do it one more time."

With those words she felt her love for him grow deeper. But while she appreciated him checking with her, there was nothing that was going to change her mind. She would let him speak his mind though.

"If you get this ink, that's it. We're permanent."

God, she hoped so. "Yes, Sir."

"I wouldn't be sitting here, claiming you with my mark, if that wasn't what I wanted. But I'm asking you, to be sure. Is this what you want?"

She squeezed his hands. "I want your mark on me so badly, Sir. Even more so if it's permanent."

He lifted her right hand, the one that would soon carry his mark and would tell the world who she belonged to, and kissed the inside of her wrist. He kept hold of it as he lowered it to the table.

"I'm going to hold your arm in place," he said giving the tattoo artist a nod. "And I don't want you looking anywhere except at me."

"Yes, Sir," she said.

It was harder than she'd anticipated to keep her eyes on him once the tattooing process began. She closed her eyes and sucked in a breath as the pain hit.

"Eyes open and on me," he commanded softly.

She opened her eyes, but only because it was him asking.

"I know it hurts." He took hold of her left hand. "Take it for me and give it back to me by squeezing my hand."

She knew he was strong, yet she hesitated.

"Now, Marie." He was still speaking softly, but that in no way diminished the authority in his command. "It's not for you to take on your own. Share it with me."

It sounded so simple, to squeeze his hand. To be honest, she didn't think it would do any good. But since he insisted, she squeezed his hand and maybe it was the placebo effect, but it didn't seem to hurt as much.

"Thank you, Sir," she whispered, and looking into his eyes, she knew that dance was no longer the only thing she could count on.

LATER THAT NIGHT, they greeted their guests at the cottage. Marie wore a simple dress of white linen. It wasn't a color she would normally wear, but Lennox had picked the outfit. She'd raised an eyebrow when he brought the gown out, but he shut down her questioning with a look.

She watched him out of the corner of her eye. He looked devastatingly handsome in his dark suit. He caught her staring at him and smiled, putting an arm around her and pulling her close.

"Looks like Fulton and Andie have arrived," he said, indicating the couple walking up the driveway.

"Are you going to talk to them about . . ." She let the sentence drop off. There were too many people nearby who might overhear, and now wasn't the right time to bring it up in public.

"Yes. I'll probably pull them aside in a bit." His arm tightened around her. "You'll have to come with me."

"Of course, Sir." Then to Andie and Fulton, she said, "Hey, guys. Come on in."

"Oh my god," Andie said holding out her hands. "Let me see it!"

Smiling, Marie held her wrist up for her friend to see. "It's still got ointment on it and it's all pink." But she described the design since it was still bandaged.

Andie oohed and aahed. "It sounds gorgeous."

Marie agreed. "I know. I love it."

Andie looked up at Fulton. "I want a tattoo."

Fulton shot a *now see what you've done* look to Lennox who just laughed and held up his hands. "Don't blame me, the tattoo was her idea. All I did was design it."

Fulton looked down at Andie. "We'll talk about it later."

"Speaking of talking," Lennox said, obviously wanting to change the subject. "We need to chat sometime tonight."

Fulton must have noticed the somber tone of his voice, because his head shot up. "Everything okay, boss?"

"Yes, just something I need to take care of."

"Okay," Fulton said. "Just let me know when you want talk."

Lennox and Marie went around the rooms, speaking to their guests. She knew most of them since a good number had been associated with the academy in one way or another over the years. Only a handful she didn't recognize and they were associates of Lennox from the real estate world. Marie was surprised that she didn't feel uncomfortable, especially with so many people in attendance. For once it seemed she didn't mind being the center of attention. Even if she wasn't naked.

"Why the giggles?" Lennox asked. "Is something funny?"

"I was thinking how it was funny that I don't mind being the center of attention today. I'm not even naked," she said with a smile.

He laughed at that. He seemed to be laughing a lot lately. It made her happy.

He leaned over as if he were about to whisper something scandalous. "I can always ask you to get naked, you know."

"I know you could." She just knew that he wouldn't. At least she didn't think he would.

He winked at her, which made her think he considered doing it. Most people in attendance were in the kink world, so it wouldn't be inconceivable of him to do so. Probably just highly unlikely.

When he took her hand and led her to the front of the room where most people had gathered, she had to wonder if he wasn't going to have her undress after all. He didn't indicate that she should kneel, so she just stood beside him as he got everybody's attention.

"Ladies and gentlemen. Friends and colleagues." Marie watched as Lennox flawlessly commanded the room. "Thank you so much for coming today to help Marie and me celebrate our union as Dom and sub. As many of you are aware, our journey has not been easy. Nor has it been short. We had to work, oftentimes very hard and without knowing if we would be successful in the end. But instead of breaking us apart, our journey has made us closer.

"This morning, our union was further solidified when Marie

willingly took my mark upon her wrist. There are no words to describe what this means to me. Through all my troubled days, she has been my steadfast rock. And yes, I invited you all here tonight to celebrate, but also to stand with us as we continue our new journey. But before I do that, I have to do one thing."

He turned to face her and she realized she had no idea what he was getting ready to do. Nor could she name the emotion she saw in his eyes. He took both her hands and gave them a gentle squeeze.

"Marie," he said. "I love you. And I've told you this before, but perhaps you'll humor me and let me say again. I could not have made it through all that I have without you by my side, and that has taught me that I never want to try."

Keeping both of her hands in his, he knelt down on one knee. She sucked in a breath. What was he doing? Could it be?

He was smiling now, though she saw some tears building in his eyes. He let go of one of her hands, and took something out of his pocket. Her free hand flew to her mouth at the sight of a small ring box.

"Marie," he said. "I love you. Please be mine in every way possible. Will you marry me?"

Her cheeks were wet with tears. Whatever she thought he might have been about to do, this was not it. Yet she'd never been happier. She nodded and whispered, "Yes. A million yeses."

Wearing a grin from ear to ear, he stood up and slipped the ring on her finger. She didn't even have a chance to see it, because he held her hand and lowered his lips to hers as the entire room erupted in applause.

"Lennox," she said. "I love you so much. You have made me so happy. Thank you."

"I should be the one thanking you." He shook his head. "Without you, I would still be living in the past. Holding on to a ghost. Unable to move forward."

She didn't have anything to say to that, so she lifted her hand and caressed his cheek. He turned his face and kissed her palm.

"Did you see your ring?" he asked.

She smiled through her sniffle. "No."

He took her hand and held it up so she could see. It was a beautiful solitaire, elegant in its simplicity, and everything she would have wanted in a ring. Had she ever thought about having one, that is.

"I love it. It's beautiful."

He whispered in her ear. "Not as beautiful as you."

They could talk no more because all at once they were surrounded by their friends and academy family, all wanting to congratulate them and see the ring.

Marie breathed a sigh of relief when Andie made her way through the crowd a few minutes later and was able to drag her away to a quiet corner.

"Wow. Talk about a big day and a half." Andie held up Marie's hand and gazed at the ring. "That is gorgeous. He did well."

Marie looked at the front of the room where Lennox was chatting with several men. "Yes, he did."

"So now I get to tell Fulton that I want a ring and a tattoo."

Marie laughed. "Are you ready for a ring and a tattoo?"

"Nah, not yet. Maybe soon." Her friend grew silent then and

Marie felt the tone of the conversation change. "Do you know why Lennox wants to talk to us?"

"Yes, but I think it's best that you hear from him."

"Something tells me I'm not going to like what I hear."

"Trust me when I say it's for the best. And everything is going to turn out all right."

She wasn't able to say anything else, because at that exact moment, Lennox approached with Fulton following close behind.

"Why don't we slip upstairs into the studio?" Lennox asked.

They walked up the stairs to the studio space that she knew was oftentimes still painful for Lennox to enter. He had come a long way, but he wasn't completely there yet. They'd decided together not to change the studio, in the hopes that the room, filled with children from the community, would continue to bring healing to them both. As they walked to the open-air room, they caught sight of easels filled with children's drawings and paintings. Only then did Lennox relax, which allowed Marie to do so as well.

"First of all," Lennox started. "I'm sorry if my invitation to chat caused you any stress. I just wanted to make sure we talked tonight. Especially now that Marie has agreed to marry me."

He leaned over and gave her a quick kiss.

"You know I took some time off at the end of last year to do a bit of consulting work. And to be honest, I thoroughly enjoyed it." When Lennox looked her way, she smiled and nodded for him to continue. "Marie and I have decided to take a year off. We're going to spend some time alone together. We're also going to travel and do some consulting work."

Fulton and Andie both stood, shock evident in their stunned expressions.

"I never planned to make a career out of the academy," Lennox explained. "It was something I did to try to make up for Winnie's death. And while it has done well, it's not my burning passion."

Andie was the first to overcome her shock enough to speak. "I can understand that. Cooking is my burning passion. Well, next to Fulton, that is. I can't imagine going even one day without cooking or baking or being in the kitchen. So I think it's good for you to go off and find what you want to do."

Fulton, of course, was more practical. "What does that mean for the academy? The summer session starts in a week and we're already at capacity for fall."

"That's what I wanted to talk to you two about," Lennox said. "I know Andie has moved into the lighthouse with you and I was thinking it would make sense for you two to be acting heads. I think it'll be good for a couple to be in charge."

"You do?" Fulton's arms were crossed as he glanced toward his sub. "What do you think, Andie?"

Andie blew out a breath. "I don't even know what to think. It's so much to take in. The two of you not being there for starters. For a year. It just won't be the same."

"I'm sure we'll pop in every now and then," Marie said. She'd known their plan to step away would come as a shock, but she was also almost completely positive that once they thought about it, they'd think it was a good plan.

Lennox put his arm around Marie's shoulder. "Of course we'll stop by. And it goes without saying, but I'll say it anyway. If either of you ever need one of us, for anything, we're only a phone call away."

"Damn," Fulton said, but there was a grin on his face. "This is not why I thought you wanted to talk."

"And there would be a significant salary increase as well," Lennox added. "For both of you."

"It's not about the money, you know," Fulton said.

"Oh, I know." Lennox winked. "But it doesn't hurt either, does it?"

Fulton laughed, but didn't deny his words. "How about this? Let Andie and I think about it, and we'll get back to you by the end of the weekend."

The two men shook hands. "Deal," Lennox said.

"Where are you going to travel to first?" Andie asked.

"An old friend of mine is getting married." Lennox looked over at Marie. "She and her soon-to-be husband have moved to New Orleans. We're going to head out that way and probably stay a week or so."

Marie had spoken to Rachel several times in the last few months and had grown to like the woman very much. She had yet to meet her fiancé, but she knew Lennox talked to him. It had been ages since she'd been to the gulf coast, and for once in her life, she was looking forward to being away from the island.

Lennox slipped his hand in hers, and leaned down for a kiss. No, Marie didn't mind being away from the island. She had learned that it wasn't the island that she wanted, it was Lennox. And her home was wherever he was.

Epilogue

Terrence Knight couldn't keep his eyes off the strawberry blonde in the corner. He couldn't quite decide how old she was, though. At times she looked to be about eighteen, but she moved seductively and sensually in a way that made her appear older. Besides, it was a private BDSM club. He knew the owner, and the owner would not allow anybody under the age of twenty-one into his club.

"Can I get you something?" the bartender asked.

"How about the name of the strawberry blonde down there?" Terrence asked.

The bartender looked him up and down, but didn't seem to recognize him. As one of the most sought after actors in Hollywood, Terrence had gone through great pains to disguise his appearance for tonight. His agent told him he didn't care if he went to a BDSM club, as long as he wasn't recognized. Terrence's insistence that confidentiality reigned supreme fell on deaf ears.

Which was why he was sitting at a bar at a BDSM club wearing a wig and two days' worth of scruff along his jaw. He doubted anyone would look twice at him and he didn't think they would recognize him if they did. Probably they would think he looked vaguely like somebody, but would be unable to pinpoint exactly who.

"You look awfully familiar," the bartender said.

Terrence flashed him a grin. "I get that a lot, must have one of those faces, you know?"

The bartender made some sort of noncommittal, grunting noise in his throat. "Yeah."

Terrence waited. Had the bartender forgotten that he had asked about the girl?

The man behind the bar picked up a wet rag and began to clean the wooden bar. "Not sure who she is." He wasn't looking at Terrence as he spoke, but rather focused his entire attention on the wooden bar he was cleaning. "This is only her second time coming here."

"She looks awfully young." Terrence glanced at her again. His breath caught in his throat when he saw her look up and meet his gaze. Her eyes were the palest blue color and looked stunning in combination with her hair.

"You know the owner's very strict about who gets in."

"Yes, I know that." Terrence didn't mean to insult anybody by his statement. "If she's in here, then she's at least twenty-one."

The bartender nodded but didn't look up.

"You know what she's drinking?" Terrence asked.

"Tonic water. With lime."

Terrence kept a smile to himself. The fact that she wasn't drinking alcohol might mean that she was looking to play. He had a very strict rule: he would never play with anybody who had been drinking. In his opinion, even one drink was one drink too many.

"Is she here with anybody?" he asked the bartender.

The bartender tilted his head and glanced over his shoulder quickly. Terrence couldn't shake the feeling that the man knew more than he was letting on.

"No," he said. "She comes alone. Both times she's been here. Last time she didn't play with anybody."

Terrence wasn't sure if he was passing along a warning or just handing out helpful information. He nodded. He wasn't sure he wanted to play tonight anyway.

Well, he wanted to play, but he hadn't decided yet if he was going to do anything with that desire.

Tonight, he told himself, it would be enough to talk to her. That was all. Though he really didn't believe it.

Terrence left the tip on the bar and saluted the man still cleaning the bar top. With his gaze firmly on the strawberry-blond woman in the corner, he slowly made his way to her. She was talking to a group of three women he recognized as submissives from his previous visits, but she looked up as he drew closer.

The conversation stopped completely when he stood before her.

"Hey," one of the submissive said. "Has anyone ever told you, you kinda look like Terrence Knight?"

He kept his eyes on the strawberry blonde as he answered. "Once or twice."

Up close, she was even more gorgeous. She dropped her gaze to the floor.

"Look at me," he whispered in a low command. He knew there were Doms who wanted a submissive to always look down. He wasn't one of them. He thought a person's eyes gave away too much information to not be aware of them.

She lifted her head and he was taken aback by her coloring. The paleness of her eyes when paired with the slightly red hues in her hair made her look like a naughty angel. He quickly shut down that line of thought, telling himself no good would come from fantasizing about her. At least not right now.

Her skin had a delicate complexion, and either she never went out in the sun or she covered herself with sunscreen.

"My name is John," he said.

John was actually his middle name. Whenever he wanted to go somewhere and fly under the radar, he used the name John.

He frowned, realizing she hadn't said anything in response.

"Your name?" he asked.

She looked at him with wide eyes. He cursed inwardly. Surely to goodness she wasn't innocent.

"If that simple question is too much for you, you may want to rethink being here." He didn't say it to be cruel. The truth was, if she was that mousey, there were Doms at the club who would eat her alive. He told himself he was trying to spare her some heartache.

"Ronnie," she said, with a slight lift of her chin. "My name is Ronnie. And I apologize for not answering you more quickly. You reminded me of somebody."

"Terrence Knight." He nodded. "I get that a lot."

She smiled. It wasn't a normal smile. The smile she gave him said that she knew what he was doing, she was well aware of his game, and that she wanted to play. "No," she said. "Not him. Someone else entirely."

He had a feeling she could be fun to play with. "Ronnie? Is it short for something?"

"Yes."

He laughed when she didn't explain further. "Can I get you a drink, Ronnie?"

"You may, but I'm only drinking tonic water with lime." She'd twisted her barstool away from the group of submissives and she only faced him now. Her gaze was sharp and unrelenting. She uncrossed her legs and left her knees slightly parted. "I never drink alcohol when there's a potential for play."

"Neither do I." His opinion of her was changing rapidly. Yes, he'd originally been drawn to her looks, but standing in front of her with her legs parted just enough to be a subtle sign she would be willing to play, he was starting to see there was so much more to her.

She sucked a sip of tonic water through her straw and the sight of those full, red lips around the piece of plastic did crazy things to his cock. She blinked innocently while taking another sip.

Oh yes, this one would be trouble.

He stepped almost in between her legs, invading her space on purpose. "Are you going to play tonight?"

"Maybe, if the right Dom happens to pass my way."

He nodded to a group of nearby couches. "Would you like to go have a seat and talk with me about what you're looking for?"

She tilted her head and gave him another once-over. "Okay."

With a smile that looked more natural this time, she hopped off the stool and headed for a couch.

Watching her, Terrence had the craziest feeling he knew her from somewhere. It hadn't hit him until she flashed that smile. The real one. But he felt it rather improbable that he could have met her and not remembered. Maybe she'd been an extra in one of his movies. That was more likely, but for some reason, she didn't give off the actress vibe.

Either way, she had made it to a couch and was waiting for him. He had more important things to attend to at the moment.

He walked over to the couch where she sat. She scooted over as he took a seat beside her. He opened his mouth to talk, but before he could get a word out, she started.

"I'm not new to the scene," she said. "But I'm new to this club. That's why you've never seen me before, in case you're wondering."

"I wasn't." He kept his answer short. From just the few minutes he'd been around her, he had the feeling Ronnie would always try to top from the bottom. She needed a firm Dom.

He had never been as firm with Andie as he needed to be. Hell, he never got a chance to scene with Andie. He'd enrolled her at RACK Academy, and she had fallen for that Fulton guy.

It'd been too long since he'd been in this situation. At a club, with a willing submissive. His fingers itched with the need to dominate her.

"What I am wondering," he said, "is what you're here for tonight. What are you looking for? What do you need?"

She seemed pleased with his direct approach, and he wondered what kind of Doms she'd played with before who had not given her directness. "I like impact play. A little bit of humiliation. No sex."

His cock protested. No sex?

Oh well, he enjoyed impact play, too. And he was willing to hand out a little bit of humiliation. As for sex, well, there was always his right hand.

He took a deep breath, decided on his course of action, and gave her a smile. "I believe I can give you exactly what you want, Ronnie. Let's chat a bit more and then we'll see, shall we?"

HOURS LATER, HE packed a satisfied and very much more subdued Ronnie into a cab. He'd offered to drive her to her house once he cleaned up, but she resisted. If she hadn't given him her phone number, he'd have thought she wasn't interested in seeing him again.

Still, he couldn't help but feel the slightest bit rejected. Something was off, but he couldn't put his finger on what exactly gave him that vibe.

"Good scene?" a familiar voice asked.

He looked up from packing his toys back into his bag to find Lennox standing nearby with Mariela at his side.

"Lennox. Man." Terrence gave him a one-armed hug. "How are you?" He didn't speak to Mariela since they were at a club and Lennox hadn't given him permission.

"I'm great." Lennox turned to look at Mariela, and at her smile, he lowered his head for a kiss.

Terrence chuckled. It was so good to see Lennox in love. If anyone deserved a long stretch of blissful happiness, it was Lennox. "I can see that. When's the wedding?"

"We're still discussing. I want a small and intimate ceremony. Marie wants to stop by a courthouse." Lennox shook his head.

"Which probably means we'll be stopping by a courthouse. Though we do have a wedding to attend in New Orleans, and I'm hoping that'll change her mind."

The look she shot him very clearly said *not likely*.

"So, how was the scene?" Lennox asked again. He knew how hard it had been for Terrence to get back into the scene after his breakup with Andie.

"It was good. Enjoyed Ronnie. I can't shake the feeling something is off, though."

Lennox didn't say anything. In fact, it was so unlike him that Terrence glanced up to see if something was wrong. His friend had turned pale.

"What?" Terrence asked.

"Ronnie?" his friend asked. "You played with Ronnie?"

He was definitely missing something.

"Yes, do you know her?"

"Do I know her? No. But I know of her father. Perhaps you've heard of Senator Lewis?"

It took a second or two for that information to sink into his head. Senator Lewis was a very vocal, very right-wing conservative politician from either Alabama or Mississippi. He was the spokesperson for the ultraconservative viewpoint. And rumor had it, the wealthy senator had ruined quite a few careers in his time.

And Terrence had tied up his daughter and beaten her.

Granted, she had asked for it, and he'd given her multiple orgasms. Yet somehow he doubted that would go over very well with Senator Lewis.

"Fuck," Terrence said. Another thought crossed his mind. "Wait a minute, how old is she?" He didn't think it was his imagination that he had remembered reading about her during the last election. He was quite positive she'd been under eighteen then.

His hands started to shake. What if she was underage? Suddenly, information that the club's owner never let anybody in who was under twenty-one didn't matter much. After all, everyone made mistakes. Although his was turning out to be colossal.

"She just turned nineteen," Lennox said immediately, and Terrence breathed a huge sigh of relief.

"At least she was legal. I was worried there for a minute." Still, nineteen was much too young for him. And for the club. What had the world come to? Was he going to have to card future play partners?

"Somehow, I doubt pointing out of the fact that his daughter is legal will have much bearing on Lewis if he finds out about this."

"He's not going to find out, though," Terrence said.

"Let's hope not." Lennox slapped him on the back. "Come have dinner with Marie and me."

Terrence agreed, but even a nice dinner with his friends did little to quell the sense of foreboding. His fears were confirmed when he checked his voicemail from the restaurant and listened to a message from his agent.

"Call me when you get this. Do not go home. There's a shit-storm brewing and your name's written all over it."

Continue reading for a special preview of

THE
FLIRTATION

Available now from Headline Eternal!

On Sunday Lynne was merely bored, but by Monday she knew she had to get out of the penthouse or she'd go crazy. What she needed, she decided, was new lingerie. Lingerie always made everything better.

As far as addictions went, she thought her obsession with lingerie was relatively harmless. She limited how much she spent, though it did help that the Wests paid her well. And she usually tried to buy when the designers were having a sale. No one else knew about her addiction, because her love life was nonexistent.

Late Monday morning, she called for a cab and made her way to what had been her favorite shop for upscale lingerie when she lived in the city. She felt like a kid at Christmas, thinking about what she'd look for. Knowing she had sexy things on underneath her clothes always made her feel more confident and secure. For her first week of school, she thought a simple bra and panty set would work.

Once she made it into the store, she waved hello to the sales associate on the floor, smiling brightly when the woman scurried over to her.

"Lynne! I thought you had fallen off the face of the earth. Where have you been?" She leaned closer and whispered, "You missed our annual clearance sale. That's not like you."

"I know. It killed me to miss it. I'm living in Delaware now, but I'm here in the city for the summer."

"Delaware?" The saleslady looked at her in shock. "Why?"

"Job. The law firm I was working at let a lot of people go." She shrugged. "I was one of them. But I have a great job now, and I love it. Delaware has been nice."

"As long as you're happy." She pointed toward the back of the store. "Got some new corsets you should check out."

"I'll go look." She adored corsets. Maybe she should get a corset and forget the bra and panties. Either way, it didn't hurt to look. She walked to the corset display, surprised to find another customer already there. Not wanting to disturb her, she scooted behind her to look at the corsets to her left.

"Lynne?"

She stiffened and turned in surprise. "Anna Beth?"

The tall woman with dark hair stood with one hand on her hip. "Look what the cat dragged in. It *is* you."

Lynne gritted her teeth. She supposed she should have felt a fondness toward Anna Beth. After all, she was the one who'd given her the final push to actually attempt the BDSM lifestyle. But she didn't. The woman was a total bitch.

Anna Beth's look was cruel. "You still reading those ridiculous books, or did you become woman enough to handle a real Dom?"

Lynne would never forget the day Anna Beth had caught her reading a BDSM romance in the employee break room. She'd shaken her head and said reading about it was fine, but living it was so much better. She then went on to brag about hot Dom after hot scene after hot sex, shutting up only when the break room was invaded by a senior partner. Later that afternoon, Anna Beth had left a card on Lynne's desk with the name and address of the club she frequented.

There had been no way in hell Lynne would want to go to Anna Beth's club. Instead, she had gone home and joined an on-line BDSM group. From there she'd met Simon. She supposed she had Anna Beth to thank, and she hated feeling like she was indebted to her.

"Actually," Lynne said, "I broke up with my Dom. I've moved to Delaware and didn't want to do a long-distance thing."

It wasn't the truth, but she wasn't about to say Simon didn't think she was submissive, and besides, Anna Beth would never know any different.

"Delaware?" Her nose wrinkled. "Why the hell would you move from New York City to Delaware?"

"The firm let me go, remember? I had to go where I could find work."

"Too bad you don't work in IT like I do. Two words: job security." She cocked her head to the side. "So, why are you here today?"

"I'm taking classes this summer."

Anna Beth's eyes rolled. "Not here in the city, doofus. Here in this store."

Why was she still standing there, letting Anna Beth talk to her like she was? Because she was too damn nice—that's why. "I'm just looking."

"Me too. I'm looking for something my Dom will like."

The bitch had a Dom. Lynne almost felt sorry for him. "That's nice."

Apparently, that was all the encouragement Anna Beth needed. "We haven't been together long. We've played together a few times, but Saturday he came in and sat at the bar like he was looking for someone. Then he looked at me and said, 'Come here, girl' in this sexy-as-fuck voice." She stopped talking for a minute and fanned herself.

Lynne really didn't need or want the play-by-play. "Good for you. I'm glad you found someone." *And may the Lord have mercy on his soul.*

Anna Beth nodded. "Rumor is he's hung up on his last girl-friend, who must've been a real bitch, but after that scene? Let's just say it's time for him to forget her, and I'm the one who's going to see to it that he does."

Lynne had no doubt she could do it. She remembered her as stubborn as all get out in the office, never taking no for an answer. Glancing at the black lace corset in the other woman's hands, she didn't think any man alive would stand a chance against Anna Beth. Putting the corset and Anna Beth together was a deadly combination. "I'm sure you'll have him on his knees in that corset."

But Anna Beth shook her head. "I'm not about to have him on his knees. That defeats the purpose. As long as I'm on my knees, that's all I care about."

Lynne didn't bother to tell her it was a figure of speech. Instead she decided she'd been friendly enough and could leave without seeming rude. "Good luck with that. I hope it works out. See you around."

Anna Beth's eyes lit up. "The thing is, he's a sadist."

She paused as if waiting for Lynne to show some sign of shock, but it didn't come as a surprise to Lynne. She'd been around the Wests, as well as their friends, long enough that she knew BDSM was practiced in many different ways.

She'd heard Nathaniel once talk about a submissive he'd played with before he met Abby. That relationship hadn't lasted long, he'd said, because the woman had needed more pain than he felt comfortable giving. Lynne respected him for that, though she always wondered about the sub. What exactly were her limits? How far did she want to go?

And sometimes, in the dark of night, she wanted to taste that world.

"Nice," Lynne said.

"It's beyond nice. It's incredible." Anna Beth's eyes grew dreamy as she talked about the scene. "He was so careful. First, he used a flogger, and from there, he went to a whip. Damn. Just thinking about it makes me horny as hell. Of course, it hurt, too, but that made it so much better. Because the pleasure that came after was like nothing I've ever experienced."

Lynne believed her. It was easy to tell from her blissed-out smile that she was telling the truth. Seeing Anna Beth so happy and content made Lynne just the tiniest bit jealous. But she stuffed that inside, refusing to let it take hold. One look at Anna Beth made it clear she wouldn't have noticed anyway. She was too lost in her memories or, by the way she fingered the corset, her future plans. She snapped back to the present and looked irritated that she'd said so much.

"Not that I expect you to understand. I mean, seriously, you're basically still a newbie. A sadist would eat you for breakfast." Anna Beth laughed and turned to leave. "See ya!"

After Anna Beth left with her purchases, Lynne wandered around the store, not as excited as she'd been before. She didn't want to look at the corsets, and the bra and panty sets now seemed boring. She blinked back tears. Shopping for lingerie was stupid anyway. No one would ever see it on her. What did it matter?

She couldn't hold back the memories of the few times she'd undressed for Simon. The way his sharp eyes had traveled up and down her body, taking her all in. At the time she'd felt as if he were memorizing her. Had he? Did he ever think back to their time together . . . and if he did, would he remember how she'd stripped for him?

No matter how many times she told herself it was time to move on, she found she couldn't. She'd tried pursuing a vanilla relationship after Simon, and halfway into the date, she'd known it wouldn't work. Though she knew numerous people in BDSM circles who would jump at the chance to set her up with someone, her heart wasn't in it if it wasn't Simon. Instead, she'd settled for neither kink nor vanilla. Anytime she felt lonely, she'd remember how it all started.

They had chatted online for two months before she'd agreed to meet him in person. Even then, she'd met him in a public place and had a friend go with her. Most people she'd mentioned her meeting to had told her she was out of her mind to meet a guy she knew only from the Internet.

Excerpt from THE FLIRTATION

At times before they first met, she'd thought she might be crazy to have said yes. She only had to watch the news to hear all about how easy it could be to open yourself up to danger. But she didn't feel in any danger with Simon. Ever. He had a calming presence about him that immediately set her at ease.

The day they'd met in person, finally, he'd asked her to dinner, and though her friend had gone with them, she'd ended up leaving before the entrées arrived. Simon had been kind, and later, when they'd progressed to where they'd talked about BDSM, he was patient and gentle.

Which was why it had come as such a surprise when he'd broken up with her.

She often thought back to their time together, trying desperately to figure out what she'd done wrong. He'd known from the beginning that she had no experience as a submissive. They had even gone to Nathaniel and Abby's Hamptons estate to watch a scene. She had been mesmerized by the two of them. And when it was over, Nathaniel had carried Abby out of the room and Simon had taken her out to their pool and they'd talked.

It was that day that she'd finally begun to understand and accept that she was a submissive at her core. She'd told Simon the same thing and he'd looked so happy.

Yet it wasn't but a few months later that he'd left.

"Lynne?"

She looked up. The saleslady was watching her with worried eyes. "Are you okay? Do you need help finding something?"

Lynne looked around. Somehow, she'd made it to the pajama section. Strange. While she loved pretty undergarments, she'd never bought fancy pajamas before.

291

Suddenly, she knew exactly what she was going to buy. It was time for something new. Time for her to leave the past behind and move forward. It was time for a new Lynne. And New Lynne wore naughty pajamas to bed.

She turned and smiled at the saleslady. "Actually, you *can* help me find something."

Discover The Submissive series from
New York Times bestselling author

TARA SUE ME

beginning with

TARA SUE ME

THE
SUBMISSIVE

THE WORLDWIDE PHENOMENON
Before there was **Fifty Shades of Grey**...

Abby King yearns to experience a world of pleasure
beyond her simple life as a librarian—and the brilliant and
handsome CEO Nathaniel West is the key to making her
dark desires a reality. But as Abby falls deep into
Nathaniel's tantalizing world of power and passion, she
fears his heart may be beyond her reach—and that her
own might be beyond saving...

HEADLINE
ETERNAL

HEADLINE
ETERNAL

FIND YOUR HEART'S DESIRE...

VISIT OUR WEBSITE: www.headlineeternal.com

FIND US ON FACEBOOK: facebook.com/eternalromance

CONNECT WITH US ON TWITTER: @eternal_books

FOLLOW US ON INSTAGRAM: @headlineeternal

EMAIL US: eternalromance@headline.co.uk